Shadows Deep

Also by Michael D. Graves

THE PETE STONE SERIES
To Leave a Shadow
2016 Kansas Notable Book

Shadow of Death

All Hallows' Shadows
2021 Kansas Notable Book
Midwest Book Award Finalist
J. Donald Coffin Memorial Book Award

Shadows and Sorrows

Human Shadow

———

Green Bike, a group novel
with Kevin Rabas and Tracy Million Simmons

Shadows Deep

Michael D. Graves

Meadowlark Press, LLC
PO BOX 333, Emporia, KS 66801
Meadowlarkbookstore.com

Shadows Deep
Book 6 of the Pete Stone Series
Copyright © 2025 Michael D. Graves

Cover photo by Dave Leiker
daveleikerphotography.com
Cover design by TMS, Meadowlark Press
Interior design by TMS, Meadowlark Press
Printed in the USA

Resale and Bulk Orders: Contact info@meadowlark-books.com.
https://www.meadowlarkbookstore.com/resale-and-bulk-orders

FICTION / Mystery & Detective / Private Investigators
FICTION / Mystery & Detective / Historical
FICTION / Crime

Library of Congress Control Number: 2025948485

ISBN: 978-1-956578-88-1

This is for Tracy Million Simmons,
who has believed in Pete Stone from the beginning.

"... dream of the soft look
Your eyes had once, and of their shadows deep ..."
—William Butler Yeats

"Evil thrives in shadows.
The gumshoe strives to make shadows safe."
—Pete Stone

Death arrived on a raw Thursday in March. Lightning gashed the gray canopy over the city. Rain drummed onto the rooftop. I stood frozen, chilled by the weather and chilled by whether I had the moxie to go on. The figure lay in the fetal position, clothed and curled, back toward me. His left arm was twisted at an odd angle, his suitcoat pulled down at the shoulder, a lump of trash dumped in a bathtub and forgotten.

Another murder, another victim. Who knew the numbers? How many since Cain slew his brother, Abel? The past mirrors the present. What was, is, and always will be. Change the dates and change the names—the stories remain the same.

A boom of thunder urged me to get on with it. I placed a finger on his neck and checked for a pulse I knew I wouldn't find. I tugged on a shoulder. His head rolled back, mouth agape in a silent scream. He hadn't gone quietly. He'd fought when they worked him over. The ripped shirt, buttons torn away, lay open to reveal cigarette burns—make that cigar burns—spread over his torso and up his neck. Yeah, he'd struggled. His death made a statement. This wasn't a mere slaying. This was torture.

Black, empty eyes stared out from the brown face. I stared at the weapon that took him out of this world, the coup de grâce, the last thing those black eyes witnessed—the knife piercing his chest.

♦♦♦

Thursday

March 30, 1939

Chapter 1

The storm had rolled in earlier that morning. I'd been in my office. Clouds gathered in the west, over the concrete and neon skyline. Lightning flashed on the horizon, and thunder rumbled. The show unfolded in black and white as I watched from my window in the Lawrence Block Building. Pedestrians three floors below hunched their shoulders and stiff-legged for doorways ahead of the downpour.

"Coffee's ready," Agnes said.

"Thanks, kiddo," I said. "I'll take it in the vein."

"You'll take it in a cup."

Agnes handed me coffee along with the morning edition of the newspaper. She glanced out the window.

"What a perfect day to stay indoors," she said.

"Agreed," I said.

"Percy asked me to lunch," she said. "If this keeps up, our meal will be seafood."

Percival Gillman, Agnes's husband, worked as cashier of the Fourth National Bank. Heavy rain camouflaged the towering structure only a block away.

I sat down behind my desk, lit a Chesterfield, and sipped coffee—hot, black, and bitter. The headline in the morning edition read, "Brinkley is Denied Damages." Dr. John R. Brinkley was back in court. He'd filed a libel suit against a critic. He claimed damages to his reputation, as if damaging his reputation were possible. The court agreed and sided with the critic. A jury of his peers labeled Dr. Brinkley a charlatan.

The doctor with iffy medical credentials achieved notoriety for his bold assertions of curing male impotence by transplanting goat testicles into patients. Gullible suckers hazarded hard-earned dough for the promise of virility. Patients often suffered ailments. Several of them died. Hounded by authorities and outraged victims, Brinkley ducked for cover. The brazen culprit went into politics. He ran for governor of Kansas—twice—narrowly losing both times. I had to tip my fedora to the quack. Goat transplants or God-given, the man had a pair.

The outer door opened, and Agnes squealed. She greeted a visitor whose familiar voice I recognized. I folded *The Wichita Eagle* and tossed it onto my desk. I stood as Agnes ushered in Ellis Waldo, an old friend. We shook hands.

"Waldo, it's good to see you. Sit. Talk to me," I said. "I didn't expect a soul to brave this weather."

Waldo lowered himself into the customer's chair and rested a sodden newsboy cap on his knee.

"I'll bring coffee," Agnes said.

Her comment brought smiles. Years earlier, Agnes waitressed at a downtown hotel where Waldo operated his shoeshine stand. That was before they each lost their jobs. Agnes served coffee to Waldo in the main dining room against the objections of a petty manager. The man found it offensive to have a Negro sitting in the midst of the hotel's genteel guests. He warned Agnes not to serve the shine man, but she ignored the order and continued to serve her friend. The manager fired them both. Waldo moved his business to the Hotel Eaton, down the block from the Lawrence Block Building. Agnes gave up waitressing and went to work for me, Pete Stone, private investigator.

Agnes returned with coffee.

"Here, Waldo," Agnes said. "Light and sweet, just like you drink it."

"You remember," Waldo said.

He sipped from the cup and murmured his thanks. Agnes hugged his shoulders.

"It's not often you come to my office," I said.

"No, Mr. Stone, I usually see you in my office," Waldo said.

He forced a grin that didn't reach his eyes. Ellis Waldo preferred being addressed by his last name. He never called me Pete. It was always Mr. Stone. I lit a cigarette and waited while he gathered his thoughts. Waldo sipped his coffee and placed the cup on my desk. He pulled a handkerchief out of his coat pocket and ran it over his nape and brow. He folded the handkerchief, tucked it away, and picked up the cup again. Then, he spoke.

"Ralph has disappeared," he said. "I can't find him, and his mother's worried. I don't suppose you've spoken to him?"

Ralph was Waldo's son, also a private detective.

"It's been over a week, closer to two," I said. "Is he on a case?"

Waldo shrugged and said, "He could be. I don't know. He doesn't live under our roof. He's his own man. His mother worries, though. We haven't heard from him for over a week, same as you. That's not like Ralph."

"Maybe he took some time off," I said. "Is there a lady friend?"

Waldo smiled.

"He sees ladies, yes, but not a particular lady."

"You say it's been over a week. When exactly did you see him?"

Waldo didn't hesitate.

"It was at our supper table, Wednesday last," he said. "Mother served navy bean soup over cornbread. Ralph was quiet that night. He's usually talkative. Sometimes he discusses his work, you know, without divulging a confidence. He talks, and I listen. He doesn't tell us everything happening in his life. Not all things are meant for our ears. That night, though, Ralph seemed upset. That's why I'm worried. When he spoke, he said things I didn't understand. It was like he was talking to himself."

I leaned forward.

"How do you mean?"

"He used words like, 'no more,' 'not again.'"

"What do you suppose he meant?" I said.

"I don't know. I asked him to tell me what was troubling him. He looked at me in a strange way, like he'd just come awake. He apologized, and that was that."

"Do you think Ralph is involved in something dangerous?"

"I have no idea," Waldo said.

"Has he been threatened?" I said.

Waldo thought before speaking. A low rumble came from above, and rain pelted the window.

"I wonder," he said and paused. "I wonder if there was ever a time when Ralph didn't feel threatened."

"What did he say after he snapped out of it and apologized?"

"He didn't say much of anything after that. He ate his soup. We all ate without much conversation. After the soup, Ralph folded his napkin. He turned down his momma's vinegar pie. Ralph's sweet tooth rarely passes up his momma's dessert. He said he had to be going, and he hugged us goodbye. We haven't heard from him since."

"That was Wednesday evening," I said. "Today's Thursday, eight days."

"I've played his words over and over in my mind," Waldo said. "Something is troubling that boy."

"No phone call, nothing, since that night?" I said.

"Not a thing. I tried his phone and got no answer. I waited another day, then I went to his place. I have a key, and I let myself in. His apartment was empty. Nothing looked out of place, but he was gone. That was on Saturday. These last few days have crawled by. He hasn't called. He hasn't shown up. Nothing, not a word. A week isn't a long time, and normally I wouldn't worry, but those words he used. Those words worry me. I can't shake the feeling that something isn't right, that Ralph is in trouble or in danger. Now, I'm here. I hate to be a bother, but if you have anything to offer, I'd sure appreciate it."

Ralph would probably surface in the next day or so wearing a crooked grin and a sheepish look. That wasn't what Waldo wanted to hear.

"Why don't I take a look at Ralph's place?" I said. "Maybe I can spot something you overlooked."

Waldo opened his hand. The key he'd been holding rested in his palm.

"I checked his rooms, but I didn't snoop. I didn't look into drawers and closets," he said.

"Did you go to his office?" I said.

Waldo looked down and shook his head.

"Ralph doesn't keep an office these days, not for a month or so," Waldo said. "Things haven't gone so well lately, I suppose. He couldn't keep up with the rent."

Waldo raised his head. I took the key and wrote down Ralph's address.

"I'll rest easier after I hear from you," Waldo said.

He donned his cap, placed both palms on the desk, and stifled a groan as he pushed himself upright. He pulled a wallet from his coat pocket.

"I intend to pay you for your time," he said.

I waved the back of my hand.

"Ralph is my friend, Waldo. We're also partners when the case calls for it. I'll run over to his apartment this morning and report when I have something. You'll be at the Eaton?"

"I'll be there," he said. "I won't be busy, though. Nobody shines their shoes during a rainstorm."

Waldo shook my hand and left. Agnes came into my office wearing a frown. I shared Waldo's concerns with her.

"What are you going to do?" she said.

"I'm going to visit Ralph's apartment," I said.

"Did you mean what you said? Do you think he'll show up soon?"

"Ralph is a responsible man," I said. "He'd never intentionally worry his parents. He's also young and bulletproof, like all young men are. I'll see what I can find."

I glanced out the window.

"If you don't hear from me soon, alert the Coast Guard."

I slipped into my trench coat.

"I'll be waiting," she said. "Percy and I agreed to try lunch tomorrow. Neither one of us wants to get out."

The downpour hadn't let up. I turned up the collar on my trench coat and exited the building. My Jones Six Roadster was parked at the curb, halfway up the block on Douglas. I hustled down the walk and climbed aboard the car. By the time I got behind the wheel and closed the door, I felt like I'd fallen into the river. I stomped water off my shoes onto the floorboard, wiped my handkerchief over my face, and pulled away from the curb.

Traffic was light, and few people were afoot. Ralph Waldo lived in the McAdams neighborhood, north and east of downtown. I drove east. At the Mead intersection, a women holding an umbrella and carrying a paper bag waited to cross Douglas. No one was behind me. I braked to a stop and waited. She waved her thanks and crossed in front of the roadster.

Down the way at Cleveland, I made a left. At Ninth, I slowed and turned right. I stopped in the middle of the block in front of a two-story frame house. A row of shops ran along the other side of the street. I parked behind a Chevy sedan. Ralph's Ford was nowhere in sight.

From the curb, I saw that the house was divided into four units, two entrances off the porch on the lower floor, and stairs leading to upper apartments on either side of the house. I couldn't make out the numbers through the rain, so I hustled up the walk and ducked under the porch roof. Apartments one and two were down. Three was up to the left, and number four, Ralph's apartment, was up to the right.

I climbed the stairs and knocked. If Ralph had returned, I didn't want to walk in on him. No one answered, so I inserted the key in the lock and opened the door. I stepped inside the chilly, dark room and listened. Water ran down my trench coat and dripped into a puddle on the linoleum. I called out Ralph's name and got no response. Rain pounded overhead, and thunder rumbled.

I scanned the shadows and flipped a switch on the wall next to the telephone. A light over a table revealed a living room/kitchen combination and two doors to the right, both ajar. Those rooms were dark. To the left, an easy chair sat beside a window that looked out the front of the house. On the other side of the chair, an end table held a lamp, a radio, and reading material.

I lifted a thin volume of poetry inscribed, "To Ralph with Love, Dad." A scrap of paper bookmarked a poem, "The Weary Blues," by Langston Hughes. Words were underlined in pencil.

"I heard that Negro sing, that old piano moan—

'Ain't got nobody in all this world,

Ain't got nobody but ma self . . .'"

Beneath the book, an outdated issue of *The Negro Star* displayed portraits of Baptist Church leaders on its front page. Ralph had penciled several letters in the margin above the newspaper's masthead: M-DC-DX. I noted the letters in my book. Roman numerals? I wrote their Arabic numeral equivalents in my book: 1,000; 600; 510. If they were numbers, their significance meant nothing to me.

At the kitchen table, I peeked at the contents of two envelopes. One contained a flyer that advertised menswear, and the other was an overdue utility bill. The envelopes were addressed to P.O. Box 9892. I noted that number in my book.

The first door on the right opened into the bedroom. The bed was made and nothing out of place. A lamp and an alarm clock sat atop a nightstand. The alarm had been set to 6:00 AM. I pulled the chain on the lamp and lit the room.

A dresser in the corner held skivvies, undershirts, socks, ties, and assorted items. I removed clothing, found nothing noteworthy, and put everything back in order. I looked under the bed for a suitcase or travel bag and came up with nothing but dust bunnies. A bedroom window looked out over the backyard and an alley. No cars were parked below.

In the closet, a suit coat and suit pants hung on separate hangers. A couple of shirts and another pair of slacks hung alongside. An overcoat was draped over a hook on the wall. Brown brogues and a pair of house slippers sat side-by-side on the floor.

I turned out the pockets of the slacks and came up with nothing. In the coat's inside pocket, I found a receipt from a hat shop in the Delano District, dated ten days earlier. That was two days before Ralph had supper with his folks. I slipped the receipt into my book.

I moved to the bathroom. Ralph may or may not have left with a packed suitcase. If his toothbrush and razor were missing, that would tell me something. I opened the door and pulled the chain on a bare bulb. I didn't bother checking for toiletry items. All I saw was the body in the bathtub.

Chapter 2

Ralph wasn't always a private investigator. He had ambition. Like all young men, he wanted money and what it would buy. That's what I thought, anyway, before I learned what he really cared about. I recalled a long ago conversation.

"What do you want, Ralph? What drives you out of bed in the morning? What drives you to fight the fight?"

He raised his eyebrows.

"What do I want? You sound like my dad. He's always asking questions like that."

"What's your answer? Money? Women? A new car?"

"Who doesn't want those things?" he said.

That answer came too quickly.

"You're holding back," I said. "Those are things other people want. You're not other people. You want something more."

He closed his eyes and shook his head from side to side.

"I doubt you'd understand," he said.

"Try me."

He looked at me, then turned his eyes and looked at something only he could see.

"I want what you have," he said, "nothing more."

"Not many people envy me," I said. "I wear off-the-rack suits and worry if I'll make next month's rent."

"That's not it," he said. "I want to open a door and walk in. Walk in with no concern over do I belong or who might be offended.

That's what I want. I want to walk in and order from the menu. I want to walk in and buy the suit without getting the eyeball from the tailor. I want to walk in and drink a beer. I want to look out that window, not in the window."

When he was younger, Ralph ran with a shady crowd and got on the wrong side of the law. He peddled drugs and dope for a double-breasted criminal too high up in the social register to dirty his own hands with the stuff. Customers were average joes along with politicians, celebrities, and other public figures.

That was the way with the mucky-mucks. One consumed illegal dope. Another mucky-muck provided the illegal dope. The biggest dope of all was the schmuck in the middle, the guy who lived on the street. The guy who carted the stuff and bore the risk of getting caught. Most peddlers lived on the fringes—the jobless, the homeless, the poor saps who lacked the foresight to be born into wealth.

With my help, Ralph broke free of that life. He gave his employer the heave-ho and began working for me. Ralph was dubious at first, not sure if he was cut out for detective work. Every man faces a hurdle from time to time. When doors slammed in his face, I pointed out that Ralph could enter doors that were closed to me. Ralph stayed with it. His intelligence and observational skills made him a natural for detective work.

Ralph discovered that some people dropped their guard in the presence of a Negro. They whispered secrets. They shared knowledge. They ignored the Negro in their midst. Ralph mingled and moved in crowds unobserved. He gathered clues on the sly.

Eventually, he became a licensed private eye and opened his own agency. It was a risky proposition, as is any new business. According to Waldo, Ralph struggled to make ends meet. Detective work came with no guarantees. A sleuth was up one day and down the next. A steady paycheck was never in the cards. Ralph's residence was no castle, but a detective didn't bunk in the hoosegow, either. At least, he usually didn't.

I gazed down at the body and pondered questions. First, who was the corpse in the bathtub, and second, where was Ralph Waldo?

I checked the pockets in the dead man's suit. A license in his wallet ID'd him as Amos Johnson, Kansas City address. Johnson carried a sawbuck and three singles, thirteen dollars, when his luck ran out. Other pockets held loose change, an opened pack of Lucky Strike cigarettes, and a book of matches in black and silver from the El Capitan Club, a jazz joint at Eighteenth and Vine in Kansas City. Nothing offered a clue as to what Amos Johnson was doing in Wichita or how he ended up dead in a bathtub.

I dialed the telephone. I owed Waldo a call before the police arrived with questions I couldn't answer. The clerk at the front desk of the Hotel Eaton recognized me and sent a pageboy to retrieve the shine man. Waldo came on the line, and I gave him a report.

"Do you know this Amos Johnson?" I said. "Was he a friend of Ralph's?"

"He might have been. I don't recall the name," Waldo said. "Ralph has friends I haven't met. This man was murdered? What about Ralph? Do you have anything on Ralph?"

Waldo didn't mask the worry in his voice.

"Nothing yet. We'll find something. I'll be on it, and the police will be on it, too. I'll give them a call."

Waldo rang off. I dialed a number I'd dialed many times before.

"McCormick," the voice said.

"Mac, it's me. There's been a murder. I've got a body," I said and gave him the address. "Don't bugle the cavalry until you get here."

Lieutenant Thaddeus McCormick, Wichita police detective, listened, then mumbled something unintelligible.

"Take the cigar out of your mouth, Mac."

"I said, a duck would drown in this weather."

"A duck would do fine in this weather. That poison rope you smoke will perish. That's not a bad thing."

He said something vulgar and hung up. I made one more call, this one to Agnes. She was concerned when I gave her the news, but Agnes acted the pro. She didn't waste time asking questions that had no answers. I assured her I'd have more later.

After I hung up the telephone, I walked downstairs. Unit number two was directly below Ralph's place. It looked dark and unoccupied. I knocked on the door and got no answer. A face appeared in the next doorway, unit number one.

"Mr. Little works days," an elderly lady said.

I turned toward the Chevy at the curb.

"That car belongs to me," the lady said. "Mr. Little drives a Packard. Are you a cop?"

I held out my identification. The woman opened the door and read it.

"You're a private detective. Ralph Waldo is a private detective," she said. "You've been snooping around upstairs, haven't you? There's trouble up there, isn't there? Is it Ralph Waldo? Is that man in trouble? Answer me."

A roof overhead didn't prevent rainfall from splashing onto the porch.

"May I step inside?" I said.

She looked me up and down. She didn't like what she saw, but she relented.

"Wipe your feet," she said.

I crossed the threshold and stepped onto a throw rug.

"Sit over there," she said and motioned to the kitchen table. "Now, tell me what's going on."

I gave the lady a rundown of what I'd found and didn't hold anything back. The discovery of a body upstairs would soon rattle her world.

"Lord, Lord," she said. "I run a respectable house. Lord, Lord."

"You're the landlady?" I said.

"Since my husband died. Eleven years ago, that was. Never had no trouble, neither, no sir, not like this. The occasional deadbeat, but no trouble like this, no sir."

"Who else lives in the house?" I said.

"Mr. Little lives next door. He operates a warehouse on Mosley. He pays his rent regular. Never any trouble."

"Does he live alone?"

"All my apartments are singles, furnished, one occupant."

"What's Mr. Little's first name?"

"Leo. Leo Little."

I entered his name in my book.

"Do you know the name of the warehouse?"

"Just the street it's on."

"Okay, who occupies number three, upstairs?"

"That apartment is empty."

"How long has it been empty?"

"Just over a week. The man who lived there came and went."

"He came and went. What can you tell me about him?"

"Not hardly a thing. He moved in only a couple of weeks ago. He brought two suitcases and nothing else. He paid a full month's rent. Then one day, he up and left. Never said hi, how are you, or kiss my butt. He just left."

"With two suitcases."

"One was hardly a suitcase at all, just a small bag. It was black like a doctor carries. This man was no doctor, though. I don't get that trade. This man was brawn, not brains."

"Two weeks was all he stayed? You didn't speak to him during that time?"

"Only the day he arrived. He paid for the month, I gave him the key, and that was that."

"What was his name?"

"He said his name was Smith," she said and rolled her eyes.

"Did Smith have a first name?"

"Yes, he did. His first name was Mister."

"I'd like to look inside number three."

"Why?"

"I'm just curious."

She muttered something and rose from the table. She took a key off a hook beneath a cupboard.

"Don't you track up that floor with muddy shoes," she said. "Wipe your feet. And bring that key back to me before you leave."

I stepped out onto the porch. A dark sedan turned the corner and pulled up at the curb. Lieutenant Thaddeus McCormick exited the vehicle. He pulled his fedora low, gripped his raincoat by the collar, and scooted up the walk. He stepped onto the porch and stomped his feet.

"You owe me a cigar," he said.

"I'd give you a nickel, but then you'd owe me three cents," I said.

He swore softly and said, "Where's the body?"

"Up this way."

We climbed the stairs and went inside.

"Where am I?" Mac said.

"Ralph Waldo's place."

Mac gave me a look.

"What brings you to Ralph Waldo's place?"

"In a minute," I said. "Take a look."

I led him to the bathroom and showed him the body. Mac studied the face, the burn marks, and the knife in the chest.

"Jesus," he said.

"Killer left a calling card," I said.

"We'll check the knife for prints," Mac said. "The killer would be a fool to leave any. Who's the victim?"

We moved to the kitchen table. I forked over the victim's wallet and personal effects. Mac studied the contents of the wallet.

"Who's Amos Johnson of Kansas City?" he said.

"Beats me," I said.

He picked through the other items and read the cover on the book of matches.

"So, why are you here, Stone?"

I told Mac about Waldo's visit to my office and his concern for Ralph's whereabouts.

"Waldo was here looking for Ralph on Saturday. He checked the apartment. Nothing was out of place then, but no Ralph. The body showed up sometime after Saturday."

I voiced what we already knew.

"Ralph didn't do this," I said. "Whoever tortured and killed this man did it someplace else. There's no sign of struggle, no blood trail. He or they killed Johnson, then lugged the body up the stairs and dumped it in the tub."

"That doesn't clear Ralph Waldo. If this is his place, he's involved," Mac said. "You're right about one thing. No one murders a man and dumps the corpse in his own bathtub."

"Those stairs are no bargain," I said. "I figure two men."

"Sounds right. Was the door locked when you got here?"

I assured Mac the door was locked.

"I used a key to get in," I said. "The lock on that door is as old as the house. It wouldn't slow down a guy with a pick."

"Ralph went missing a week ago Wednesday?" Mac said.

"That's the last time his family saw him."

"Eight days," Mac said. "That corpse isn't eight days old. The coroner will tell us when he died, but Amos Johnson was alive eight days ago. Someone went to a lot of trouble to put that body in the bathtub. Who and why? And why leave the murder weapon in the victim?"

"Someone delivered a message."

"A message meant for Ralph."

"A message Ralph never received. He would've split before the body arrived."

"Who else lives in this house?" Mac said.

I gave him a rundown of the tenants.

"Leo Little lives directly below in number two. The landlady vouches for him, regular with his rent. She's next door in number one."

"Little may have heard something," Mac said.

"I'll pay him a visit," I said.

"So will the police. That leaves the apartment on the other side of that wall."

"Number three. The previous tenant moved out about the time Ralph disappeared. According to the landlady, he showed his mug little and spoke even less. I have a key."

"Let's take a look," he said.

"Let me go first," I said. "I want to try something."

I took a water glass from Ralph's cupboard and gave Mac instructions. Then, I walked downstairs, crossed the porch, and climbed up the other stairway. Number three was a mirror image of Ralph's place. The door opened onto the kitchen, living room to the right, bed and bath to the left. The common wall separated the apartments' living rooms/kitchens and bathrooms.

I placed the rim of the glass against the common wall and pressed my ear to the bottom of the glass. I tapped on the wall. Mac spoke in a normal voice. I heard, "Four score and seven years ago…" After a sentence or two, I tapped on the wall again, and Mac went silent. A moment later he joined me. I held up the water glass.

"It sounded like Honest Abe was right here in the room with me," I said.

I moved to the bathroom and inspected the wall. I stepped into the tub and ran my fingers over the tiles. I left the bathroom and looked over the kitchen/living area. It could have been Ralph's place. The same easy chair sat alongside the same window with the same table and lamp next to the chair. Everything identical, only in reverse.

"What are you looking for?" Mac said.

"The landlady said the tenant carried a small bag, like a doctor's bag. I heard your voice through the wall with a water glass. A guy with a stethoscope could pick up a mouse fart."

"You're reaching, Stone."

"Yeah, I'm reaching. All I've got is a fistful of nothing."

I looked through the window streaked with rain to the street below. A Buick coupe idled out front. It hadn't been there when Mac arrived. A match flickered, and the tip of a cigarette glowed. The driver looked up my way, a woman with dark hair. She stared a moment, then turned away, and the coupe rolled to the west. Where was Ralph Waldo, I wondered? Was he still alive?

Chapter 3

McCormick made the call from Ralph's place. I waited downstairs on the porch. I returned the key to the landlady and assured her we hadn't left footprints in number three. Mac came down the stairs, checked his watch, and took a fresh cigar out of his pocket. An unmarked police car came around the corner and pulled up at the curb. Mac tucked the cigar back into his pocket.

Two men in civvies exited the car. One strapped a canvas bag over his shoulder and slipped a camera under one arm. The other one toted a black bag, powder, ink, and pads for collecting fingerprints, I figured. The coroner arrived next. Attendants in white coats pulled a stretcher out of the back of their vehicle.

The landlady stood in her doorway and watched Mac lead the way up the stairs. An *Eagle* reporter hustled up the walk and called out to McCormick. Mac ignored the reporter who trudged up at the rear of the parade and disappeared inside. Moments later Mac came back down alone and told the landlady he wanted to talk to her. They went inside.

That made five people upstairs gathering evidence and dealing with the corpse, and a sixth person taking notes. Two people downstairs huddled behind a closed door. I felt as relevant as yesterday's newspaper. I made my exit.

The rain had stopped, but the sky remained overcast. If the sun still existed, it hid behind clouds. I drove over to Mosley and rolled south toward downtown. Aged clapboard and brick buildings suitable for light industry, repair shops, and such occupied sites along the street. Empty lots overgrown with weeds added an air of desolation to the neighborhood. Signs next to doorways, many hand-painted, identified businesses.

South of Fourth Street, a single story structure with a shingled roof caught my eye. A sign read "L.L. Storage." My keen detective instincts kicked in, and I pulled over.

Lightbulbs encased in wire dangled from the ceiling and illuminated lumber, bricks, and roofing materials stacked on the concrete floor. Crates identified electrical supplies, paint, and other building supplies. Workers in dungarees maneuvered carts and shifted inventory from here to there. A rail-thin man with a brush cut and a prominent Adam's apple pushed a loaded dolly.

"Leo Little," I said.

"In the cage," he said and gestured with his head. "He doesn't like to be bothered." The Adam's apple bobbed and came to rest. He moved away.

The cage allowed its occupant a view of the floor and its inventory. Leo Little heard his name and looked up. He watched me approach.

"You heard him," Little said through chicken wire. "I'm busy. Unless you got something you want stored, beat it."

Sitting on a stool, Little threw back his shoulders. He wore a bowtie, horn-rimmed glasses, and a chip on his shoulder. I wondered which one generated the most snickers among employees. I slid my card through an opening in the wire, and he scanned it.

"You're a private detective," he said. "Why would I want to talk to a private detective?"

"It's about the dead body I found in your apartment building," I said, and I didn't lower my voice when I said it.

Heads turned. Leo glared from his cage. He made a notation in a small booklet and tucked the booklet into a wallet on the desktop, one of those long wallets fit for a breast pocket. He left his wallet lying on the desk and came out from behind the wire. He selected a key from a ring and locked the cage.

"Over here," he said.

We walked across the floor where he unlocked a door. We entered a windowless office, and Little closed the door. He moved to a chair behind a desk and motioned me toward another chair.

"Okay, let's have it," he said. "What body?"

"Upstairs over your apartment," I said. "I discovered it this morning."

"Upstairs? Ralph Waldo?"

"Ralph is missing. Somebody stashed the victim in his bathtub," I said. "The man's name was Amos Johnson. Does that ring a bell?"

Little frowned.

"Amos Johnson. I met the man. He's a friend of Ralph's, or was."

"How'd you meet him?"

"At the apartment. They came down the stairs as I was leaving. Ralph introduced us."

"I take it you didn't care for the man," I said.

"Not when I learned he peddled drugs. I don't cotton to that stuff. I didn't understand why Ralph hung around with the guy."

"How'd you learn Johnson sold drugs?"

Little paused.

"My men were loading a truck on the dock. I watched them at work. One of the men said he needed some air. He didn't say he needed a piss or a smoke. He said he needed air. That sounded funny. I gave him a minute, then went out back to check. He was standing next to this Amos Johnson. They had their backs turned, but a blind man could see what was going on. When my guy returned, I told him to take a hike and don't come back."

"How did he take it?" I said.

Little wrinkled his brow.

"He smiled," he said.

"How about Johnson? Was that the last time you saw him?" I said.

"That was the last time I saw either of them," he said. "The user was found dead behind a bar, curled up in a ball. Overdosed on heroin. Now, you tell me Johnson's dead. The scales are balanced in my book."

"Last night, did you hear anything unusual?" I said. "Any commotion or disturbance upstairs?"

"I didn't hear a thing. It was lights out for me at ten, just like every night. Go to sleep at ten, up and at 'em at six."

Who could hoist a body and navigate the stairs without making a racket? Some guys wake up if a cricket coughs. Others sleep through a tornado.

"Any idea where Ralph might be?" I said.

"I haven't seen Ralph all week," he said. "He comes and goes, never on a schedule."

"How's business?" I said. "That's a load of material you have stowed under your roof."

Little gave me a look. I'd bumped the chip on his shoulder.

"What kind of question is that? You wondering why a guy who owns a business lives in a dump on Ninth Street?" he said.

"I'm just making conversation."

"Yeah, conversation," he said. "I own the building. What's underneath that sagging roof is worth a fortune, but everything belongs to folks who live in finer neighborhoods than mine."

"Owners of construction outfits," I said. "You warehouse building materials. That's good for you, too, isn't it, construction in Wichita? The city's shaking off the doldrums, coming out of the depression. Everybody benefits."

Little stood up and opened the door.

"I've got work to do. Take your patter down the road," he said.

From Little's warehouse, I drove downtown. Pedestrians along Douglas carried umbrellas to ward off rivulets of water that dripped off eaves and awnings. At St. Francis, chandeliers inside the Hotel Eaton lit up the lobby. Guests lounged on divans and chairs. I rolled past the Lawrence Block Building at Emporia and continued to the west.

The Broadview Hotel towered over the Arkansas River. I crossed the bridge and drove into the Delano District. Past the Handley intersection, I pulled up at a shop tucked between a diner and a used furniture store.

The sign over the door read, Harlow's Hats. The bell tinkled when I opened the door. A man holding a clipboard and a pencil turned my way and winced.

"Howdy," he said. "You caught me just in time. I was getting ready to close." He took a gander at my fedora. "That soggy muskrat has seen better days, no offense."

"None taken. You could say the same about the soggy guy underneath it," I said.

He stuck out a hand.

"Harlow Hubbard."

I shook his hand and gave him my name.

"Harlow Hubbard. Your folks were fond of alliteration?"

"My folks wouldn't have known the word," he said. "My old man loved football. He played it in his youth and reminisced the game in his dotage. He wanted his son to play and thought goalposts for initials might inspire me."

"Did H.H. play football?"

"I broke my leg during my first season. The break healed, but the twisted knee never did. It still acts up on a day like today. I gave up football and became a hat man instead."

"Harlow's Hats," I said.

"I kept the goalposts," he said.

I pulled Ralph's receipt out of my pocket and handed it over to Harlow Hubbard.

"I'm trying to locate a pal," I said. "He bought a hat from you. That receipt is dated before he went missing. I wonder if you recall him?"

Hubbard studied the receipt. He lifted his head, gazed at the ceiling, and tapped his pencil on his teeth.

"This pal of yours, a Negro fella?"

"That's right."

"I recall that young man," he said, then grinned and shook his head.

"Something funny?" I said.

"Why are you looking for him?" he said. "How do I know you're his pal?"

I handed him my card.

"I'm a private investigator. Ralph Waldo is the name of the man who bought your hat. He's also a detective, and he may be in danger. If he is, I intend to help him."

"A private detective," he said. "That fits, certainly better than that Stetson fit your friend."

"How do you mean?"

"That fellow, Ralph you say? He was dressed like you, in a suit and a fedora, although his hat wasn't as waterlogged as yours. The clothes fit the man."

With a slight limp, Hubbard moved to a shelf and lifted a buckskin-colored cowboy hat.

"This Stetson is identical to the hat your friend bought. Now, this is a fine hat, one of my best sellers. It looks good on a cowboy, and it fits a certain businessman. It doesn't fit every man. You friend wore a nice suit, but that hat looked ridiculous on him. It didn't fit him."

"Why he was buying a cowboy hat?"

"He didn't volunteer, so I asked him. I didn't want a disappointed customer."

"What did he say?"

Harlow eyed the muskrat on my head. Then, he turned and lifted another hat off the shelf, a gray fedora with a black hatband.

"Try this on."

I did and looked in the mirror.

"It's a swell topper," I said.

"Three dollars buys the fedora and the answer to your question," he said.

I forked over three singles.

"What did Ralph say?"

"He said he needed cowboy regalia. He said, 'I'm headed to Hollywood. Ad astra per aspera.'"

"Hollywood? And the state motto?" I said.

"That's right."

"To the stars through difficulties," I said.

Chapter 4

"The Birds won another one. This is gonna be their year. I can feel it," Tom said. "Wait and see."

My pal Tom spouted the same prognostication every preseason. He'd been a St. Louis Cardinal fan since he was a shirttail kid scratching dirt in the Ozarks. He took over the farm when his dad died. Then, when his mom passed, he declared he'd had his fill of farming. He gave up the plow, married his gal, and the newlyweds left Missouri. Tom and Mabel migrated to Wichita and opened a bar, Tom's Inn on Seneca. Tom pulled the stick at the bar and served up cold beer. Mabel served hot food from the kitchen in back.

"This is spring baseball," I said. "It's too early to make predictions. The season is weeks away."

"Johnny Mize got four hits today. The Birds slaughtered the Senators."

"The Washington Senators don't have much. They finished under .500 last season," I said.

"I know. So did the Cardinals," Tom said. "Mark my words. This is their year."

"How about a beer?"

Tom tilted a glass under the tap and filled it with Storz beer. He placed a coaster in front of me and centered the glass on the coaster.

"That's a good looking hat you're wearing," he said. "So, why the frown?"

"I went looking for a pal today and stumbled onto a dead man. The pal's still missing."

Two guys in dungarees took stools at the other end of the bar. One raised two fingers, and Tom nodded. He delivered glasses of Storz, pointed out the menu on the wall, and returned. He lit a cigarette and leaned over the bar.

"Do I know the pal?" he said.

Tom's brow furrowed when I answered. He knew Ralph, and he shared my concern for his safety. Mabel came out of the kitchen and chatted with the men in dungarees. Then, she came my way, and I pecked her on the forehead.

"You're ice cold," she said and patted my hand. "I swear, Pete, sometimes I wonder about you. Cold beer isn't what you need. It's hot soup for you to ward off that chill."

My only nourishment that day had been beer, black coffee, and Chesterfield cigarettes.

"Soup it is. You always know best, Mabel," I said. "Give me a minute to make a telephone call."

Mabel toddled back into the kitchen. Tom gave me change for a dollar bill, and I went to the telephone booth in the corner. The operator placed a long distance call to Kansas City. Aaron Bernstein ran a numbers racket and belonged to the Jewish mob. He stood beside me that time I went up against killers who'd taken my friend's life. Aaron Bernstein was a bookie and a pal, a man I trusted. I spoke into the telephone, and he greeted me with a familiar line.

"How's my favorite Cowtown cop?"

"Ducking the rainfall, hat in hand," I said.

I gave Bernstein the lowdown on the missing Ralph Waldo and the body in the bathtub.

"Ever heard of Amos Johnson?" I said.

"No, don't know him," Bernstein said. "Give me what you've got."

"I have a home address on Euclid," I said and gave him the number. "I also have a matchbook from the El Capitan Club."

"I know the El Capitan," he said. "If he was a regular there, someone will know him. I've got business tonight. I'll drive through the guy's neighborhood and swing by the club. Give me some time to nose around. I'll get back to you."

"Thanks, pal. If I'm out of the office, Agnes will have the helm."

"Aaron the errand boy, at your service," he said and rang off.

Mabel carried a tray laden with food and shuffled from the kitchen. I got off the stool and took the tray.

"Mabel, you shouldn't be carrying that," I said.

"The doctor says I should do what I can," she said. "I'm getting stronger."

Mabel had suffered a stroke the year before. Thanks to rapid medical attention, she'd come through the ordeal with her faculties intact. Still, the stubborn woman had limits. She served the men at the end of the bar, and I carried the tray to my stool.

I looked at the fare and grinned. Navy bean soup over cornbread, the meal Ralph's mother had served a week ago Wednesday night.

"Mabel, this is perfect," I said, and it was. I spooned soup and told her it was delicious. When she returned to the kitchen, I pointed to my glass, and Tom refilled it. I ate while Tom chatted about the Cardinals. He bragged on Johnny Mize and Joe Medwick, both fine hitters. I countered his comments by heaping praise on Joltin' Joe DiMaggio, the New York Yankee's star center fielder. Favoring a Yankee was always good for getting Tom's goat. He stared with an open mouth. Then, he looked down at the floor and shook his head.

"A Yankee fan, right here in my bar," he said. "You're breaking my heart, Pete."

I finished the soup and chased it with one more beer. The soup warmed my insides, and talking baseball was a welcome diversion from worrying over Ralph Waldo. Tom had owned his tavern since before I hung out my shingle as a private eye. He'd heard my stories and taken in hundreds of others. In my book, years of working the stick and listening to every Tom, Dick, and Schmo who unloaded his troubles across the bar qualified the man as a certified head doctor.

Some nights we'd chat for hours. I enjoyed the evening, but the day had been a long one. The warm meal and cold refreshment caught up with me. My eyelids drooped.

"Mabel's got the coffee pot on," Tom said.

"Ixnay, Tom. Thank Mabel, but I have to call the game. A bed is crooning my name."

I settled up and said goodnight. The sky remained overcast and gloomy. Stars and moon were invisible when I boarded my roadster at the curb. According to the newspaper, the moon waxed and glowed bright. Cloud cover rendered that report moot.

I drove north on Seneca, and headlights flashed in the rearview mirror. I crossed the river and turned right on Central. The headlights stayed with me. In a half-dozen blocks, I turned left on Waco and drove north. The headlights followed me. At Eleventh Street, I made a left. The headlights went by and continued north on Waco. I couldn't make the vehicle in the dark.

I drove over to my place and rolled past. I circled the block and saw nothing suspicious. Lights glowed in windows, and the streets were dark and quiet. I closed the circle and pulled up at the curb in front of the two-story house near the corner of Eleventh and Lewellen. I lived on the upper floor. I killed the motor and lit a cigarette. The motor ticked, a dog barked, and a screen door slammed. I got out of the roadster and tossed the butt into the street.

A hedge ran along the sidewalk between the two-story house and the bungalow next door. I neared the stairway that rose alongside the house, and leaves rustled behind me. As I started to turn, two pairs of hands grabbed my arms from behind. The assailants pushed me forward and drove my face into the wall. My new fedora went flying, and my nose was shoved into my skull. Blood ran onto my lips.

The downstairs porch light cast a glow. A brown fist squeezed my left arm. A white fist squeezed my right arm. Its owner grabbed my hair and yanked. Foul breath stank of whiskey and cigarettes. A voice hissed in my ear.

"Back off, gumshoe. Don't go sticking your nose where it don't belong. Get me? You don't want you should be wearing a wooden kimono."

"Is that the offer you made Johnson before you tortured him and ran a knife into him? Am I next, a two-for-one deal with the undertaker?" I said.

The owner of the brown hand punched me in the midsection. I doubled over, and my nose dripped blood on a pair of black and white spectator shoes.

"Don't bleed on me," he said and gave me another blow to the gut.

I caught my breath and ran my tongue over my lips.

"You might ease up on the fists," I said.

"Don't crack wise or you'll get a real beating," he said.

"Thanks for the warning. It isn't often a stranger takes interest in my welfare. Why don't you jerks give up? It's late. I'll just call the cops, and they'll give you lovebirds a nest in the clink. How does that sound, Mister Smith?"

Spectator shoes shuffled his feet and uttered a hoarse whisper.

"I'm gonna stick him."

"Shut up," said his clever companion. "This is a warning, Stone. Next time we won't be so easy on you."

They turned me loose. My knees buckled, and I sagged to the steps. I rolled to my side, and my soup came up. I coughed my throat clear as salt and pepper disappeared into the shadows.

Friday

March 31, 1939

Chapter 5

I woke up on my bed, lying atop the covers, a crumpled suit for pajamas. Dark spots stained the pillowcase. I lay still and recalled the previous night's events. I had collapsed on the stairs. Then I dreamt I climbed a mountain. Somehow, I made it into my bedroom.

I pushed myself upright. The groan in my ears sounded distant, like it belonged to someone else. I dropped my legs over the side of the bed, and my feet came down on my trench coat balled up on the floor. Something dark lay alongside the coat. My eyes focused on my new fedora. My midsection felt tender, but breathing came easy. Smith and Company had spared my ribcage.

I shuffled six miles to the bathroom and pulled the chain on the light. The mug in the mirror stared back, nobody I recognized. If I'd been packing heat, I'd have plugged the culprit in the glass right between the eyes. Dry blood caked the stubble of beard. A gentle touch with fingertips determined that my nose was bruised, not broken. No blood in the toilet brought another ray of hope. No blood and no breaks, a great day to be Pete Stone.

A bath, a shave, and a pressed suit took longer that morning. I moved like a man twice my age and apologized to no one for it. I was alive. In the kitchen, Eight O'Clock Coffee warmed my insides. The clocks chimed nine times, so I telephoned Agnes and told her I was running late.

By the time I stepped outside and closed the door behind me, I gave myself long odds on an early tombstone. I gulped the morning air. The storm had moved on, and the eastern sky looked bright. The steps were steeper that day, but I made it to the bottom.

I unbuttoned the top on the roadster and folded it back. Sunlight and an open sky were just what the doctor ordered. Fresh air brought hope and a fighting chance.

Sidewalks on Douglas, barren the rainy day before, were alive with pedestrians that Friday morning. Customers entered and exited banks and stores. Hinkels Dry Goods at Main and Douglas displayed men's hats in a window. My body took a beating the night before, but my lucky fedora came through unscathed.

I mulled over my conversation with Harlow Hubbard. Ralph said he was off to Hollywood. Going to Hollywood seemed both improbable and impossible. What would compel Ralph to travel halfway across the country? Also, I figured he lacked the wherewithal for such a trip. Hollywood? Why did he keep that tidbit from his family? Ad astra per aspera. To the stars through difficulty. Was that a reference to movie stars?

My shoes needed a shine. I'd stop to see Agnes first, then visit Ellis Waldo. I drove east on Douglas and pulled up at the Lawrence Block Building. I crossed the lobby and climbed the stairs. On the second floor landing, I paused to catch my breath. Then, I continued to the third floor.

Agnes looked up from her desk when the door opened and didn't speak. She put down her pencil and studied me. Then, she tore a page off her writing pad and handed it over.

"You just missed Aaron Bernstein," she said.

"I'll call him back."

"Don't bother. He was going to bed. That man keeps the oddest hours. He lives like a vampire."

I read the note aloud.

"Amos Johnson lived alone on Euclid in a one-bedroom rental. Neighbors zipped their lips when they heard he was dead. One old man called him a thief and said he wasn't surprised someone did him in. He slammed the door in my face. The guy who runs the neighborhood liquor store opened up. Johnson was a regular customer, and the store owner liked him. Johnson wasn't married, but he talked about a sister.

"A bouncer at the El Capitan Club pocketed a fin before he gave me the score. Johnson hung around with musicians. He and Charlie Parker were palsy-walsy, and Johnson reserved a table when Bird played a gig at the club. Johnson dealt dope, small-time operator. The Lincoln didn't buy the name of the kingpin who supplied the dope. You owe me a dog and a beer."

Bernstein's mention of a kingpin gave me pause. There was no doubt that salt and pepper had done in the unfortunate Amos Johnson. They hadn't acted on their own. Someone else called the shots. I was alive because no one had given the order to bump me off.

Agnes stared and raised an eyebrow when I finished reading.

"That new hat looks swell, but it doesn't cover your nose," she said.

"I slipped in the bathtub."

She sniffed.

"Your nose looks like a bruised tomato. You've been in a scuffle. You've been hurt. Fess up."

"It's nothing to fret over, sweetheart."

Agnes drummed her fingers on her desk.

"If Lucille sees you like that, you'll have some real explaining to do," she said.

Lucille was my gal, and Agnes was right. Lucille worried about my safety.

"Lucille is going out of town for a few days," I said. "I'll be hunky-dory by the time she returns. Let it go."

The drumming on her desk continued.

"You could be a poker player," I said. "What do you say we nix your salary and play poker instead? How would that be?"

"You'd go bust in a week," she said. "Then, where would I be?"

"I believe you," I said. "Okay, here it is. A couple of critics took issue with my investigation. They delivered their criticism with enthusiasm."

"What you're saying is a couple of thugs didn't want you snooping around, so they worked you over," Agnes said.

"That's one way of putting it."

"What are you going to do?"

"I'm going to get a shoeshine."

I tipped my lucky fedora and left.

The Hotel Eaton was at the other end of the block, on the corner of Douglas and St. Francis. My new topper and pressed suit made for a dapper reflection as I passed store windows. Shined shoes would complete the look. Also, I had questions for Waldo.

A half-dozen elderly ladies approached the entrance just as I did. They each toted a copy of *Appointment with Death,* an Agatha Christie mystery. They chatted about Hercule Poirot and his latest case. I held the door, tipped my fedora, and smiled. They passed through the entrance one-by-one, smelling of lilac.

"Thank you."

"Chivalry lives."

"We're the Mystery Matters Book Club."

The last lady said, "Thank you, young man." I returned her smile and did not question her eyesight.

The usual suspects lounged in the pillared lobby. Scattered on overstuffed couches and chairs, sheltered patrons removed from quotidian life on the streets basked in hushed elegance. Dowagers in muted grays and blues huddled and whispered in confidential tones. Gentlemen in tailored threads scanned magazines and newspapers. An overhead fan spirited away fumes from pipes and cigars. The scene played out miles away from honking horns outside.

I passed by the doorway to the restaurant and the marble staircase that rose to rooms above. I paused at the desk to thank the clerk who'd paged Waldo for me the day before. The clerk palmed my quarter and nodded his appreciation. The girl at the tobacco stand tipped her head when I walked by, and the barber next door waved his clippers.

Waldo was settling up with a customer when I arrived, so I stepped up into the empty chair. The customer paid and moved a few feet away to the barber's window. He hovered within earshot and watched the barber through the glass. Waldo sat down on his stool and gave me the once over.

"Well, aren't you the cat's meow, sporting a new hat and a sharp suit," he said. "You're looking fine from the ankles up, all except that shoe leather," and he added in a lowered voice, "and that nose."

I eyeballed the man at the window and kept the conversation banal.

"Rescue my shoes, Waldo. They need your attention."

A man exited the barbershop, and the man who'd been waiting went in. No one else was nearby. I brought Waldo up to date on my investigation. Waldo brushed my soiled shoes and listened without interruption.

"Ralph bought a cowboy hat," I said. "He told the hat man he was going to Hollywood. Then, he said, 'ad astra per aspera.'"

Waldo worked polish into the leather with his fingertips.

"Hollywood? Ad astra per aspera?" Waldo said.

"His words."

"The boy's talking in riddles," Waldo said.

He brushed and wiped in silence. He polished and buffed and shined. He popped his rag.

"I don't suppose you'll be telling me how you got that nose?" he said.

"Nothing to worry about, Waldo. I can take care of myself."

"I'm sure you can, Mr. Stone. Still, it troubles me. I'm an old man. I've lived a good many years. I've seen tough times, you know that, but along the way I've managed to sidestep violence. Now, both my son and my friend are in the thick of it. My son is connected to a murder. He may or may not be alive. My friend has been hurt. And here I sit, an old man shining shoes. That doesn't sit well with me. No, sir, it does not."

"Don't dwell on violence, Waldo. I intend to find Ralph. I intend to help him when I do."

Waldo popped his rag a final time. Foot traffic picked up. Another gentleman lingered outside the barbershop. I rose from the chair.

"Can you step away for a minute?" I said.

Waldo placed a hand-written sign on his stand that read, "Back in 20 minutes." The restaurant off the lobby was quiet. The waitress invited us to pick our own table. We sat in the corner next to a window that looked out onto the sidewalk. I ordered coffee for two.

"What do you make of that Hollywood comment?" I said.

"Ralph never mentioned Hollywood to me," Waldo said. "I'm surprised. I don't see how he could travel to California. He hardly manages to hang onto nickels and dimes. He doesn't have the money for a cross-country trip."

The waitress arrived with our coffee and moved away. Waldo added cream and sugar to his cup. I sipped mine and lowered the cup.

"Maybe Ralph didn't have to travel to the coast," I said. "I think he's right here in Kansas. He never left."

"How do you mean?" Waldo said.

"There's been news about a to-do shaping up out west, in Dodge City."

Waldo lit up.

"Yes, it was in the papers," he said. "A cowboy picture, *Dodge City* it's called. The newspaper said Hollywood is coming along with it. The stars are coming to Kansas, ad astra. I read that and put it out of my mind. Dodge City, Kansas, might as well be Hollywood, California, to this old man."

"Ad astra per aspera," I said.

"To the stars through difficulty," he said. "What could interest Ralph in Dodge City?"

Waldo furrowed his brow. I lit a cigarette.

"One step at a time," I said. "First, I have to find him. That movie premieres April first. That's tomorrow. Stars and studio executives arrive in the morning. I'll be at the station in Dodge City when their train pulls in. That last night at the dinner table, you said Ralph behaved strangely. He said, 'no more,' 'not again.'"

"That's what he said."

"Has anything else come to mind?"

Waldo thought that over and shook his head.

"No, nothing unusual."

"Ralph wrote some letters on a newspaper. They may be Roman numerals," I said and showed Waldo the note in my book. "Does M-DC-DX mean anything to you?"

"I don't recall Ralph saying anything that connects to those letters. I don't know what they mean."

"It may have been an idle doodle, notes to himself," I said. "I'll keep digging. Do you carry a photograph of Ralph? It would help."

Waldo flashed a wry grin. He pulled out his wallet and handed over a worn, creased photo. I looked at it and grinned myself.

"A mug shot," I said. "Perfect."

"I carry that as a reminder of where Ralph's been and how far he's come."

Just how far had Ralph come? I pondered that question.

"The cops took that picture," Waldo said. "Ralph was headed down a dark path back then. That was before you stepped in, Mr. Stone. It was you who got Ralph out of that mess."

Something stirred inside, in shadows deep where bad memories sleep. I pictured Ralph Waldo wandering down that dark path.

Chapter 6

It took a couple of hours to line up the ducks. I stepped through the paces, thankful for activity that prevented me from dwelling on my bruises. Agnes listened to my plan, head cocked. She frowned and drummed her fingers on my desktop. Drumming her fingers was becoming a habit.

"I can't stop you from going after Ralph," she said. "I wouldn't try. That doesn't mean someone else won't try to stop you. Watch your back, detective."

"You really care about me, don't you, Agnes?"

"I care about my job. If anything happened to you, I'd have to go back to waitressing."

She conceded a smile when she said it.

"Think of this as a weekend getaway," I said. "I'll be back Monday."

"Lieutenant McCormick called," she said.

She left my office, and I dialed the telephone. Mac gave me the coroner's findings.

"Based on body temperature and state of rigor mortis, the coroner figures Johnson died ten or twelve hours before you discovered the body. That makes it Wednesday evening. Thursday's rain came in just before dawn. The body and clothes were dry with no exposure to the storm. The killer didn't leave muddy footprints."

"It's killers, plural," I said.

Mac listened to my report on the goons who roughed me up the night before.

"Someone's trying to get your attention," Mac said.

"Johnson was tortured, then knifed sometime late Wednesday before the storm," I said. "The killers would've moved the body in the dark, probably after midnight. They finished the job before the rain arrived. What about fingerprints?"

"The murder weapon was clean. Perps either wiped it or wore gloves. They didn't touch the wallet."

"The moon was bright Wednesday night," I said, "if it wasn't behind the clouds. Did the landlady see anything?"

"No. She says she never met Johnson. She's not a night owl. She turns out her light at ten o'clock."

"Maybe a neighbor saw something," I said.

"We're canvassing the neighborhood," he said. "What do you have?"

I gave Mac what Aaron Bernstein had told me. Amos Johnson was a small fry drug dealer. I figured Mac already had that, and I was right.

"That squares with the report we got from KCPD," he said. "What else do you have? Anything on Ralph Waldo?"

There was no reason to divulge my plan to visit Dodge City, a trip that might turn into a wild goose chase.

"Nothing yet," I said. "I'll have something next week."

Mac hung up, and I dialed my gal, Lucille. She and her sister had made plans to visit their mother in Oklahoma. They'd drive down to Woodward that afternoon. I told Lucille I'd be out of town on a case and wished them a safe journey. I didn't tell Lucille where I was going and who I was looking for. She knew Ralph and cared for him. If I gave her the details, Ralph's disappearance would only add a worry line to her forehead.

"We'll have dinner and swap stories next week," I said.

I hung up the telephone and keyed the lock on the bottom drawer of my desk. I retrieved my Smith & Wesson .38 and checked the cylinder, six cartridges. I slipped the gun into my coat pocket. Agnes hugged me at the door and raised an eyebrow.

"You're taking your gun," she said.

"Just a precaution," I said. "I don't expect to use it."

"You never expect to use it," she said. "Pete, one last thing."

"I know. Watch my back."

"No, silly. Get me Errol Flynn's autograph."

"What a two-timer," I said.

Agnes winked and closed the door behind me.

My roadster was parked at the curb. I rolled toward my place, then changed my mind and circled the block. I turned east on Douglas toward Union Station. Ralph's Model A Ford had a lot of miles on it. The train or bus would be more reliable than his car on a trip out of town. I coasted through a parking lot next to the train station and spotted Ralph's Ford in minutes. He'd left town on the train.

At home on Lewellen, I tossed a clean shirt, a pair of skivvies, and a shaving kit into a bag. Dodge City would be packed with out-of-towners, and I didn't count on a bed for the night. I'd make do in the roadster.

I paused at the doorway and listened to the heartbeat of the house. My clocks would go silent before I returned, but I dotted the i's and crossed the t's, anyway. I took the necessary moments to wind the Black Forest cuckoo clock, the Seth Thomas grandfather clock, the Austrian Zappler Animated clock, and a dozen others. Then, I left.

I tossed my grip into the roadster and drove out of Wichita on that last day in March. By the time I reached the city's outskirts, the sun had peaked. I enjoyed the breeze with the top down. A meadowlark trilled its tune from a fencepost and ushered me along the way.

Dodge City lay some 150 miles west of Wichita. I mulled over the case as I passed through Goddard and Garden Plain. Waldo's comment stayed with me, "You got Ralph out of that mess." I also recalled Ralph's comment at that supper, "Not again."

When I neared Kingman, both the gas gauge and my stomach signaled low on fuel. Coffee had gone down easy, and solid food beckoned. I reached a filling a station and pulled up at the pump. A man in bib overalls and a frayed ball cap walked out with a black and tan terrier pup trailing behind. The man lifted the hose on the pump and raised a brow.

"Fill 'er up," I said.

The pup squatted on his haunches and stuck out a pink tip of tongue.

"That's a handsome roadster," he said. "Jones made a fine car. I admire those spoked wheels. What year is she?"

"1919. She's twenty this year," I said. "She's no longer a debutante, but she's still a looker."

He hung up the hose and lifted the hood.

"Oil's fine," he said. "1919? Was that the year Jones closed their doors?"

"They closed the next year. A fire took them out," I said.

I jutted my chin toward a diner next door where a Chevy pickup and a dusty Ford were parked.

"Is the chow decent?"

"It's the best in town," he said.

"Does the owner pay you to say that?"

"No, but she'll kick me out of bed if I don't."

I touched the brim of my hat.

"Park her in the shade when you're finished," I said.

The diner's doorbell tinkled, and a dozen eyes looked my way. A trio of women sat around one table. Their spouses sat around a nearby table. It was a scene reminiscent of a church social, men on one side, women on the other.

They stopped talking and took notice of the most interesting character they'd seen in some time, yours truly. Their brief appraisal determined I wasn't that interesting after all. Heads turned back to conversations.

They wore weathered and patched clothing suited for labor. The men's hands were knuckled and veined, strong enough to fist a pitchfork, gentle enough to coax milk from a cow's udder. The women had square hands with short nails, hands that worked the griddle and hoed the garden, did the laundry and the mending. I walked between the tables and took a stool at the counter with my back to the room.

"The silver-tongued devil next door recommends your food," I said to the lady with "Shirley" embroidered on her apron.

"That silver-tongued devil had better recommend it. He's been forking it down his neck for twenty-five years," she said.

I congratulated her on her marriage and ordered a hamburger and coffee. Shirley disappeared into the kitchen. Voices behind me talked over each other in conversations meant to be shared table-to-table. Jim and Sally were the topic of discussion that day, neighbors not present and therefore subject to gossip.

"Jim pressed old Ned Farley to milk his cows while he's gone, can you believe that?"

"Ned Farley's about as dependable as the weather."

"Sally didn't give Jim much choice in the matter. Sally told Jim this was once in a lifetime, and she was not going to miss it. She was plumb tired of arguing about it, too. Either Jim was going to drive her to Dodge City or she was going to hitch a ride on her own. She'd stand alongside the road and show a little leg if that's what it took."

That brought laughter.

"Delbert Butcher, you hush your mouth," a woman said.

"I didn't say it. Sally did."

More laughter.

"Remember that gal in that movie, Myrna Loy? When she lifted her skirt above her knee and tried to catch a ride?"

"That was Claudette Colbert."

"I thought it was Myrna Loy."

"It was Claudette Colbert in *It Happened One Night,* with Clark Gable."

Shirley appeared with my hamburger.

"You do it all here, waitress and cook?" I said.

"I do today," she said. "I have a gal, but she called in sick. Gin flu would be my guess."

The bell tinkled again. A brunette stepped through the doorway, one long leg at a time. Heads turned, and conversations stopped. The woman paused and surveyed the room. Her gaze shifted from face to face. She wore a green dress, matching cloche, low heels, and a look that would trigger a brawl in a monastery.

Her brown eyes met those looking her way. She stared back. Then, she placed one foot in front of the other and glided toward a table in the corner.

A female voice said, "Delbert, if you don't put those eyes back in your head, you're going to turn into a pillar of salt."

Even Delbert's wife laughed.

Shirley moved to the corner table and took the brunette's order. A few moments later she came out of the kitchen carrying a bowl of peaches with cottage cheese and a pot of coffee. She poured coffee for the lady. Then she refilled cups with coffee and glasses with tea for the others.

The locals drank coffee and tea. Most took their lunch at home. Folks hoarded nickels to buy beverages and enjoy a social hour with friends, a respite from daily drudgery. Shirley understood and didn't begrudge pouring refills.

My burger was fresh, hot, and delicious. Shirley had added a dollop of coleslaw to the plate. My last chow was Mabel's bean soup from the night before, and I'd tossed that when the goons worked me over.

"Your husband's a straight shooter," I said. "This burger hits the spot."

Shirley leaned over and spoke in a softer voice.

"Those folks gossip about Jim and Sally, but we're all friends here. They're good people, just jealous. Me, too. I'm jealous. Can you imagine the excitement we're missing in Dodge City? I'd give an arm to see that."

Shirley's husband came through the door with the terrier tagging along behind.

"Carl, don't you know enough to keep that mutt outside?" Delbert Butcher said. "Your wife ought to throw you out on your ear, cur and all."

"What do you mean, cur? This is a purebred guard dog. Killer goes where I go." Carl looked down and spoke to the pooch. "Sic 'em, Killer."

The terrier yipped and stuck out his tongue and wagged his tail. Everyone laughed. Carl shrugged and took the stool next to mine. Shirley poured iced tea into a glass and placed it in front of her husband.

"An even dollar will do it," Carl said to me. "Stop in again when you pass through. I admire that roadster."

"Will do," I said.

I drained my cup and settled up for the fuel and the food. The brunette watched me move toward the door. I smiled, and touched the brim of my hat. Her gaze stirred me. I vowed to avoid monasteries.

Chapter 7

Where was the connection between Amos Johnson and Ralph Waldo? I chewed on that question and pondered the bitter answer as I drove. At one time or another, they each dealt dope. Maybe Bernstein got it wrong. Maybe Amos Johnson had been a standup citizen. Maybe he loved his mother, coached youth baseball, and sheltered stray dogs. Maybe pigs fly.

The miles rolled by. Other questions gnawed at me. If Ralph was safe, why did he disappear? Why the Stetson? What drew him to Dodge City, if that's where he was? He didn't leave on a lark.

Smith and his anonymous pal murdered Johnson. They dumped the body in Ralph's bathtub. They acted on orders, but whose? Someone in the shadows called the shots.

Ralph had fallen on hard times. He no longer kept an office. Running a business is tough, any business, including a detective agency. Ralph had the temperament and skills for the work. That didn't keep doors from slamming in his face. Narrow-minded folks didn't cotton to a Negro snooping around in their lives, probing into the privacy of people in decent society. Excellence at his craft held little water when it came to making a living. A man needed jingle in his jeans to survive. A man needed to earn a buck. Ralph needed bread and eggs on the table and a roof over his head. If he had packed it in as a detective, what was he doing now to earn that jingle?

I couldn't shake my recollection of Ralph's former employer, a two-bit twit in a three-piece suit. The devil in disguise sported tailored pinstripes, a Borsalino fedora, and a gem on his pinkie finger that might've been copped from the Crown Jewels. Fumes of French cologne wafted over the man but failed to cover the stench of rat.

The man's MO was simple, park his pompous ass in a watering hole, entertain a bevy of bimbos, and ride herd on the ponies who delivered drugs to his clientele. While the music played and the dancers swayed, he plied a blonde or three with hooch, puffed on his cigar, and waited for the dough to roll in.

Ralph Waldo was once one of those ponies. He carried marijuana or whatever the market demanded and bore the risk of getting caught, all for chump change. If Ralph got caught, he knew to keep his yap shut. A tour in the clink was temporary. There was no coming back from a bullet behind the ear or a bath in the river.

One evening, I spotted Ralph's former employer. The king and his court were at the Kaliko Kat, a nightclub on Broadway. I watched as he delivered instructions to Ralph Waldo. Ralph tucked a paper bag inside his jacket and left. That didn't sit well with me, so I approached the throne. A muscled goon intercepted me, but I grabbed the goon by the family jewels and decked him with a roundhouse.

The king watched his bodyguard go down and chuckled. He applauded and offered me employment on the spot. The man's name was Reginald Dexter. I declined Dexter's offer and promised him he'd get the same treatment I gave his bodyguard if he didn't loosen his grip on Ralph. A couple of pals on the police force backed up my threat and added one of their own—strictly off the record: leave Wichita or get shipped out in a box. Dexter didn't take it well, but he left town.

♦ ♦ ♦

Verdant fields of winter wheat thrived outside Wichita. Green fields gave way to gray dust and tumbleweeds as I pushed on. For a decade, harsh winds, unreliable moisture, and a relentless sun had beaten down crops and farmers alike. As the Dirty Thirties drew to a close, hardy souls broke ground and planted seed, but that number of souls had dwindled. Fewer farmsteads survived the end of the decade.

Traffic picked up. At Pratt, Greensburg, and crossroad junctions, cars and trucks fell into the caravan moving west. We inched toward Dodge City. Neighbors and strangers tooted horns and waved. Hollywood's cattle-call resounded through the countryside. Folks responded, eager to play extras in the once-in-a-lifetime extravaganza.

East of Mullinville, I picked up Highway 154 and drove northwest, past Fort Dodge, then bumped over the tracks into Dodge City. Traffic clogged busy streets, not only cars and trucks, but cowboys on horseback, and horse-drawn wagons and stagecoaches.

Before the Great Depression hit, Dodge City had boasted a population of ten thousand citizens. A decade later, population estimates were closer to eight thousand. Those numbers meant nothing that day. Visitors would increase the population a dozen times over during the next few days. Each visitor would be another stalk in the haystack. Somewhere in that haystack was a single needle I intended to find, a needle named Ralph Waldo.

Movie stars on a train christened the Warner Brothers Special drew closer. Citizens and visitors couldn't wait. Crowds motored over streets and strolled along sidewalks, anticipating the arrival.

Farmers, cowboys, and businessmen wore Stetsons, pearl-buttoned shirts, and boots with pointed toes. Wide belts with silver buckles held up their jeans. Overalls and suits remained in the closet. Men scratched newly-grown beards and twirled waxed mustaches. Ladies wore bonnets decorated with ribbons. Their bright skirts flowed over billowed petticoats. They strolled in twos and threes beneath frilled parasols.

Jack Warner was no fool. He recognized an opportunity when he saw one. Warner welcomed the lieutenant governor of Kansas with open arms. The dignitary traveled from the Sunflower State to the coast to personally deliver a message to the movie mogul. An invitation written on a buffalo skin, above the signatures of the mayor, the governor, and other officials, offered to premiere the studio's latest movie, *Dodge City,* in the very town featured in Warner's film.

The wheels turned in Warner's head, and he saw dollar signs. Imagine the publicity, the press, the photographs. The country had seen nothing like it. Those bums in advertising couldn't hold a candle to this. They squandered his dough on still photos and press releases, yesterday's news. What a yawn. This was big, big. Reporters and photographers from both coasts would descend on Dodge City. They'd file stories in real time, hot off the press. Their bylines would be read in every jerkwater town in America. The publicity would thrill readers, spur them into theaters, and best of all, the publicity would be free. Moviegoers in every state would line up to see the cowboy picture.

Warner accepted the lieutenant governor's invitation with a beaming smile. He chartered a train and dispatched his stars to Dodge City, Kansas.

For the next few hours I canvassed the town, on foot and behind the wheel, and talked to anyone who would listen. A pair of men, Negroes in jeans and straw hats, approached the corner at Walnut and Second. I showed them the picture of Ralph.

"This is a friend of mine," I said. "I wondered if you've seen him. He's working in town this week."

They looked at the picture and gave me a wide-eyed stare.

"You carry a mug shot, and you say you're this man's friend?" one said.

"That's right," I said.

They didn't believe a word. They said nothing more, just shook their heads and hustled across the street. Other folks reacted the same way. Some were leery of an out-of-towner. Most were too preoccupied and excited to fret over a missing person.

Several men lounged in the shade of an elm in front of a stone house on Vine Street. Some sat on chairs and stretched their legs. Some sat on an overturned bucket or a crate. The group circled a metal washtub where a block of ice and bottles of Grain Belt beer floated in water. Drinking in public was generally frowned upon, but the mood was light, and cops weren't eager to write citations. Dodge City cops and others on loan from Garden City, Cimarron, and neighboring communities strolled the walks in pairs and looked the other way. A quiet beer among friends was just fine.

I handed the photo to a man holding court from a chair.

"What's it, Schmidt?" one of the men said.

Schmidt said, "A wanted man, I reckon. Am I right? Is this man wanted?"

"Only by me," I said. "He's not in trouble, but he's gone missing from Wichita. I believe he's here in town."

"You picked a helluva weekend to lose a man in Dodge City," another man said.

That remark elicited chuckles. Schmidt handed the photo to the man seated next to him. Each man gave it a cursory glance and passed it on. The last man handed it back to me. Someone mumbled, "sorry," and swigged his beer. No one recognized Ralph.

I fared no better in the rest of town. Local citizens were too busy preparing for the big day to worry about a missing person. They'd filled spare rooms with cots, and every bed available was taken by boarders. Hand-lettered signs in windows read, "No Vacancy." The bustle and the signs in the windows didn't change as I moved to neighborhoods away from the center of town.

Dodge City lay nestled along the Arkansas River. I motored up and down streets that ran up and down hills. I buttonholed pedestrians with no luck. Downtown, I chatted with pedestrians and store owners, but no one was interested in talking to a private eye, not on that day.

Floyd Herring was the proprietor of a 24-hour waffle house next to the bus depot. His sign boasted air conditioning inside. The day before, the downpour in Wichita had left me chilled. Twenty-four hours later in Dodge City, the sun shone, and cool air was welcome. I went inside and ordered a cup of coffee. I lit a Chesterfield and slid Ralph's photo across the counter. Floyd held the photo and shook his head.

"Sorry, I couldn't say. He could have been here. I've seen hundreds of new faces, more than I've ever seen. I've never been busier. To tell you the truth, I hardly see customers' faces at all. My head hits the pillow, and all I see are waffles. I'm not complaining. All this hoopla has been a shot in the arm for my bank account and many another, too. I just can't be certain about that fellow."

I thanked Floyd and finished my coffee and cigarette. So it went, up and down the street. The sun set and lights came on.

Moonlight shone over the train depot when I pulled up under a gnarled black locust tree. A chipped grindstone was propped against a log beneath the tree. I nosed the roadster close to the grindstone and killed the engine. Limbs overhead were quiet, but I could expect birds at dawn. I buttoned down the top on the roadster.

I went into the Fred Harvey Hotel. More signs in the windows read "No Vacancy." "No Vacancy" had become a local mantra. The hour was late. At the front desk, a harried clerk worked to appease a lodger upset with his accommodations.

"The room I reserved was to be en suite," the customer said. "En suite, a room and a bath. My room does not have a bath. The only bathroom on the floor is down the hall."

"That bathroom is for your convenience, sir. You are welcome to use it," the clerk said.

"That bathroom is open to the hoi polloi," the lodger said. "That is unacceptable, young man. That is not en suite."

"I'm sorry, sir," the clerk said. "Our en suite rooms are occupied. Every room in the hotel is occupied. I'm sure you understand. The room you have is the best we have available this evening."

"I do not understand at all. Someone altered my reservation. I intend to seek accommodations elsewhere, at another hotel. Tell me what other hotels are available in this town."

"We have a number of fine hotels in the city, sir, the Lora Locke, the O'Neal, the Dodge House, and others, but, sir, every hotel in town is full," the clerk said. "You'll not find another room anywhere for miles. Please accept our apologies and stay with us. May I offer you a complimentary meal in our restaurant for your inconvenience?"

The two men continued head-to-head. I left them to iron out the details and entered the restaurant. The hour was late, but the dining room bustled with patrons. Waitresses hoisted trays and glided from table to table. I spotted a table for two and took a chair.

"Coffee?" the waitress said and filled my cup.

A trio of elderly gentlemen occupied a table nearby. They turned when I came through the door, gave me the old up-and-down, then went back to their conversation. One of the men faced my direction and glanced over, then turned to his companions when I made eye contact. The dapper fellow wore a suit with a vest and a tie. He had white hair, a matching mustache, and a lean, hard look on his leathery face.

Diners at the next table giggled and fawned over their food, open-faced sandwiches on dark bread. The waitress followed my gaze.

"That's the house specialty," she said. "Well, it's the house specialty this week."

"What is it?" I said.

"It's called the Midnight Frolic. It's caviar and boiled eggs on rye, topped with tomato, Roquefort cheese, olives, and let's see, oh, yes, pickles and onions. It's very popular."

"Caviar in western Kansas?" I said. "Did they pull those fish eggs out of the Arkansas River?"

The waitress looked miffed, so I smiled and winked. She returned my smile.

"We borrowed the recipe from the chef at the Lora Locke. He created it long ago, a local hit. People have come through town for years asking for it." She leaned over and whispered, "Especially high-rollers and wannabes."

I wondered which category the foursome next to me fell into.

"Caviar and I are not complete strangers, but we rarely appear at the same table," I said. "How does it taste?"

The waitress reddened.

"I've never eaten it. I can't afford the two bucks," she said.

"No need to be embarrassed," I said. "You appear to be a prudent woman."

I glanced over at the couples. They'd probably eaten fresh farm food all their lives and never tasted caviar, let alone a two-dollar sandwich. The night was special, and the sandwich was a sinful treat.

"I'll have bacon, eggs, and toast," I said. "Make it hen's eggs."

The waitress wrote down my order and gave me a thumbs up. A diner had left a copy of *The Dodge City Globe* at my table. An advertisement portrayed Olivia de Havilland holding a match to Errol Flynn's Chesterfield cigarette. Errol looked pleased. Why wouldn't he? Olivia de Havilland had never lit my Chesterfield cigarette.

I struck a match and lit my own cigarette. I soothed my bruised ego with caffeine and nicotine. Since my arrival in town that afternoon, I'd gone to bat more times than the Bronx Bombers in the World Series. The Yankees often hit the ball, but I'd struck out every time. Ralph Waldo remained in the shadows.

The waitress arrived with my late-night breakfast and refilled my cup. The three men stood up and said their goodbyes. Two men moved toward the door. The third man with the white hair and mustache looked my way. He walked over with his cup and saucer, placed them on my table, and sat down.

"Mind if I join you?" he said.

I chewed a bite of eggs and shrugged.

"Have a seat," I said to the man already seated.

"I see you're not much for fish eggs," he said. "Can't say as I blame you. I'm a meat and potatoes man myself. Have been for eighty-five years. I've always preferred food over cuisine. You don't say much, do you?"

"I'm just enjoying my chow—and waiting," I said.

The man furrowed his brow and said, "What are you waiting for?"

"You've been eyeballing me since I walked in," I said. "You have something on your mind you want to say. You didn't come over here to talk about fish eggs."

"I was right. I made you for a cop the minute I laid eyes on you," he said.

He reached across the table and stuck out a hand.

"Hamilton Bell's my name. Folks call me Ham."

Bell's handshake was firm.

"Pete Stone," I said, "Private investigator out of Wichita."

"Yes sir, I said to those fellows, that man is a cop. That man didn't come here to see a picture show."

"I've heard of you," I said. "My dad told me stories about you when I was a kid. You're quite the lawman."

"I was in my day, tall hog at the trough. That was long ago. I was a lawman for three dozen years, marshal, sheriff, and a deputy before that. Not many men lasted thirty-six years in the law, not in Dodge City they didn't. Many a man lived a quick life in the early days. That was before we got civilized. I knew Wyatt Earp and Bat Masterson. I was there the night Bat's brother, Ed, was murdered."

Bell paused and sipped his coffee.

"Listen to the old coot yammer," he said. "In spite of the way I go on, I'm not prone to braggadocio. I just wanted you to understand who you're talking to. I have one question, Pete Stone. What are you doing in Dodge City?"

We locked eyes. I sipped my coffee. Neither of us blinked.

"Still the lawman?" I said.

"You know better than that. Once a lawman, always a lawman. If you're asking me do I have any authority these days, the answer is no. I'm long retired." He leaned forward. "On the other hand, if I was to snap my fingers, this dining room would be crawling with cops. You know how that would go. The police would haul you downtown, set you down under a hot lamp until you felt more inclined to talk."

The waitress arrived and refilled our cups.

"Thank you, Marjorie," he said to the waitress.

Ham Bell spoke the truth. His words carried weight in Dodge City.

"I'm happy to talk," I said. "I've been talking all day to people all over town. I just don't like to be pushed. I'm looking for a missing person."

I handed over Ralph's picture.

"I've shown that to lots of folks, but no one has seen him. It's more likely they've seen him but don't recall him. Folks have their heads in the clouds at the moment."

"That's the truth," Bell said. "Folks right now don't talk about anything but Hollywood, Errol Flynn, or that picture show. Most of it is gossip. Is this man wanted?"

"Not by the law. That picture was taken long ago," I said. "His name is Ralph Waldo, and he's a private eye. When we work together, he's my partner. When we don't work together, he's my friend. I have reason to believe he's here in town. He might be on a case or he might be hired labor helping your town get ready for tomorrow. I believe he's in danger. I'm not the only one looking for him. I intend to find him before someone else does."

"Who else is looking for him? Why would he be in danger?"

"I don't know the answer to your first question. As for the danger, a couple of goons stepped on me in Wichita. They warned me off my investigation."

"And you didn't listen because you don't like to be pushed. I didn't think you were born with that schnoz. Why would a couple of goons give a whit about a private eye and a missing person?"

Ham Bell's gaze didn't waver. An owl would lose a staring contest with the man.

"They were more interested in the body," I said.

"Aha," he said, "of course, the body."

"The goons who worked me over tried to frame Ralph Waldo for murder. They left a body where it would be found."

"So, the police are involved."

"Lieutenant McCormick is the homicide detective on the case," I said.

"Lieutenant McCormick," Bell said. "I know Thad. He's a good man."

Bell looked at the photograph, then at me.

"You're telling the truth," he said. "You're not telling me everything, but you're not lying, either. I'd have to be a fool to think you've told me everything. You'd be a fool if you had."

"I've been roaming your streets and looking under rocks since I arrived in Dodge. So far, I've found nothing. White folks are too busy to talk, or they're not interested, or both. Negroes clam up.

They don't trust a stranger. Meanwhile, Waldo's missing. He's close by."

"Your man could be living under anybody's roof," he said. "There's lots of out-of-town labor here, men and women, preparing for the big do. We have bigots in this town same as other places, but Dodge City is no sundown town. People here don't judge a man by his color. Most people don't anyway. In my day, cowboys of every color drove cattle into town, whites, Negroes, Mexicans. Even Indians drove cattle. By the time they reached Dodge City, cowboys were so covered with trail dust skin color didn't matter. All that mattered was the color of their money."

Ham Bell sat back. We relaxed and filled an hour. He discussed the old days, and I took it in. I'd passed muster with the retired lawman, so we smoked tobacco and swapped stories. Bell was orphaned young, but he was resourceful, and he made his way to Kansas in his teens. He'd sold jewelry in Pennsylvania and earned money by cleaning clocks. Bell lit up when I told him about my collection of timepieces.

"How'd you come to acquire an Austrian Zappler Animated clock?" he said.

"I was on the lookout for a man, and the trail took me to Hot Springs, Arkansas. I spotted a curio shop in the center of town that had a Seth Thomas banjo clock in the window. The clock lured me inside. I own a Seth Thomas, but I wondered if the owner had other clocks for sale. Carina disappeared behind a beaded curtain and returned with the Zappler cradled in her arms. It was trimmed in gold and ivory, intricate detail, hand-crafted with delicate precision, and it was nestled under glass. It was love at first sight."

"You bought it on the spot."

"No, I didn't. It was out of my price range. I told the lady I didn't have the money to buy it. Carina said not to worry. She was sure fortune would smile on me. She promised to hold the clock until the cash found me. She knew I wanted the clock, and she wanted me to own it. Carina turned out to be an oracle. Fortune did smile on me.

Before I left Hot Springs, I came into a windfall, and I bought the clock."

"Good for you," he said. "Things worked out. What about the man you were looking for? Did you find him?"

Ham Bell fixed me with that steady gaze.

"Yes, I did," I said.

What I didn't mention was that the man I had trailed to Hot Springs that long ago day was Ralph Waldo. Ham Bell pulled a pocket watch from his vest and announced it was after midnight.

"I'm not as young as I once was. I'd better get some shut-eye," he said. "Tomorrow's a big day. Good luck with your search, Pete Stone. Tread lightly. Citizens are excited about the festivities, but lawmen around here are edgy. We're not accustomed to having this many folks in town. We don't want any trouble."

"Neither do I," I said.

We settled our bills and called it a night. Outside, I approached my roadster and spotted a figure in the shadows. Someone sat atop the grindstone near my car. That someone watched me. I stopped several feet away and waited. The shadow stood erect. Long legs and curves told me the figure belonged to a woman. Although I couldn't see her face in the shadows, I knew the woman was stunning. Even in the dark, I was sure she wore a green dress and a matching cloche. The woman spoke.

"We need to talk," she said.

Chapter 9

I froze when she spoke and waited for my eyes to adjust. I scanned the scene and peered into dark corners. Only a day had passed since the salt and pepper tag team had mashed my nose against the wall and used my torso for a punching bag. I was wary of sounds in the dark and strangers who lingered in the shadows. Neither leggy dame nor hired hit men would get the drop on me that night.

"Put your purse on top of the fender and step away," I said. "Hold up your hands and keep them where I can see them."

The lady did as I said.

"Move closer, into the moonlight."

She stepped out of the shadows, one long leg at a time. Moonbeams haloed her hair and revealed a slender neck and shining face. Her beauty would make Aphrodite weep with jealousy. The aroma of Tabu came with her. I recognized the scent because a salesgirl had touted it for Lucille's birthday gift. I'd chosen Joy instead.

"Who are you and what are you doing here? Why did you follow me to Dodge City?" I said.

Her face broke into a wry grin.

"Is something funny?" I said.

"Slow down, cowboy. Ease up on the twenty questions. May I lower my hands?" She did so and said, "I left my six-shooter in my other bra. I only want to talk."

I listened to crickets and sounds of the city. Patrons moved through hotel doorways, and low voices came through open windows. I heard nothing suspicious nearby. If anyone lurked behind a parked car, they remained silent. The lady traveled alone. I moved forward, toward a pair of eyes aglow in the moonlight. Once upon a time, long ago in another place, those deep, dark pools might have swept me in.

"That's better," she said. "Gotta cigarette?"

I pulled a pair of Chesterfields from my pack and discovered my matchbook was empty.

"I have matches in my purse," she said and turned toward the roadster.

I rested my fingertips on her arm.

"Let me," I said.

Her wry grin returned.

"Aren't you the gentleman?" she said.

I rooted around and found matches, no gun. I lit our cigarettes.

"Now for some answers," I said. "Who are you and why are you here?"

"I'm nobody of note," she said and blew smoke into the night. "My name is not important. I'm not looking to make a new pal."

"No dice, lady," I said. "Who are you?"

"My name is Stella Grace. And you are Pete Stone. There, now we're pals."

"We're not pals," I said. "Stella Grace. Stella is star. 'To the stars through difficulties.' Is that you?"

She didn't reply.

"You saw me earlier today," I said. "If you tailed me from Kingman, I'd have spotted you. Yet, here you are. Why? I don't like being followed. Did someone tip you I was here?"

"You're certainly full of yourself," she said. "You act like Pete Stone is the only person who rolled into this burg today. Haven't you've noticed? These hills are crawling with people. They're like ants in the sugar bowl. Maybe I traveled here like everyone else for hundreds of miles, to see those Hollywood stars. I didn't tail you. We did see each other earlier. You traveled west. I traveled west. Where else would we be going? You didn't drive forty miles outside of Wichita to eat a hamburger at a diner."

"How did you find me?"

She glanced over her shoulder at my roadster and looked back at me. That grin was becoming a permanent fixture.

"How many people drive a 1919 Jones Six Roadster?" she said. "You're about as difficult to spot as a float in the Easter parade."

A two-door Buick was parked a few feet away.

"I spotted that coupe in Wichita, from the window of an apartment on Ninth," I said. "It was raining, but I made out a brunette at the wheel. You looked up at the window, gave me the eyeball, and drove off. Today at the diner, you gave me the once over. You still haven't told me why you're here, and don't tell me you're mooning after Hollywood actors. I don't buy it. You're cagey, but you keep popping up. You said we needed to talk. Talk."

She dropped her cigarette butt and ground it beneath her shoe.

"I'm here to meet someone arriving on the train," she said.

"Who?" I said.

She shook her head and said, "It's no one you know. You're looking for someone. I'm waiting for someone."

"How do you know I'm looking for someone?" I said.

"I nosed around," she said.

Agnes knew I was looking for Ralph Waldo, but this dame didn't get anything from Agnes.

"You talked to Harlow Hubbard," I said.

"The hat man," she said. "You walked out of his shop wearing a new fedora. A detective leaves a murder scene and visits a warehouse. Then, he goes shopping for a hat."

"So, you were following me," I said.

"That was yesterday," she said. "Nothing added up. You wanted more than the hat. You wanted information. After you left the store, I talked to the hat man. A lady can get information, too, if she asks the right questions."

Stella Grace could've gotten the number to Harlow Hubbard's bank account and a mention in his will if she'd gone for them.

"You're looking for Ralph Waldo," she said.

"How do you know Ralph?"

"I've never met him," she said.

"You idled your coupe in front of Ralph's place, the scene of a murder, and you never met him. How did you know it was a murder scene?" I said.

"May I have another cigarette?" she said.

I held another match for her and allowed her time to come up with an answer to my question.

"I didn't know it was a murder scene, not until I arrived there," she said. "I knew Amos Johnson from when we were kids. I knew what he did for a living. I've been afraid it would end badly for Amos. I've never met Ralph Waldo, but Amos talked about him. Amos visited Ralph at his apartment. I was looking for Amos and thought he might be there. Instead, I found you and the cops crawling all over the place. It wasn't hard to figure what had happened."

"Is the person on the train connected with this?" I said.

"The person on the train is Miriam Johnson, Amos's sister. She's a bit player in Hollywood. She doesn't know about this. I telephoned her yesterday, and her roommate answered. Miriam had left on the train for Dodge City, the train due to arrive tomorrow. She doesn't know that her brother is dead."

"Yesterday, you tailed me. Today, you're not tailing me, but you've been on my heels. That stop in Kingman was a coincidence? I don't buy it. I don't know what your game is, but, lady, you serve up more screwballs than Carl Hubbell."

"Who's Carl Hubbell?"

"Pitcher, New York Giants. Doesn't matter," I said. "Talk straight."

"You have a reputation," she said. "You're unorthodox, but you're dogged. You get results. You're looking for Ralph Waldo, and you won't stop until you find him. I've told you the truth. Amos's death came as a shock, but it was no surprise. He ran with bad company. You're afraid Ralph Waldo is in for the same. You have reason to be afraid."

She came closer.

"You've already been roughed up," she said.

An owl hooted.

"Who wants Ralph Waldo dead?" I said.

"The same person who murdered Amos Johnson would be my guess. We're both looking for answers."

"How well did you know Amos Johnson?"

"We were close as kids. We went different directions, but our paths crossed from time to time. I never forgot him."

"You say his death was no surprise," I said. "Did you warn Amos?"

Stella paused a beat.

"Amos knew the risks. He did what had to do to survive. Some of what he did was outside the law."

"He was a drug dealer," I said.

"Yes," she said. "Crime is a dangerous occupation. Danger includes more than the law. The real danger comes from fighting among themselves. The king of the hill is always vulnerable."

"Amos Johnson's home was Kansas City. Is that where the king resides? Who's vulnerable in Kansas City?"

"Who isn't? Whoever is on top," she said. "The crime scene shifts. The political scene shifts. Those interests overlap. The political pyramid in KC is shaky. Tom Pendergast will be out soon. When he topples, others will follow."

"And others will climb the hill," I said. "Johnson crossed someone. The law didn't stick a blade into his chest. Who did Amos cross, and how does Ralph figure into the puzzle? What was the connection between Amos and Ralph?"

"I want answers same as you," she said. "All I'm saying is watch your back, and don't block me out."

"Why would I do that? We just met."

She stared at me.

"Dim light is good for you," she said. "It shadows that nose job. You could almost pass for attractive."

I wasn't swallowing that bait. Nothing was going to happen between Stella and me. I wasn't dead below the waist, but I wasn't dead above the neck, either. I had a special lady in my life. The dame in the shadows spelled trouble.

"The sun will be up soon," she said. "Get some shuteye."

Stella Grace climbed into the coupe and disappeared into the dark. I climbed into my roadster. She'd mentioned Tom Pendergast, a well-known political boss in Kansas City and a man with questionable ethics. From a Main Street office next to the Monroe Hotel, Pendergast doled out bribes and favors to party loyalists. He'd ruled Kansas City since the mid-twenties. The newspapers predicted his days as a politician were numbered. His reign was under siege.

Whispered rumors developed into open speculation. Pendergast was in failing health. Pendergast and the governor were on the outs. Pendergast was under investigation for tax evasion. The Feds were cracking down on corruption. Pendergast had fallen out of favor with the mafia. Hyenas smelled blood, and they'd be circling.

I took out a Chesterfield. The black and silver matchbook I'd taken from the lady's purse glittered in the moonlight. The cover read, "El Capitan Club, 1610 E. 18th Street," a twin to the matchbook in Amos Johnson's pocket.

I struck a match. The flame illuminated the inside cover of the matchbook. A number was scribbled in pencil, 9892. That was Ralph Waldo's post office box number.

Stella Grace knew Amos Johnson, but claimed she hadn't met Ralph Waldo. Yet, she knew Ralph's street address and carried his P.O. Box in her purse. Was she concerned for Waldo's safety or was my pal next on the hit list? Was Stella Grace devil or angel?

Dawn drew near. The night would be short, but the day would be long. Since there was no room at the inn, my roadster would have to do for a bed. I tossed the cigarette butt into the shadows, and pulled the fedora over my eyes. The lights went out, and I drifted off to sleep.

Saturday

April 1, 1939

Chapter 10

Was it the pink sky on the horizon, roaring motors and grinding gears, or my own aching frame that woke me? Odds were split. Pick 'em. Whatever brought me around that morning was a cruel April Fools' prank. The victim was a beat up private eye, and he wasn't laughing.

I pulled myself to a sitting position, surveyed the landscape, and fell back against the roadster's seat. Staying on the move the day before had allowed me to ignore my body's bruises. It was time to pay the penalty for a few hours' respite. The demons regrouped and left me stiff and sore.

I gripped the steering wheel, pulled myself up again, and got my bearings. The Harvey House was lit up. Customers entered and exited the hotel, vibrant and chattering, laughing and back slapping, all of it annoying. A newsboy propped his green bike against a rail. He freed an ink-stained bag from the handlebars, slung it onto a shoulder, and went through the doors.

I exited my roadster with my grip in hand. A cardinal urged me with a cheer, cheer chirp. I moved through the door and into the hotel. An elderly couple in the hallway looked me over and gave me a wide berth. The lady gasped. Her male companion shielded her, Sir Galahad to the rescue. They watched me disappear into the Gents.

I washed and shaved and splashed on some Aqua Velva. I changed into a fresh shirt, combed my hair, and took a gander in the mirror. I wouldn't win a beauty contest, but I'd no longer frighten old ladies.

The restaurant was packed, and every table was taken. Just as well. My tender innards couldn't handle food on an empty stomach. I tipped a waitress who brought me a steaming cup of joe. I took a seat in the lobby and pulled a flask of bourbon from my grip. I spiked the coffee, lit a Chesterfield, and waited for the medicine to do its work.

When a phone booth opened up, I went inside and dropped a nickel. The operator made the connection, and the phone rang three times before I heard a voice.

"McCormick."

"Happy April Fools' Day," I said.

"Only a fool would call me at this hour on Saturday. Where are you, and why are you calling me at home?"

"I'm in Dodge City. I'm calling you at home because I knew that's where you'd be," I said. "Don't tell me you're still in bed."

"It's Saturday and it's early," he said. "You're interrupting my hurkle-durkle."

"Hurkle-durkle?"

"It's a Scottish expression, passed down by dear old Grandad. It means hunker down in bed, pull up the covers, and take an extra hour to snooze. I do that on Saturdays. Not today. You've ruined my hurkle-durkle. I should have taken the phone off the hook. Why am I talking to you?"

"I've trailed Ralph to Dodge City," I said. "I haven't found him, but I think he's close by. I'm not the only one looking for him. I'm keeping an eye peeled for Ralph and watching over my shoulder for that pair of thugs on his trail."

"One Caucasian, one Negro?"

"That's right," I said.

"We fished a pair of floaters out of the Little Arkansas that match that description," Mac said, "right down to the spectator shoes. The lads went for a swim. They'd have made it, too, if they hadn't been weighed down by that lead between their ears. Each man had been popped behind the ear with a .22 pistol. We found blood on a footbridge in Riverside park. Somebody shot them, and off the bridge they went."

"Executed," I said. "Any clues to the killer?"

"We're still investigating. The bridge is a popular stopping point for strollers and couples. It's covered with fingerprints and footprints. We've ruled out a lovers' spat," Mac said.

"Thursday night they braced me outside my place. They took me from behind. I didn't see their faces, only their fists."

"The stiffs we recovered have to be them," Mac said. "The Negro carried a blade that was a cousin to the one we pulled out of Johnson."

"I figure him for Mr. Smith, Ralph's former neighbor," I said. "Did you run this by the landlady?"

"Way ahead of you, pal. We showed her a photo, and she made a positive ID. It was Smith, all right. The landlady didn't seem upset over losing her former tenant."

"Have you talked to Leo Little?" I said.

"Little heard nothing from upstairs on the night in question. He turns out the lights at ten and falls into a coma, his words, until six o'clock the next morning," Mac said.

"That squares with what he told me. The landlady and Little could share the same light switch," I said. "Did Little seem edgy to you? I may have annoyed him."

Laughter came over the phone.

"Stone, you annoy everybody."

"Thanks, Mac. That leaves us with Smith and company. Those two killed Johnson, then someone did them in. What does that mean, and where does it leave us?"

"Those are the right questions," Mac said. "All we have to do is find the answers."

McCormick rang off, and I placed another call. This one answered on the first ring.

"Are you getting in or going out?" I said.

"Does it matter? I'm going to hire a service to screen my calls," Aaron Bernstein said. "Why is a cowboy cop calling me at this hour on a Saturday morning?"

"I thought hurkle-durkle was for Scotsmen," I said. "I didn't know Jews practiced it."

"If you called to make silly remarks, I may have to shoot you."

I told Bernstein where I was and why.

"Dodge City?" he said. "Home of the cowboy. Next, you'll be riding a hoss and yelling yeehaw."

"I met a lady last night," I said.

"You met a lady last night, and you're calling a bookie this morning? I shouldn't have to tell you this, but a gentleman calls the lady the next morning, not a hurkle-durkle Jew, whatever that is. Hang up and send her flowers. It's called etiquette. Ask Emily Post."

Bernstein's laugh sent a chill down my spine.

"Can the corn, tough guy," I said. "I need information from your contact at the El Capitan Club. What does he have on a gorgeous dame, brunette hair, long legs, and brown eyes a fathom deep? She calls herself Stella Grace. The moniker may be phony."

The phone went silent. The throb in my temple kept the beat. I counted a dozen before Bernstein spoke.

"Stella Grace is no phony. That's her name, all right," Bernstein said.

"You know her," I said.

"I know her. We danced the tango a time or two," he said. "We danced, and then we didn't."

"Let's keep the record straight. I only spoke to Stella Grace last night. We did not dance the tango," I said. "She went out of her way to warn me off my hunt for Waldo. She told me Ralph was in danger. She said if I didn't back off, I'd be in danger, too. You tell me. Can I believe what she says?"

"If the lady said it, believe it," Bernstein said. "Stella Grace will slice your chest open and stomp on your beating heart, but if she tells you Ralph is in danger, then bank on it. He's in danger. The same goes for you. A wise cowboy would work on his quick draw. You might grow an eye in the back of your head, too."

The guy next to me leaned forward. He stared to his right, westward, down a set of train tracks that narrowed to a point in the distance. He raised up and checked his watch, a routine he'd followed for the second, third, or twelfth time. The guy on the other side did the same. Folks on the platform willed a vision to appear. They twitched and shifted from foot to foot, antsy as children tugging at sleepy parents on Christmas morning. C'mon, hurry up, it's time.

The Warner Brothers Special would arrive that morning. The crowd grew dense, and elbow room shrank. What began as a gentle bump and a polite, "Excuse me," gave way to not so gentle jostling and pushing. People filled in from behind and jockeyed for position.

I looked over my shoulder and eyeballed the real show. A sea of Stetsons, fedoras, and bonnets stretched as far as the eye could see, uphill to the north and on past the Lora Locke Hotel at Walnut and Central. Two dozen robust souls perched atop the awning of a café on the corner. I pondered the load bearing capacity of the shaky structure. The young men who towered above the crowd seemed unconcerned about toppling off and dropping to the walk below.

Little ones watched their parents fidget and got caught up in the excitement. Belt-high cowboys and cowgirls, outfitted in western duds and adorned with holstered cap pistols, squirmed and tugged at their mothers' skirts and pleaded, "When's it gonna get here?"

McCormick's news of the floaters in the river meant Smith and associate wouldn't be sticking yours truly with a knife. They were out of the picture, a good thing. On the other hand, if someone wanted me toes up, another assassin might step up. Salt and pepper would be replaced by another culprit unknown to me. That was a bad thing.

I couldn't figure why someone was after Ralph. What did he possess, what did he know, that made him a threat? I had to get to

Ralph Waldo and watch my back. Bernstein was right. I didn't have a third eye. I'd keep both of mine open.

Voices rose in mumbles and grumbles. The sea of humanity parted, and a chain of open-air limousines inched toward the platform. The mayor and businessmen and local dignitaries, all adorned with newly grown mustaches and beards, waved to the crowd. A train from Kansas City arrived from the east bearing the state governor and other dignitaries. An earlier train from the east coast had passed through town during the night, loaded with reporters and celebrities. That train was to hook up with the Warner Brothers Special west of town and make a grand entrance with the Hollywood bunch.

Shortly after ten, a whistle sounded in the distance. Someone yelled, "Here she comes!" The crowd cheered. An escort of airplanes roared overhead. A shape appeared far down the track. The Warner Brothers Special, its engine wearing a broad, yellow grin, rumbled and rolled and whistled. It grew larger and larger and hissed to a stop at the platform. The band played, "Oh, Susanna," and the throng broke into song. Ornery kids lit firecrackers and whooped.

Doors on the train opened. Stars paused in vestibules and waved as a speaker at the microphone introduced each celebrity. The crowd applauded at the sight of Humphrey Bogart, Ann Sheridan, John Garfield, Alan Hale, Jane Wyman, and a host of others, all flashing Hollywood smiles. Finally, the headliner appeared, the star of the picture, Errol Flynn. The swashbuckler turned cowpoke raised his Stetson, and women shrieked. Several women yelled, "I love you!" If the tabloids could be believed, old Errol had loved more than a few of them right back.

I kept an eye out for Ralph, a near impossible task in the thick throng. Young men attired in western getups hustled to and from the train, created a path, and escorted celebrities. Others toted bags. I didn't spot Ralph among them.

Boring politicians horned in at the microphone and delivered boring speeches. Photographers pointed cameras at the stars and ignored pleas from the master of ceremony to stand back. When the last speech ended and the microphone went silent, the mass of humanity oozed away from the platform, up Central toward the Lora Locke Hotel. The Lora Locke, the fanciest hotel between Wichita and Denver, was the weekend home of the stars. Guests would freshen up and eat lunch before joining a parade and taking in a rodeo.

I stayed behind on the platform. The festivities weren't for me. The afternoon and evening would be packed with events, and the film would run all night long, over and over on several screens. Stars would circulate between the Dodge, the Crown, and the Cozy theaters to mingle with viewers and sign autographs. Everyone would have a good time, but I wasn't on vacation. I still hadn't spotted Ralph.

The young men who'd ushered celebrities stayed back, too, and loitered in the shade of a cottonwood. They looked to be high-schoolers. They'd seen to the needs of the Hollywood gang. Staff at the Lora Locke Hotel would attend to the stars there. What was next for them?

I strolled over to show them Ralph's picture. One by one, they glanced at the picture and shook their heads. Train doors down the line banged open. Someone said, "Let's go." The men shuffled out of the shade and moved toward the train. Passengers in rear cars appeared in the vestibules.

"Who are these folks?" I said to a redcap.

"They're Hollywood, same as the others, 'cept these folks don't have stars on their doors," the redcap said. "They're mostly stunt folks, extras, and such. The bigshots won't risk a star's neck shooting an action scene, and you can't shoot a crowd scene without a crowd. That's who these folks are."

The local cowboys helped passengers down from the train. They ushered guests, offered arms to the ladies, and toted luggage.

I buttonholed one of the ushers and said, "Where are you taking these people?"

"They're staying at the Trail Inn," he said.

The Trail Inn was located a few blocks from the station, on the corner of Avenue A and Chestnut. Baggage handlers loaded luggage into waiting vehicles. Most of the passengers waved off the vehicles and chose to stretch their legs the short distance to the hotel. People strolled off in twos and threes.

I moved to fall in with the migration when another person emerged from the last passenger car on the train, just ahead of the caboose. A Negro woman appeared in the vestibule and shaded her eyes with her hand. She looked to her left and to her right. No one was nearby to help her. The vehicles had departed, and the redcap had moved to the front of the train.

She came down the steps hefting a cardboard suitcase and struggled against its weight. I walked over and touched the brim of my hat.

"May I help you with that?" I said.

The lady froze and glared. She gripped the handle with both hands and shook her head.

"No, sir. I'm doing just fine," she said and tipped her nose up. "I'll thank you to let me be."

She turned and quick-stepped to catch the group. I held back for a moment, then followed. Those at the front crossed over Chestnut at Central and followed the sidewalk east toward the hotel in the next block. The lady trailed at the rear.

Up ahead, a dark man in a cowboy hat appeared from the alley. His back was turned to me when he walked out of the shadows and tipped his hat to the lady. The man leaned over and spoke a few words, then he took the suitcase. They walked together behind the rest of the group.

I walked faster. I hadn't seen the man's face, but his Stetson was a twin to the one I saw at Harlow's Hats. I maneuvered around pedestrians crowding the walk to close the distance between us.

A dark sedan up ahead squealed around the corner at Avenue A. The driver gunned the engine. Loud pops like gunfire rang out. A woman screamed, and folks ducked. The driver leaned on the horn.

Teenaged boys leaned out the window and hooted and hollered at the crowd. They sped around the corner and disappeared.

A pair of cops on the walk watched the car go by.

"Stupid kids," one said.

"Just backfire," said his partner.

The man in the Stetson had stepped in front of the lady and shielded her with the suitcase. He pushed his hat back and turned as the car went by. The western duds threw me, but there was no doubt the man under the Stetson was Ralph Waldo.

People around me laughed nervously and made jokes about shoot 'em up cowboys in the old west. People yapped and pointed and shook their heads. A wisecracker said, "Where's Wyatt Earp when you need him?"

I elbowed my way through the crowd toward Ralph. Another car, this one a Buick coupe, pulled over at the curb. A door opened, and Ralph and the lady climbed in. I called out Ralph's name, but the door slammed shut. The car pulled away. Ralph and his companion were gone.

Chapter 11

ollywood visitors lingered on the steps of the hotel. Others had gone inside and on to their rooms. I didn't make the driver of the coupe, but it had to be Stella Grace. The woman from the train must have been Miriam Johnson, Amos's sister. Three women chatted together on the steps. One of them asked me for a light.

"Say, do you know the name of that woman who got into that car a moment ago?" I said.

"No. I saw her on the train, but I don't know her," she said.

One of the others said, "She's pretty quiet. She didn't say much on the train, at least not to me. Her name is Miriam something or other, not the friendliest person."

The other woman spoke up.

"She's not rude, really, more like suspicious or wary. Like a little puppy that's been kicked one too many times. She wanted to be left alone."

"Is she an actress?" I said.

The woman raised her head, threw back her shoulders, and said, "Honey, we're all actresses."

Her companions laughed and slapped each other on their backs.

"That's right, sister," one said.

"You tell him, Tina," the other said.

"We answer cattle calls," Tina said. "We work all day for part-time pay and dream of that first speaking role. Then, when the picture wraps, we go back to waitressing or giving manicures or cleaning hotel rooms."

"Or whatever else it takes to pay the rent," her companion said and dropped her eyes to her feet.

"But if someone asks what we do for a living," Tina said, "We tell them the truth. We're in show business."

I thanked the ladies and walked back toward my car. I drove city streets and searched for the coupe. If Miriam was a friend to Stella, she was safe. Ralph's safety came with a caveat. I didn't trust Stella and didn't know if she was an ally. She denied knowing Ralph. Why? What was her game?

I drove for an hour up and down over the hilly terrain of Dodge City. On Spruce Street west of Central, an elderly gentleman sat on a bench in front of a red brick building. I pulled up behind a hearse at the curb and killed the engine. The man on the bench crossed his legs, placed his hands behind his head, and watched as I exited my roadster. A smile appeared beneath his white mustache.

"Well, aren't you the enigma?" he said. "A gumshoe who collects antique clocks and drives a classic automobile. Next, you'll be telling me you read a book. You're a man of mystery, Pete Stone."

Hamilton Bell teased.

"I'm no mystery, Ham, just a throwback," I said. "I appreciate things that last, and I'm slow to change. I don't jump on the bandwagon until the bandwagon has come to a halt."

A sign on the brick building bore Bell's name.

"This your place?" I said.

"This is one of them," he said. "I only told you about my life as a lawman. Along the way, I managed a business or two."

"Like the Elephant Livery Stable," I said.

Bell laughed and said, "You heard about that, did you? Folks came from far and wide to see my stable. It was the biggest structure in these parts back them. I met a lot of good folks in that stable. I owned a dance hall for a brief period, too, and I've owned an ambulance and a hearse. And I've done some other things. How did you come to acquire a Jones Six automobile?"

I told him the story of recovering stolen jewels for a former client, a man of wealth who at that particular moment was short on cash.

"In lieu of cash, he offered me the car as payment for my services. I accepted," I said.

"You were outside the Trail Inn today when that carload of youngsters created a disturbance," he said.

Bell's conversation veered quicker than a Kansas twister. Not much escaped the man.

"How could you possibly know that?" I said. "Are rowdy youngsters dragging the streets newsworthy?"

"They're not newsworthy," he said. "They're just ornery school boys who happen to be all-state athletes, the golden ticket to fame and glory in a small town. It doesn't hurt that their daddies are merchants and bankers and such. They're high strung and connected and get away with foolish antics. Those boys have had their run, and they know it. They'll graduate next month, and when they do the sun will shine on another dog's ass. Some will go on. Others have reached their peak. I didn't mean to talk about those boys. I was wondering how your investigation is going. You were asking after a woman, a gal who came in on the train and disappeared in a vehicle."

The cops on the beat must have heard my conversation and passed it on to Bell.

"I asked after the gal. I found my missing person, too, and lost him a moment later. He disappeared in that same vehicle. He's here in town, at least he was. I haven't located the Buick coupe. He came here for a reason. Someone was after him in Wichita. Maybe he needed to get away."

Two youngsters decked out as cowboys strolled toward us on the walk. A small boy, three or so, drew his cap pistol and snapped off a shot. Ham Bell ducked and pointed his finger. "Pow! Got you, Dennis."

Dennis let out a grotesque, "Argh!" grabbed his tummy, and spun to the walk in a pirouette. He lay sprawled, tongue hanging out.

"Dennis is Marjorie Hopper's boy," Bell said, "the gal who waited on you last night. That tyke was born with imagination. I wouldn't be surprised to see him in a picture show one day, if I live long enough."

Dennis's companion yelled, "C'mon!" and the little guy sprang his feet. He ran after his pal.

"I carried a gun back in my day, but I never shot a man," Bell said.

"I wish I could say the same," I said.

"I had an advantage over a private cop," Bell said. "I wore a badge. That badge gave me privilege to draw my gun. I drew before the other guy did. The toughest criminal goes weak at the knees staring down the barrel of a Colt .45. People used to say I was quick on the draw. I wasn't fast. I was first. There's a difference."

We talked a while longer. Ham Bell was a teenager back east when a cattle rancher named Henry Sitler built the first house in the area. George Hoover set up a tent saloon west of Fort Dodge and sold whiskey to the soldiers. Cattle and whiskey birthed a town.

The restless teenager back east worked his way to a new life in the west. When the railroad arrived in Dodge, Ham Bell rode in on its heels. He planted roots in Dodge City. He and the town grew up together.

After a while, we said our goodbyes. I left the gentleman sitting on the bench. My stomach needed more attention than the coffee and bourbon I'd swallowed at dawn, so I drove to Floyd Herring's 24-hour waffle house.

It was mid-afternoon, and the rush was over. People lined up for the parade that wound through city streets. Crowd noise and music a block away made its way into the diner. The band replayed, "Columbia, the Gem of the Ocean," a tune featured in the movie.

I ordered scrambled eggs and a waffle. Floyd set the plate on the counter, refilled my coffee cup, and poured a cup for himself. He lit a cigarette and leaned back on the counter.

"You're the guy who was looking for that missing fella," he said. "You're a private detective."

"I thought you didn't remember faces," I said. "You said you see nothing but waffles at night."

"That's me all right. I dream about waffles, but something happened yesterday, not long after you were here. Something that shook me. A man stopped in, not a local. He didn't pass himself off as a pretend cowboy, either. He was dressed in a suit, like you are, but this guy was brawny and unshaven. He said he was looking for a guy, too, same as you, and the description he gave me fit that fella in the picture you showed me. His tone was none too friendly, if you know what I mean."

"Did he say why he was looking for my pal?" I said.

"Nah, that's all he said, but something told me he was up to no good. I might've forgotten about it, but he did something else. The rush was over, like now, and I was in the kitchen standing over the griddle. I keep an eye on the dining room through the pass-through," he said and thumbed over his shoulder to the opening in the wall. "He was alone at the counter, and he pulled a revolver out of his jacket, checked the cylinder, and tucked it away again. The whole thing took only a few seconds, but I didn't breathe easy until he forked down his last bite and left. That cash register gets a mite hefty by mid-afternoon, and I've been robbed before."

Another customer came in. Floyd took his order and moved to the kitchen. I finished my meal, slipped an extra buck under my plate, and left.

<h1 align="center">Chapter 12</h1>

The parade ended, and the mob migrated toward the rodeo grounds. The streets were busy but passable. I continued my search for the coupe.

A rodeo in western Kansas was a common spectacle, but Dodge City officials had been under the gun to produce a quality show in a limited time. Jack Warner came to the rescue. To perform alongside local talent, Warner embellished the occasion with seasoned rodeo stars, stunt men, and horses. All arrived on the train amid promises to make the show grand.

I drove to the grounds and parked as the band played the final notes of "The Star-Spangled Banner." The bleachers were packed, and a sign at the entrance read, SRO. Standing room only looked sparse. An Illinois fellow who'd been in the news, Robert Wadlow, was reputed to be the tallest man alive at a shade under nine feet. Wadlow himself would have disappeared in that crowd.

Ralph Waldo would not be a spectator at the rodeo. If Waldo was nearby, he'd have a job to do. I strolled behind the chutes and livestock pens and nosed around. A guy in a suit and a fedora didn't blend in with cowboys, but the hands were busy, and nobody took notice. Young men who'd been on the train platform earlier helped out at the rodeo.

These were genuine cowboys, men who worked every day with cattle and horses, not drugstore variety cowpokes. The gentlemen downtown would pull off their polished boots at sundown on Sunday and don a coat and tie on Monday morning. These real cowboys wore dusty boots with rundown heels from countless tug-o-wars with lassoed calves and steers. Faces and hands were as leathery as their boots and just as scarred and dusty.

Both in the saddle and on foot, cowboys moved slowly and spoke in soothing tones so as not to startle the animals. The "yippees" and the "yahoos" were saved for the public to watch on the big screen, for those people who paid to see the beast and the buckaroo perform.

A cowboy wiped his forehead with a bandana and nodded at his partner. The pair ushered a bronco toward the chute where other hands took the reins and positioned the horse. A rider eased onto the saddle.

The bronco busted out of the gate. The rider tugged on the reins and flapped one arm in the air and brought his stirrups down on the horse's neck. The crowd roared. The horse dipped and spun. The cowboy sailed through the air, and the buzzer sounded. He landed in the dust, a half-tick out of the money. He picked up his hat, slapped it against his thigh, and waved at the applause. He'd lost, but he'd try again. I knew the feeling. I had a job to do, and Ralph wasn't around, so I left.

I stopped at all three theaters downtown and asked after Ralph with no results. Each location was prepped and ready to entertain crowds.

"Maybe he'll usher when the show starts," I said to a theater manager.

"Nah, we've got high-schoolers lined up for that," he said.

I drove through town as the light dimmed and shadows grew long. The sun winked goodnight on the horizon. I pulled up at the Trail Inn and went inside. I played a hunch, not certain if Ralph had a room at the hotel. If he did, he might stop in to freshen up before the nightshift.

I spotted the clerk and crossed the carpeted floor. Potted ferns spread their fronds at either end of the desk. I asked the clerk for Ralph's room number. The man in shirtsleeves and a tie didn't hesitate. He gave me the number of a room on the second floor. I found it at the end of the hall.

I knocked on the door, and no one answered. I knocked again and called Ralph's name. Still no answer.

Back downstairs, I leaned over the desk, summoned the clerk, and made a request. He listened with crossed arms, his expression that of a cigar store Indian. His reply was curt.

"Of course, you may not have a key to his room," he said.

"This is important," I said. "The man may be in danger. He could be in his room now, unconscious or worse. I need to check. You need to check."

"I'll be the judge of what I need to do," he said. He turned and glanced at the cubbyholes on the wall. "The room key is right here. No one is in the room. It will remain unoccupied until he returns. We at Trail Inn do not hand out keys to strangers."

"I'm not a stranger," I said. "I'm his friend."

"So you say."

"I'm also pals with Ham Bell. You know Ham Bell, don't you? If I call on Ham, he'll snap his fingers and fill this hotel with cops," I said.

My bluff didn't work. The clerk didn't fold.

"Mr. Bell and the city police are welcome at the Trail Inn," the clerk said. "You, sir, are not. Good day."

The clerk turned and disappeared behind a closed door. I rapped my knuckles on the desk and turned to leave. A cleaning woman caught my eye. She flicked a feather duster over a lampshade and the table beneath the lamp. She worked her duster over surfaces of chairs and tables and edged toward the front desk. She stepped behind the desk and dusted a counter that ran along the wall. She kept the duster moving, and with her free hand removed a key from a numbered cubbyhole.

She came from behind the desk and stowed the duster on her cart. Then, she glanced my way and moved to the stairs. I waited a moment and went up myself. The maid waited near the end of the hall.

"Was you telling the truth? Are you really Ralph's friend?" she said.

I assured her it was true. I explained I was Ralph's friend and business associate.

"Business associate? Just what business are you in?"

I gave her my card.

"So, Ralph Waldo is a detective? Well, I'll be. I've seen it all. Ralph's a nice man. I wouldn't want anything bad to happen to him."

"Neither would I."

"How about Mr. Bell? He's your friend, too?" she said.

"We had dinner just last night," I said.

"I'll bet you did. How long have you known Mr. Bell?"

"What time is it?" I said.

She studied me and chuckled. Then, she dropped the key into my hand.

"I suppose you're telling the truth," she said.

"Because I have an honest face?" I said.

"Because you're a terrible liar," she said.

I pressed a buck into her hand and thanked her. She giggled and shook her head and muttered, "Ham Bell," as she walked away. I unlocked the door and went inside Ralph's room.

The furnishings were Spartan, an unmade bed, a nightstand with only a lamp, and a couple of hooks on the wall with empty wire hangers dangling from them. Two shirts and a pair of slacks were thrown over a straight back chair. I checked the garments, and the pockets were empty.

In Ralph's grip, I found socks and skivvies, some worn, some laundered. A shaving kit contained standard grooming items, razor, toothbrush, toothpaste, and such. I returned the kit to the bag. Something caught my eye. Nestled between folded socks, the corner of an envelope peeked out. The envelope bore a Kansas City postmark. Inside was a letter inked in delicate cursive:

Ralph,

> *A.J. has disappeared. It's too late to help him. He's dead or will be soon. Those who took him suspect you to be A.J.'s accomplice. They will come for you.*
> *Leave Wichita now. Depart from Union Station and go to Dodge City. A train from Los Angeles will arrive on April 1st. Be there when it arrives.*
> *You'll have no trouble finding work. Enclosed is cash to help you along.*

> *Ad astra per aspera.*

To the stars through difficulty. Stella Grace must have written the letter, the woman who claimed not to know Ralph Waldo. Stella knew Ralph. Stella knew Amos Johnson. Did she know who did him in? Did Ralph have answers? I sat back on the bed and waited for him to return.

Chapter 13

Voices in the hallway brought me awake. A door in the distance opened and closed. The room was dark. I hadn't intended to fall asleep, but exhaustion had caught up with me. I lay stretched out on the bed, Ralph's letter on my chest. Ralph had not returned.

I pulled the chain on the lamp and checked my watch. I'd napped for an hour. I returned the letter to Ralph's bag. Then, I washed up in the bathroom next door. No one was at the front desk, so I placed the key in its cubbyhole and left the hotel.

The sky was clear, and the moon shone bright. The honeyed scent of a linden tree wafted in the evening air. The aroma conjured a memory. It took me back to my brothers and a trio of cousins, goofy kids giggling and running in the moonlight way past our bedtimes. Was that yesterday or a lifetime ago? Summer nights stretched back decades, each a mere tick on the cosmic clock, from chasing fireflies in the shadows to chasing death in the shadows.

Voices and traffic noises caught my attention. I boarded the roadster and drove over to the Lora Locke Hotel at Walnut and Central. Pedestrians mingled on the sidewalk, hoping to glimpse a movie star. Others huddled and waited for the next show at the Dodge Theater.

I went inside the Lora Locke. The glow from a brilliant, crystal chandelier bounced off a skylight and cast a warm glow over ivory-toned octagonal columns. An ivory hued ceiling was trimmed in rosewood. Seven steps rose to another floor and a fireplace flanked by potted greenery and a pair of flags, the stars and stripes on one side, the blue state flag bearing the seal and gold lettering on the other. A marble floor polished to a high gloss reflected the scene. The Lora Locke deserved its moniker as a fine hotel. It boasted the elegance of big city counterparts.

Remaining evening festivities would take place at the Lora Locke and the three theaters showing *Dodge City* throughout the night. Stars circulated from venue to venue and mingled with the locals. I'd circulate as well.

I touched the brim of my fedora and passed by a clerk at the front desk. The clerk nodded. Near the dining room, a familiar voice came from a telephone booth. The booth's door stood open, and a crowd gathered to listen, all to the apparent delight of the speaker. A slight man in a fedora barked into the receiver. His squeaky, staccato voice was recognizable to everyone within earshot. Walter Winchell dictated his next "Man About Town" column to an assistant in New York City.

"That's what I said, sweetheart, 114 cases of scotch. That's right, 114. And that was just the press corps."

The crowd laughed.

"We surged into Dodge City on a wave of alcohol. Oh, it was a swell trip."

Winchell laughed along with the crowd. Everyone joined in, even the teetotalers. Kansas's complicated history with alcohol divided its voters. Some people voted wet, others voted dry. State law prohibited the sale of intoxicating liquor, but the law allowed taverns to sell beer.

Congressmen played both sides of the aisle with a common goal, appease voters and get reelected. Governments never learned. Legislating morality was a fool's game and had been since the snake slithered into the Garden. The Sunflower State didn't suffer a lack of moralists. Do-gooders were always eager to dictate how others should live. The law said no whiskey, but Kansans imbibed sprits. Citizens enjoyed booze, and life went on, just as it had since the serpent seduced Eve, and Eve seduced Adam.

Down the hall a bell dinged, and elevator doors opened. A tall, handsome man stepped off the elevator. The movie star himself stood amidst a throng of assistants, each lady an adorable beauty. The entourage came my way.

"Excuse me, Mr. Flynn, may I trouble you for an autograph?" I said.

Errol Flynn, glassy-eyed and grinning, said, "Sure," with an elongated "shh," like a librarian hushing a noisy patron. An assistant handed him a glossy, eight-by-ten headshot.

"Make it out to Agnes," I said.

Flynn wrote, "To Agnes with Affection," and autographed it with a flourish.

"Thank you," I said. "You've just made a fan very happy."

"Give her a kiss from me," he said with a wink.

He walked away but didn't get far. A woman outside the telephone booth shrieked and yelled, "Errol Flynn!" A mob descended on the star. His assistants linked elbows to control the crowd. Flynn threw back his head and laughed.

Patrons in the dining room heard the racket and swarmed like bees. I stepped aside, then made my way toward the dining room. A waitress at the door watched the commotion. I showed her Ralph's picture.

"Have you seen this fellow?" I said.

She looked at the photo and said, "Are you a cop?"

I introduced myself and gave her my card.

"He may have been around," she said. "There's lots of temporary help now. He doesn't work in the kitchen. He may have been out back unloading trucks. I tell you, mister, I've been on my feet for twelve straight hours. At this point, I wouldn't recognize a snapshot of my husband."

Among the tables, some empty, some occupied, were two women sitting together, a Caucasian and a Negro. I walked over.

"Mind if I join you, ladies?" I said.

"You're that masher. Go away."

"Miriam, dear, this is that private detective I was telling you about." Stella Grace turned toward me and said, "Pete Stone, this is Miriam Johnson."

"How do you do?" I said and took Miriam's hand. "My condolences."

"Thank you," she said.

"Sit down," Stella said.

"I'm sorry I was curt with you," Miriam said. "Momma taught me to be on the lookout for mashers. I've been away too long, I guess. Midwestern manners don't exist on the west coast."

"No apology is necessary," I said.

The ladies accepted cigarettes. I put a third Chesterfield between my lips and struck a match, lighting theirs, then mine.

"Three on a match," Miriam said. "That's unlucky."

Stella noticed the black and silver matchbook I'd taken from her purse. She flinched, and I tossed the matches onto the table.

"There's a number inside the cover," I said to Stella, "Ralph Waldo's post office box. Put it in your address book. By the way, I read the letter."

Stella said nothing.

"I spotted Ralph Waldo this morning," I said. "He sidled up to Miriam outside the Trail Inn. They both got into your car, and the three of you disappeared. You told me you didn't know Ralph."

A waitress stopped at the table, refilled the ladies' coffee cups, and filled another cup for me.

"I met Ralph this morning," Stella said. "First time I laid eyes on him."

"You sent a cryptic letter, cash enclosed, to a man you've never met?" I said. "That hardly seems likely. Then, when you did meet him, you took him for a spin in your coupe? Is that what you'd have me believe?"

"It's the truth," Miriam said. "Neither of us met Ralph before this morning. He came to me. He introduced himself to me."

That squared with what I'd witnessed that morning. Ralph had approached Miriam.

"Amos talked about Ralph over the telephone," Miriam said. "I was in L.A. at the time."

"Okay, you met Ralph today. Where is he now?" I said.

"He's worked all week. He and others like him unloaded trucks, decorated the downtown, and carried what needed to be carried," Stella said. "He's been busy."

"This burg shipped in enough food to supply the Hollywood commissary for a month," Miriam said. "I've never seen so much food. I thought this was a sleepy little town."

"Not this weekend it isn't," Stella said.

"Ralph worked all week," I said. "Today is Saturday. I've combed the town since I spotted him this morning. If he'd been on the job, I'd have spotted him again. I think Ralph is under wraps, and I think you two dames did the wrapping. Fess up."

"Ralph is ready to leave with us," Stella said. "We expect him to meet us here any time. He and others were hired to work during the week while students were in school. This weekend, students are taking over, ushering, waitressing, and what have you," Stella said. "Ralph's work is done."

"The Negro lifts the bale and totes the baggage," Miriam said. "The white folks rub elbows with the celebrities."

"Hush that talk," Stella said. "Miriam worked today. She fulfilled her obligations to the studio, the luncheon, the parade, and the rodeo. Now, we're all going to Wichita. Miriam and I will do what needs to be done for Amos. He deserved that. You'll excuse us if we're not feeling festive at the moment."

"Ralph is meeting you here?" I said.

"That's right. He'd planned on taking the train in the morning. I offered to drive him."

"Where has he been all day?" I said.

"Holed up at the Trail Inn," Stella said.

"No dice," I said. "I just left his room. He's not there."

Stella looked at Miriam. Miriam lowered her eyes.

"He didn't stay in his room," Stella said. "That was my idea. Dodge City is crawling with visitors, too many to recognize the one who might try to harm Ralph. It seemed easier to keep him under wraps, as you put it. He stayed in Miriam's room."

"When he gets here, we'll leave," Miriam said. "He's collecting his pay."

"Where?"

"Next door, at the Dodge Theater. His boss told him to stop by this evening."

"Look, ladies. I'm not leaving town without Ralph," I said. "I'll get him to Wichita. You might as well head back now. I'll go to the theater and retrieve him."

They huddled together and agreed. I left them at the table and exited the hotel. I tossed Flynn's picture into the roadster and reached under the dashboard for my Smith & Wesson .38. Stella Grace was right. Any stranger could be the one who'd harm Ralph.

I walked over to the Dodge Theater. People waited for the next movie in a line that stretched up the block. I stepped up to the ticket booth.

"This show is sold out. You might try the Crown or the Cozy," the lady said. She swiveled her head side-to-side and leaned forward. "A floor seat at the Cozy is only a buck. We charge three dollars for a floor seat here."

I placed the photo of Ralph on the counter.

"I'm looking for this man," I said. "He's meeting his boss here this evening."

She picked up the photo.

"Is Ralph in trouble?" she said.

"You know him, good," I said. "No, he's not in trouble. Is he inside?"

"He was," she said, "but he left. He and that other fellow left together. They went out for a cigarette."

Ralph Waldo didn't smoke. The short hairs on my neck tingled.

"Who was the other fellow?"

"I didn't know him. He had his arm around Ralph, like they were friends."

"Can you describe him?"

"I can tell you I didn't care for his looks. I wouldn't date him."

"Which way did they go?"

She pointed to the corner and said, "That way."

I quick-stepped past the Lora Locke's entrance, stopped at the end of the building, and peeked around the corner. A shape on the sidewalk caught my eye. I crept closer. Ralph's bag lay abandoned in the dim light. I hugged the brick wall and inched down the walkway. At the rear corner of the hotel, voices came from the alley.

"You have one minute," a voice said. "Talk now or I plug you."

A labored reply came from a familiar voice.

"I don't have what you want," Ralph said. "I don't understand why—."

A fist slammed flesh. Ralph groaned. I clutched my gun and eased around the corner. A bulb over a doorway cast light over two shadowy figures. Gravel crunched beneath my feet, and a figure pivoted. A gun barrel glinted in the light, followed by a crack and a whistle. The gunman shielded himself behind Ralph and fired blindly into the dark.

I leapt from the shadows and brought down the butt of my pistol. The man grunted and staggered. His fedora saved his coconut from splitting open. He weaved, and I smashed a loaded fist into his face, knuckles and steel turning his nose to mush. A bullet pierced a barrel of garbage. Another swing caught him on the chin. He groaned and staggered away. His pistol landed in the alley with a thud.

I started after him and stopped. Ralph stood frozen. I called out his name. He extended his arms, fingers splayed, and backed away.

"It's me, Ralph! It's Pete! Pete Stone!"

Ralph focused wide eyes. His shoulders slumped, and his voice quavered.

"Pete?"

"Yes, Ralph. It's me."

Ralph shook. He bent over, hands on his knees, and threw up the contents of his stomach. The moment passed, and he stood up, still shaking. Ralph had been where few men ever venture. Ralph had peered into the abyss, that bottomless void, and returned from the brink.

"Pete," he said.

I caught him as he fell forward. Footsteps and voices approached from further up the alley. Gunfire had drawn attention.

"What's that noise?" Ralph said.

The man I'd decked had been swallowed by the shadows. If he avoided the men coming toward us, he'd melt into the crowd. I wanted to go after him, but I couldn't leave Ralph. I was in no mood to hang around and answer questions. I needed to get Ralph to safety, to Wichita.

"Shots up this way! Peel an eye and watch your step, boys!" a voice said.

"That's our cue, pal," I said. "Let's get the hell out of Dodge."

Monday

April 3, 1939

Chapter 14

When Agnes arrived at the office that morning, the coffee was brewed. Errol Flynn smiled out from the framed photograph propped on her desk. Agnes came into my office as I lit a cigarette. She carried a steaming cup in one hand and the Hollywood star's headshot in the other. I tucked my matches into my coat pocket. She leaned over and pecked me on the forehead and clinked her cup against mine.

"You're the best," she said.

"For the record, Errol advised me to give you a kiss," I said, "from him."

"Errol did, huh? You know how to treat a lady," she said. "You found Ralph?"

"We rolled into Wichita Sunday morning," I said, "the wee hours."

"You kept your promise. I didn't really expect this picture and autograph, but thank you. And you said you'd be back at your desk today. Here you are. That must have been some trip."

"I've had quieter weekends," I said.

"You don't look worse for the wear," she said. "Your nose looks better. You might tell me about that hand you stuffed into your pocket."

It was tough to slip the old curveball past Agnes. I rested my hand on the desk.

"Those knuckles are raw," she said. "Spare me the gory details. Just tell me the guy deserved it."

"He deserved it. He disappeared, but he was breathing through a bent schnoz. He may need dental work."

"Where's Ralph?"

"I left him with his folks. He'll lie low for a while. Then, he'll find a new address. Ralph can't go back to the apartment where killers dumped Amos's body. He doesn't want to draw attention to his parents, so he'll leave their place soon."

"Why does he have to lie low?"

"We may see an encore performance. This isn't over, Agnes. Somebody wants Ralph dead. It has something to do with Amos Johnson, a connection from their past, dealing drugs or something else. Ralph left the drug business when he began working with me. He's assured me of that, and I believe him."

The phone rang, and Agnes answered it.

"He's right here," she said and handed over the receiver. "Lieutenant McCormick."

"Mac," I said.

"You're alive and at your desk. That question's answered," he said.

"What question?"

"A pal was asking after you," Mac said. "This pal wondered if you were alive. He told me a tale of gunshots in the night, signs of a scuffle in an alley, and an unregistered firearm found at the scene. This pal of yours heard the news, connected the dots, and immediately thought of you. Why would that be Stone? Why would he think of you?"

"Because Hamilton Bell is a good cop, and Hamilton Bell hears everything," I said.

"Ham Bell. I knew you'd get it. So, now I'm the one with the questions. What kind of hijinks have you been up to, and how in the world does Ham Bell tie you to a scuffle in a Dodge City alley?"

I told Mac about trailing Ralph to Dodge City and crossing paths with the town's native son.

"Ham Bell keeps his finger on the pulse of his town. He knows everything. I came upon Ralph's would be assassin and took action. The man got away, but I got Ralph."

"Is he okay?"

"He's back home. I promised Waldo I'd find his son, and I did. That was to be the end of it, but it won't be. Somebody is after Ralph. Do you have more on those floaters you dragged out of the river?"

"Small-time losers, former juvenile delinquents," Mac said. "They began with petty theft and upped the ante to stolen automobiles and armed robbery. They met behind bars, each doing a nickel at Leavenworth. They were paroled a year ago and partnered up. The murder-for-hire tag team called themselves Smith and Jones, if you can believe that. Their real names were Moon and Boyd, Monte "Midnight" Moon and Alex "Bullet" Boyd. They killed Amos Johnson. We don't know who paid for the job."

Mac's voice trailed off.

"What aren't you telling me?" I said.

"I'll do what I can, damn the politics. There's pressure from above to close the case, tag it a drug deal gone bad, and move on. We have a victim, and we have the killers. Case closed."

"This might have nothing to do with drugs," I said. "This goes beyond Amos Johnson."

"Speaking of Johnson, a sister showed up. She identified the body and wants to claim it," he said. "The coroner's not ready to release it yet."

"Was the sister alone?" I said.

"The coroner mentioned a real looker who was traveling with her."

"Are they still in town?" I said.

"I have no idea. How do you know the sister?"

"I met them in Dodge City. The sister came in from Hollywood."

"Yeah, Miriam Johnson," Mac said. "She calls herself an actress. She waitresses and cleans houses to pay the rent on a skid row dive, but she's earned a few bucks as an extra in the movies. That makes her an actress. According to what I've got, she hitched a ride out of Kansas City when she turned sixteen and never looked back."

"Ralph and Amos Johnson knew each other back when," I said. "Johnson mentioned a sister from time to time. Ralph asked about her once, and Johnson didn't say much. Ralph thought she might be dead."

"She's alive. Her brother's dead," Mac said. "How does a small-time dealer from Kansas City end up dead in Wichita?"

"*Mors certa, vita incerta.*"

"Speak English."

"Death is certain, life is uncertain," I said.

"Whatever you say, Stone. Ham Bell asked me to call him back," he said. "Is there anything you want me to tell him?"

"Tell him I drew my gun, but I didn't fire. He'll appreciate that."

♦ ♦ ♦

M-DC-DX, letters scratched in the margin of the newspaper, were Ralph's notes, not Roman numerals. We drove across Kansas through the predawn Sunday hours. I explained how I found the corpse in his apartment. He gazed into the dark and listened in silence.

"That woman told the truth," he said. "I didn't want to believe her."

"Stella Grace mailed the letter to you."

He shrugged.

"She called me at home," he said. "I reached for the newspaper and made notes, M-DC-DX."

"Stella Grace called you?"

"It was a woman," Ralph said. "It must've been her. She gave me instructions and warned me to follow them if I wanted to stay alive. She told me I had to get out of town. A ticket would be waiting for me at the train station. She said to go to Dodge City and wait for the train from Hollywood. Dodge City, DC in my notes. Amos Johnson's sister, Miriam, would be on that train. That's the M. A room was reserved for me at the Trail Inn. People were looking for help to get ready. She suggested I get a job until the train arrived."

"When did you receive the letter?" I said.

"It arrived the day I got the phone call," he said. "She must've thought I'd ignore the letter. I would have, too, if she hadn't enclosed a C-note. She called to light a fire under me, but that money lit my fire."

"A hundred bucks? She must have dough. The letter said Amos Johnson knew too much. Someone thinks you know something," I said.

"I don't know what that would be. We had a strange friendship," Ralph said. "After I quit Dexter, Amos and I lived in separate worlds. He knew I'd moved on, and he respected that. He didn't discuss his business, except—."

Ralph went silent.

"What?" I said.

"I got another phone call," he said. "A man said he was in town, onto something, and wanted to meet. Then, the phone went dead."

"Did you recognize the voice?"

"No. The man whispered, in a hoarse voice, like he was excited but couldn't talk. I figured it was a wrong number."

"When was that call?"

"A few days before the woman called."

"Stella Grace. How does she figure into this?"

"I don't know," Ralph said. "She wanted me to go with them."

Ralph stared into the darkness.

"Some detective," he said. "I get an anonymous letter and an anonymous telephone call, and now my life is turned upside down. Those women were strangers to me. I didn't know Miriam, but Amos showed me her picture one time. She'd sent it from California, a glossy shot where she was wearing one of those old-timey gowns like women do in cowboy pictures, parasol and all.

"Why do those women care about me? Why give me money? I thought Amos Johnson was alive and well. I thought that woman who called me was setting me up to be her patsy. I thought she was setting me up to take the fall in a heist, or something worse. My imagination ran wild. I never figured I was in danger. Who'd come after me? I hadn't done anything to anybody. I made up my mind to finish my job in Dodge, collect my pay, and go back home. I collected my pay. That's when a guy stuck a heater in my ribs."

"Somebody wants you out of the picture."

"Like they took out Amos Johnson," he said.

"Somebody thinks you and Amos shared something," I said. "M for Miriam, DC for Dodge City. That leaves DX. You mentioned Dexter."

"I could be wrong," Ralph said.

"It's speculation," I said, "but you noted it."

Ralph turned toward the window.

"Amos and I were in the same business in those days. The man recruited us both. That man is the only connection I can draw between us. Reginald Dexter. We both worked for Reginald Dexter," he said.

Reggie Dexter. I'd pried Ralph from the clutches of Dexter, once before. Wichita police had ordered Dexter to get out of town and stay out. Ralph broke his connections with crime, shrugged off his past, and went straight. He'd carved out a life as a private detective. Now, that life was threatened. Dexter was back.

"Dexter," I said. "DX."

Friday

April 7, 1939

Chapter 15

"You haven't been yourself, Pete. Are you sure you want to go out? We can go another night."

"Not a chance, gal o' mine. This is opening night, and we aren't going to miss it. Here we are."

I pulled over to the curb. *Dodge City* was showing at The Miller Theater, six days after the premiere in its namesake town. Lucille read me. Ralph was safe in Wichita, but for how long? Waldo had informed me over a shoeshine that Ralph had moved into his own place.

"It's not much of a home, but he was in a hurry. He insisted he had to get out from under our roof," Waldo said.

We both knew he couldn't stay undercover indefinitely. How long could a young man stay cooped up inside four walls? He had to resume his life.

I reached for the door handle, and Lucille placed a hand on my arm.

"You're preoccupied. Is it Ralph?" she said.

"Not tonight. Tonight, it's you and me, sweetheart," I said.

"I'm glad you didn't watch the movie earlier," she said.

"I wanted to save it for this night," I said, "with my special gal."

I'd been busy in Dodge City, too busy to take in a picture show.

"I understand," she said, "but it's not just tonight. You've been preoccupied for days. Is it Ralph?"

Violence shadowed my profession. Lucille met me when her husband went missing. She hired me to find him. His body turned up floating in the river, but when the cops ruled it a suicide, Lucille didn't buy it. Her husband had been murdered. I pursued the criminal and brought him to justice.

Eventually, Lucille became my gal. She cared for me and fretted over the dangers my job posed. She'd already lost one man. She wouldn't handle losing another. She asked a question and deserved the truth, at least enough truth to avoid a lie and put her at ease.

"Someone tried to kill Ralph," I said. "I stepped in. That was six days ago. Six days, and nothing has happened. It's been too quiet."

"Quiet is good, isn't it?"

"When it stays quiet. I can't shake the feeling that it isn't over. I have to be ready, but I don't know for what."

"Ready how? What are you going to do?" she said.

I leaned over, put an arm around Lucille, and squeezed.

"What I'm going to do is enjoy the evening with my lady. I'm going to watch a shoot 'em up cowboy picture starring the handsome Errol Flynn."

"And the beautiful Olivia de Havilland," she said.

We exited the roadster and walked to the corner of Douglas and Broadway. We crossed Douglas and strolled the half block to the theater. A line of people on the sidewalk stretched from the ticket booth to the north. The film would be a sellout. Patrons shifted and glanced at their watches, craned their necks to eyeball those ahead of them, and fretted over whether there'd be a ticket available when they reached the booth.

"Oh, my," Lucille said. "Do you think we'll get in?"

"I know we will," I said.

The Miller Theater and *The Wichita Eagle* had a longstanding relationship together. Sometime earlier, the theater had treated our paperboy, Rusty, and a host of other carriers to an evening at the movies. The photograph of smiling lads in the next day's edition brought goodwill and free advertising for both the theater and the newspaper.

When Rusty delivered the *Eagle* to my office, I palmed him cash to purchase tickets in advance for Lucille and me, and tipped him enough to buy tickets for his family, as well. There would be no long line for us that night. Our ducats were in my pocket.

Lucille and I went right inside. Lucille "yummed" when she smelled popcorn. I bought a bag at the refreshment stand, and the usher found seats toward the front of the theater.

Lucille squirmed like a schoolgirl. "I'm pleased you waited to watch this with me," she said again. "You must have been the only person in Dodge City who didn't watch it the first night."

The theater filled, the lights dimmed, and the buzz of voices lowered. The screen lit up with an animated feature, Mickey and Minnie Mouse hosting a surprise party. The cartoon entertained the audience in the early going, but toward the end it devolved into an advertisement for the National Biscuit Company. More than a few patrons groaned.

A newsreel came next, followed by a blare of music. The opening credits for *Dodge City* rolled across the screen. Moviegoers cheered and applauded as each name appeared in mile-high script, Errol Flynn, Olivia de Havilland, Bruce Cabot, and the list went on. Whether the stars knew it or not, the Sunflower State had adopted each member of the cast and made each one an honorary Kansan.

Set in 1872, the fast paced story was Errol Flynn's first cowboy picture. He played a sheriff determined to clean up the lawless town of Dodge City run by a violent, lowdown killer and thief. Gun play, barroom brawls, and stampedes kept the audience on the edge of their seats. Scenes in brilliant Technicolor looked realistic, and no one seemed distracted by mountainous landscapes on the horizon. The film was shot in southern California, not the flat prairieland of western Kansas. No matter. This was a Kansas story, and its heart was in the heartland.

The good guys teetered on the edge of disaster, but at the last moment our hero swooped in and brought down the villain. Music and hoorahs ushered the victor into the sunset, his gal by his side.

We cheered the happy Hollywood ending. The lights came up, and the audience hooted and hollered. A teenager nearby bounced out of his seat and said to his pals, "Let's watch it again!" The youngsters ran out to line up for another ticket.

Lucille and I walked outside. A crowd of people huddled on the sidewalk and waited for the theater to clear. They shifted from foot to foot. "Don't tell us how it ends," one said, and people laughed. Smells of burning tobacco and fresh popcorn mingled in the air. Scattered clouds inched across the sky beneath starlight and moonbeams.

"Dinner, drinks, both?" I said.

"How about something sweet?" Lucille said. "Cake at the Eaton? It's nice out. Let's walk."

We walked with others, a laughing, chattering throng of people.

"Isn't Errol Flynn handsome?" a woman said.

"I was too busy watching Olivia de Havilland," her male companion said. The woman gave him a playful elbow.

At the Douglas intersection, a figure appeared from around the corner. A man reeked of alcohol. He weaved and bumped into Lucille. She let out an, "oof," and fell into me.

"Watch where you're going, lady," the man said.

I grabbed him by the sleeve as he turned away.

"Watch your language, mister," I said. "It was you who ran into the lady. Apologize."

He struggled, but I held him tight by the back of his collar.

"Apologize, mister," a pedestrian said.

Others chimed in.

"Yeah, say you're sorry."

"Let me go," he said.

He pivoted and swung a left hook over my head. Bumps on the sidewalk are common, but this guy was going to apologize. He scanned the onlookers.

"Apologize," I said.

He hung his head and said, "Sorry, lady. My mistake."

I released him, and pedestrians moved on. The man didn't go far. He backed off a few paces and stopped under a streetlamp. He brushed his sleeve with his fingertips and straightened his hat and his collar. Then, he looked up and gave me a gander of his sour puss, the cut above one eye, the bent nose. He threw back his shoulders and grinned, a gap in his maw.

"See you around," he said.

"Wait!" I said.

The man squirmed upstream through the crowd. I followed. He crossed Broadway in the middle of the block, and disappeared around the corner at First. I turned the corner and saw no sign of him. I peered into doorways and shadows and came up empty. He was gone.

Lucille was alone in a crowd. I hustled back to her, and she gripped my elbow.

"Pete, what a horrid creature," she said. "Why did you leave me? Do you know that man?"

I shook my head and said, "I don't know him, but we've met."

The incident dampened the evening. We walked three blocks from Broadway to St. Francis in near silence. Lucille asked for a cigarette, and I lit hers and mine. I considered my options as we walked and mentally kicked myself. The goon got close to us and slipped away.

I opened the door at the Eaton. In the lobby, a man and a woman sat together on a couch. The woman read a magazine, and her companion puffed on a pipe. The clerk at the desk waved, and I touched the brim of my fedora.

A familiar waitress greeted us, and Lucille gushed about the movie.

"Oh, I can't wait," she said. "We're going tomorrow, Saturday matinee."

She seated us next to a window. We declined the menu. Lucille ordered chocolate cake, and we added coffee for two.

"Sweetheart, I'm going to shake the tree," I said.

"What's that mean?" Lucille said.

"I have to go out of town, just for a day," I said. "That guy could be anywhere, and I can't sit and wait. There's also another guy in Kansas City I need to see."

"Should I be worried?" Lucille said.

"I'd feel better if you left town, too, until I get back."

The waitress brought coffee and cake. Lucille tasted a bite, closed her eyes, and said, "Ambrosia." She forked a bite of cake and reached across the table.

"Taste this," she said.

I nibbled.

"Ambrosia," I said.

"You're impossible," she said. "Who doesn't like cake?"

"Cake is swell, if there's nothing else," I said. "I just never understood the fascination. Cake can't stand up to Mom's apple pie or Aunt Vera's lemon meringue."

"Pie over cake. That is so wrong," she said. "My sister already asked me to visit. I'll stay over for the night. They're decorating eggs."

"Eggs?" I said.

"You heathen," she said. "Sunday is Easter. She asked me to go to church with the family and stay for dinner. I'll be fine."

Lucille ate cake while I smoked and sipped coffee. When she finished, the waitress removed her plate and refilled our cups. Lucille opened her purse.

"I'm going to freshen up," she said. "I hope I remembered my lipstick."

She looked inside her purse and started to stand, then sat back down and pushed her purse away.

"Oh, god," she said. "I'm think I'm going to be sick."

She held her napkin to her face and shook her head, back and forth. I reached for her purse and looked inside—a brush, a key ring, a beaded wallet, and other ordinary items. Nestled on top of a handkerchief was one item that didn't belong. Lying atop a handkerchief was a single tooth.

Saturday
April 8, 1939

By late morning, I'd reached the outskirts of Wichita, my roadster pointed north. It had been one week since locating Ralph in Dodge City; nine days since discovering Johnson's body in the bathtub.

Lucille had been shaken the previous night. The goon with a gap in his grin had planted his dislodged tooth in her bag, a calling card meant for me, a card that said, "This isn't over. We'll meet again."

I held Lucille in my arms until she fell asleep. That morning, she scrambled eggs while I made coffee and toast. Lucille telephoned her sister and confirmed the visit, then packed a bag. I made phone calls while she packed.

Lieutenant McCormick listened to my report on the incident with the assailant. He assured me a car would patrol Ralph's neighborhood. Ralph said he'd stay alert and not leave his place for next day or so.

We left Lucille's place together. She blew a kiss and drove off. At my place on Lewellen, I bathed and shaved and changed into a pressed suit. Then, I left town, too.

At Newton I picked up Highway 50 and headed northeast toward Kansas City. I had questions that needed answers. I rolled through Peabody and on to Florence. Only a couple of years earlier, our country's president had visited Florence on one of his famous whistle stop tours. Franklin D. Roosevelt delivered an address from the rear platform of his campaign train and assured the crowd that the economy was coming back. Voters responded and elected him to another term in office.

An hour later I reached Emporia and drove through the downtown intersection at Commercial Street. To the east, a city auditorium was going up, a massive structure scheduled to open the following year. Building new schools, churches, libraries, and auditoriums did more for the confidence and welfare of a community than a politician's promises. I had to tip my fedora to FDR. The economy was looking up.

Past Exchange Street I rolled into a Sinclair station and pulled up at the pump. An attendant in a white shirt and bowtie said, "Fill 'er up?" and I touched the brim of my hat. I stepped away and smoked a cigarette. The young man wiped the windshield, checked the oil level and tire pressure, then hung up the hose. He swished his rag around the gas cap and cleared away drops of fuel.

"Ninety cents, sir," he said.

I handed him a dollar and told him to pocket the dime. He smiled and said, "Thanks." A few blocks down the road, a diner beckoned. A train in the distance blew its whistle and rolled alongside a grain elevator. I went inside the diner, empty that midafternoon, and took a stool at the counter.

"How's the coffee?" I said.

"Hot and fresh," the lady said and reached for the pot. "Anything else?"

I sipped the coffee and declared it delicious.

"This'll do," I said.

A carousel behind her showcased golden-crusted pies.

"Say, you wouldn't have a slice of Mom's apple, would you?" I said.

She glanced behind her and said, "Well, let's see. I'm a mother, and I baked those pies. Is that good enough?"

"Sold," I said.

The coffee was fresh and hot, and the homemade pie was delicious. I ate it with relish.

"For a moment there, my legs were back under Mom's table," I said. "Thank you. I'm glad I stopped in."

"I appreciate that," she said. "Most travelers shovel food into their faces with no more than a grunt. Most figure a kind word isn't necessary."

"Next time you bake a pie for your youngsters, remind them to thank their momma," I said. "I wish I could."

◆ ◆ ◆

The city noted for lively music and tasty barbecue grew up at the confluence of the Kansas and Missouri Rivers. The Kansas City jazz district was on the Missouri side of the river at Eighteenth and Vine. Some called it the jazz hub of the country. Musicians from far and wide dropped by to jam in local night clubs. Businesses thrived in the neighborhood, many owned and run by Negroes.

Amos Johnson had lived a few blocks east of the jazz district on Euclid. I passed through the Vine intersection and continued on Eighteenth Street. A rib joint on the corner teased me with a pleasant aroma of barbecue. I turned into the neighborhood of single family clapboard houses, brick apartments, and small businesses. Aaron Bernstein had knocked on doors and asked after Johnson. He'd gotten the cold shoulder for his efforts. Neighbors didn't talk about Johnson. At least, they didn't talk to a white man come calling.

A sign on the roof of a liquor store read, "Ernie's." The establishment had bars on the windows and a weathered bench along the wall. A dark-skinned man with Popeye forearms and a Bluto expression sat cross-legged on the bench. A hand-lettered sign in the window said, "OPEN." I parked at the curb.

Popeye eyeballed me. A cigarette dangled from lips beneath a bent nose and cauliflower ear. I got out of the roadster.

"How're the Monarchs looking this year?" I said. "You think Satchel's ready?"

The man's puss wrinkled into a frown. His yellow-nailed fingers pulled the cigarette from his lips. He glared.

"What you be talkin' about?" he said.

"Pitcher? Satchel Paige?" I said.

Satchel Paige had hurt his arm in the Mexican League the year before. The Kansas City Monarchs was the only franchise in the Negro Leagues who bet on his comeback.

"You yapping nonsense," he said.

"Not a baseball fan, huh?" I said. "Is Ernie in?"

"Why don't you go through that door and see for your ownself?" he said.

I went through that door. Bernstein had talked to the owner, but I had more questions. A dark man with gray hair and a shiny face sat atop a stool behind the counter and read a newspaper. He glanced up when the bell tinkled, looked my way, then turned back to the *Kansas City Star*. He gnawed on a toothpick as he read.

"The nice man out front suggested I might find Ernie here," I said. "Would that be you?"

Ernie read the obituaries.

"You from Kansas?" he said without looking up.

"Does it show?" I said.

He removed his toothpick, inspected its purchase, and wiped it on his sleeve.

"I get Kansas trade," he said. "Kansas trade keeps me off the breadline. One day that governor of yours will grow weary of Jayhawk dollars making a one-way trip across the state line. One day your Congress will change the law, and you folks will buy your whiskey at home. Then, I'll retire. I'd sooner retire now, but I can't afford to. Business is too good. What'll it be? Bourbon? Scotch? Gin?"

I hadn't intended to buy whiskey, but old Ernie had a point. Whiskey was a tough bargain in the Sunflower State.

"Bourbon, Four Roses."

He wrapped the bottle in brown paper. I motioned to the obituaries.

"Lose someone?" I said.

"Not this day," he said. "I check every day looking after friends. I look for my own name, too. So far, so good."

I handed over some bills.

"Amos Johnson died," I said. "What can you tell me about him?"

The cash register dinged, and the drawer slid open. Ernie slipped the money into the tray and slammed the drawer shut.

"Amos Johnson. That's twice in one week a white man darkens my door and twice a white man asks me about Amos Johnson. The other white man was dressed better than you. You look like a cop."

I gave him my card. He took it with the tips of his forefinger and thumb, read it, and dropped it on the counter.

"My guess is you know all about that other white man. My guess is you've already spoken to him," he said. "What brings a private eye up from Wichita to pester me with questions about Amos Johnson? What did that boy do to stir up this interest?"

"Amos Johnson got dead," I said. "He was murdered. Another man is marked for the same, unless I stop the killer. You knew Johnson, and Johnson had a sister."

"Amos did talk about his sister," Ernie said. "I don't recall a name."

I didn't buy it. "Miriam? Miriam Johnson? Does that ring a bell?"

Ernie looked up to the side, his hand over his chin.

"Maybe it does," he said. "What about her?"

"She grew up in the neighborhood, same as her brother," I said. "This store didn't go up last week. It's been here a while."

"Since before the Depression and Prohibition before that," he said.

He reached for cigarettes on the register, looked inside, and crumpled the empty package. I offered a Chesterfield and held a match for both of us.

"Who's this other man the killer has in his sights?" he said.

I gave him the details on Ralph.

"This young Negro is a friend and a detective, same as you?" he said. "Ha. Do I look like the stork dropped me on my head?"

"I'm not here to argue," I said. "The other guy told me you knew Amos Johnson. You've been in the neighborhood. You know Johnson's family."

"My granddaddy opened this store," he said, "Grandpa Ernie. Ernie Junior was my pop. You're talking to Ernie Three. I grew up right here, lifting and hauling crates of booze, off and onto trucks, here to there, wherever they needed to be. Before I could drive, I rode my bicycle and delivered hooch. Prohibition kept customers from coming into liquor stores. It didn't keep them from drinking. I've been around. I know the neighborhood."

"It's too late to help Amos," I said. "He got on the wrong side of someone, and it cost him his life. If I get a handle on who Amos crossed, I'll save another man's life."

Ernie eyes didn't leave my face as he crushed his cigarette butt in an ashtray. Air whistled through his nostrils, one breath, then another, and another.

"Those obituaries I read, many of those folks are Negroes," he said. "Some from the neighborhood. Some die under what are called suspicious circumstances. Sometimes a cop drops in to ask questions, do I know so-and-so, do I know anything about how he died? Then, the cop disappears, and the whole thing is dropped. We bury the dead.

"No one cares. The cops ask questions, pretend to do their job, and we move on. Now, a private cop out of Wichita shows up and asks about one of ours. Goes out of his way like he cares. You can appreciate my skepticism."

"I care," I said.

"Yeah," he said. "Miriam Johnson's been gone for years. She had enough of life in the neighborhood and hit the road, hitchhiked to the west coast the story goes. I don't care to dwell on how a sixteen-year-old girl made it to the coast with no money. Amos bragged she was in the movies, but that was smoke. I never saw her in a picture.

"Their mother didn't miss her. Mother didn't miss Amos either for that matter. Amos had been living on the street since he was a kid. Daddy got kicked out of the nest for tomcatting when they were babies. He died under suspicious circumstances."

He drummed his fingers on the countertop.

"How about Stella Grace?" I said. "She grew up here, Caucasian."

"Stella Grace?" he said. "Can't help you there."

"What else have you got?" I said.

Ernie rapped his knuckles on the counter.

"I'd take another cigarette if you can spare one."

I lit a cigarette for Ernie.

"Amos worked for a man who values his privacy," he said, "a powerful man who provides narcotics to select customers. Marijuana and cocaine from what I understand, maybe more. It's a chancy business, especially for the man on the street. A man on the street is prone to taking the big sleep in an alleyway."

Ernie took a long drag on the cigarette.

"I can tell you who Amos worked for," he said. "If that man finds out I yakked about him, it'll be me in those obituaries. Then, you'd have to deal with my brother. You don't want that. Your name would be in the obits, too."

"Reginald Dexter," I said. "Johnson had a history with Dexter."

Ernie's eyes went wide, and he coughed into his fist.

"You already know. What do you intend to do?" he said.

"I intend to talk to Reggie," I said.

"You have a death wish."

"I met him long ago. Don't worry. Your name won't come up," I said. "I wouldn't want anything to happen to you. I'd hate to face that guy on the bench."

I picked up my bourbon, and Ernie laughed.

"That guy on the bench is the nice brother," Ernie said. "My other brother is the mean one."

Chapter 17

The doorman at 1610 E. Eighteenth Street wasn't keen on admitting a white guy dressed like a cop. He stood with feet spread shoulder-width and filled the doorway, equal parts beef and bravado.

"What you be doin' here? What you be wantin' to stir up trouble for?" he said. "The El Capitan Club ain't no place for you."

"You'll get no trouble from me," I said. "I'm looking for lively jazz and a quiet drink."

"Don't jive. How do I know you're speakin' the truth?"

"I'm telling the truth," I said and palmed him a fin. "Honest Abe."

He glanced at the bill and said, "I can always count on dear old Abe. Frees the slaves and opens the doors. Come right on in."

He stepped aside. A waitress showed me to a table for two. I ordered bourbon on the rocks. A man at the entrance looked over the room.

"Make it two," I said.

Aaron Bernstein gave me the high sign and worked his way to the table. We shook hands, and he took a seat.

"You look too prosperous for a bookie," I said. "Your look is all wrong. It's bad for business."

"What's that mean?" he said.

"A doctor or a lawyer, sure, you want a guy dressed like a winner. Who wants to deal with a bookie who looks like he never lost a bet?"

"Wrong, sucker. People respect prosperity. If I dressed like a cop, nobody would come near me," he said.

Bernstein wore a bespoke suit, double-breasted wool, silk tie, and matching handkerchief. The scar on his chin only enhanced his image. He looked like he'd stepped off the pages of *Esquire*.

The waitress arrived with our drinks, and we clinked our glasses. A solo pianist tickled the keys and tables filled. Other musicians arranged themselves onstage.

"Thanks for coming," I said.

"You called. I came," he said. "What's up?"

"Amos Johnson worked for Reginald Dexter," I said. "I'm trying to get a handle on why Dexter would want Johnson dead. Do you know Dexter?"

"Lots of people know Dexter. I know his people. How do you know him?"

I gave Bernstein a rundown of Ralph Waldo's former association with the drug dealer and how I freed Ralph from Dexter's clutches.

"He and I remain at odds," I said.

"So you went toe-to-toe with Dexter?" Bernstein said and laughed. "The cowboy knows no fear. That was back then, Pete. Getting close to Dexter is tougher these days."

"How so?"

"Nobody sees Dexter unless Dexter wants to be seen," he said. "When he visits a club like the El Capitan, he's surrounded by a cadre of lieutenants and goons."

"He must be doing well," I said.

I caught the waitress's eye and raised two fingers. Bernstein removed a pocket humidor from his jacket.

"Montecristo," he said. "Cuban."

He snipped the ends off a pair of cigars and held a flame to each. I took a long draw and savored the Cuban tobacco.

"Fine threads. Fine tobacco. I'm in the wrong business," I said.

Bernstein laughed and said, "Wanna bet?"

"Not with you," I said, and he laughed again.

The waitress brought fresh drinks.

"Dexter's into more than narcotics these days," Bernstein said. "He's branching into legitimate businesses, or businesses that appear legitimate."

"Legitimate? He must have an angle," I said.

"He's made connections in high places," he said, "political connections."

"That's the angle," I said. "Legitimate business and politics. Oil and water."

John R. Brinkley came to mind, the corruptible goat doctor and wannabe governor.

"Dexter and politics," I said. "How do you know so much about him?"

Bernstein puffed on his cigar and grinned.

"People talk. I listen," he said.

"What's Dexter's business?" I said.

"This and that. He owns an outfit in your neighborhood, something called Craft Construction."

"In Wichita? Can't be. The cops ran Dexter out of town long ago." I said.

"I didn't say he wielded a shovel in the city. He's just the owner. He has people run the day-to-day," he said.

"He'll have an insider downtown, I'd wager. City contracts could make a man healthy in a hurry," I said.

A Negro couple, dressed to the nines, sat down at the next table. The lady wore silver satin and a glittering tiara. Her escort sported a brown zoot suit and a fedora adorned with a flamingo feather. He looked my way and arched an eyebrow. I raised my glass. He did not acknowledge my gesture.

"Dexter's aligned himself with the German American Bund," Bernstein said.

I lifted my bourbon and swallowed.

"There's no limit to the depths a man can sink," I said. "We're sipping aged whiskey and smoking premium tobacco. Why do I have a bad taste in my mouth?"

The German American Bund, Nazi sympathizers, had brought Aaron Bernstein and I together. Criminal members of that organization murdered my friend who worked for Stearman Aircraft at the time. I met Bernstein, a Jewish mobster working undercover with the FBI. They rooted out Bund loyalists attempting to undermine the aircraft industry. Aaron Bernstein had risked his life for me. Together we attained justice for the death of my pal.

"We stomped the Bund in Wichita," he said. "We knew we didn't finish them off. Your boy, Dexter, attended that little celebration in Madison Square Garden. He rubbed elbows with the mucky-mucks. The Bund leader, Fritz Kuhn, was there."

"Twenty-thousand Americans celebrated Adolf Hitler and George Washington. They waved American flags and swastikas," I said.

Musicians settled onstage. A woman in red took the microphone and belted out "Georgia on My Mind." A man I recognized took me by surprise. Ivan S. Baker, jazz drummer and poet from Wichita, spotted me. He pointed his drumstick, and I hoisted my glass in salute.

"Stella Grace," I said.

Bernstein's expression didn't change. He fixed his eyes on the woman in red. She closed her eyes and swayed. He drew on his cigar and blew a cloud of smoke.

"Stella Grace," he said. "What do you know?"

"She was tied to Amos Johnson, long ago. She showed up in Dodge City when I was there. She'd warned Ralph Waldo that some-one was after him, and she warned me to watch my back. I met her and Johnson's sister, Miriam, an actress of sorts. That was a week ago. I can't figure Stella Grace, devil or angel?"

Bernstein pondered the question.

"Stella herself couldn't answer that. I thought I knew her. I didn't. We met right here in this club. We danced on that floor," he said and pointed.

"The lady was a swan in high heels, graceful, gliding. No dame I ever met carried herself like Stella. We raised the temperature that hot summer night. The temperature didn't drop after the music stopped, either. We played house. Days became weeks. We played our roles, but the script didn't hold up. We ran out of lines, and we each dropped back into character. We were together then. Then, we weren't."

"Does she still live in Kansas City?"

"She disappeared. One day, I kissed her goodbye. When I returned, she was gone. I haven't seen her. Then again, I haven't looked for her."

Bernstein went quiet. The music played.

"Dexter and I need to have a chat," I said.

"Maybe you didn't hear me," he said. "Nobody talks to Dexter unless Dexter wants to talk."

"I heard you," I said. "Dexter will talk to me. He'll want to talk to me."

The band kicked into high gear. Couples swayed and jived on the dance floor. Bernstein and I drank and smoked. A pleasant warmth swept over me. My mind emptied of all thoughts but one. Dexter will talk to me.

Sunday

April 9

to

Monday

April 10, 1939

Chapter 18

The clocks chimed. The telephone rang. Or was it the telephone, then the chimes? Who called at this hour? The sun had barely shown its face. A sliver of light crept into the gray room. The clocks went silent. The telephone did not. I trudged to the kitchen. The Black Forest cuckoo said six.

"Hello?"

"Hello, darling. You sound awful. I wanted you to know that I'm home."

The fog lifted.

"You shouldn't be at home," I said. "You were going to your sister's. Come to my place, and we'll spend the day together."

Lucille's laughter tinkled through the receiver.

"Look out the window, Mr. Detective. The day has come and gone. You heathen, you slept all day, didn't you? Sis and her family invited me to Easter service. We hid the colored eggs and ate ham and scalloped potatoes for dinner. I just got back home. I'm going to brew a cup of tea, soak in a hot tub, and go to bed. Call me tomorrow. You can explain why you slept away an entire day."

We rang off. I put on a robe, lit a cigarette, and stepped onto the porch. My roadster was parked in its usual spot at the curb. The sky had a funny hue, dark to the east, a halo of sunlight to the west.

What happened the evening before? I didn't leave the club right away. I switched from bourbon to coffee before Bernstein and I parted ways in the late evening. I drove through the night, Ottawa, Emporia, on to Newton, and south to Wichita. Everything was clear.

I arrived home before sunrise, went straight to bed, and slipped into a coma. The realization jolted me. I'd been out for better than a dozen hours. Worry and stress had taken their toll.

Sunday evening, I relaxed in my chair. I drank Eight O'Clock coffee, pondered Reginald Dexter, and considered the rattlesnake. Comparisons between Dexter and the rattlesnake seemed unfair—to the rattlesnake. The rattlesnake is honest, true to its nature. It doesn't pretend to be anything but what it is, stealthy, venomous, and a threat to all creatures.

Dexter acted the pretender, a shapeshifter who courted the vulnerable to his advantage. Men like Amos Johnson or Ralph Waldo fell under his spell. Should they become disloyal, no longer useful, the shapeshifter delivered a fatal strike. Death was the penalty. His world was divided into two camps, winners and losers. Winners survived, losers died.

Dexter hid in the shadows, like the snake. He had to be drawn into the open if I was to learn why he had Ralph in the cross-hairs.

I poured brandy into a snifter and reached for a paper sack on the counter. Lucille had surprised me with a tasty assortment of mixed nuts, roasted and salted, purchased at a store downtown.

"It's called the Nifty Nut House. Isn't that cute?" she said. "The aroma of roasted nuts is delicious. I bought two sacks from a nice man, Mr. Muckenthaler. His store's on Broadway, not far from the Miller."

Sack in hand, I retrieved my copy of Louis Untermeyer's *Modern British Poetry* from the bookshelf. In the comfort of my chair, I munched on nuts, sipped brandy, and thumbed the leaves of poetry. I paused at a William Butler Yeats offering, "When You Are Old," and read it slowly. Then, I read it again.

> When you are old and gray and full of sleep,
> And nodding by the fire, take down this book,
> And slowly read, and dream of the soft look
> Your eyes had once, and of their shadows deep;

The open book weighed heavy on my lap. I nodded and dozed and dropped into shadows deep.

◆ ◆ ◆

Ralph Waldo had a new address. He no longer lived in the building where Amos Johnson's body had been deposited. Remaining at an address known to an assassin was not feasible. On Monday, I drove to my office in the Lawrence Block Building. I'd visit Ralph at his new home later. First, I sipped a cup of joe with Agnes. She glowed with her news and delivered it rapid fire.

"Oh, did you see it? Percival took me. It was wonderful. What did Lucille think? Did she love it? She loved it, didn't she? I thought it was wonderful. Percival's been such a good sport. I put Errol's picture next to my bed, but then I thought that was too much, so I moved it to the mantel. That movie deserves an Oscar. Don't you think? Oh, to think, you actually met Errol Flynn in the flesh. Did the audience applaud when he came on the screen? Everyone applauded when we watched it. What was your favorite part?"

Agnes went on. She asked a question, answered it herself, and went on. I drank coffee, smoked a cigarette, and marveled at my star-struck gal Friday. When she came up for air, I held up my hand. I told her I had to go to work, donned my fedora, and left.

I drove north and east toward Ralph's old place on Ninth. I braked but didn't stop. Nothing had changed except the addition of a "For Rent" sign staked along the sidewalk. The two downstairs units remained occupied, the landlady's and Leo Little's.

An elderly woman in a worn winter coat pushed a cart. The coat was too heavy for the weather. She gave me the eyeball from behind a pile of blankets and clothing when I rolled past her.

I drove on to the intersection at Fourteenth and Madison and pulled up at a faded boarding house with another "For Rent" sign, this one tacked to a gray picket fence missing teeth. The remaining pickets listed like sailors following a two-day liberty. Porch steps creaked beneath my step. A lace curtain covered the glass panel on the door. I tapped on the glass. A moment later, a brown hand turned the knob and disappeared.

I went inside and followed Waldo's instructions, up the stairs, second door. I tapped again and waited. The door cracked open.

"Yeah?"

"It's Pete," I said.

The door swung wide. I slipped inside. Curtains were drawn on the single window. I flipped a switch on the wall and got nothing for my effort. An empty socket hovered from the ceiling. My eyes adjusted to the dim light. The bed was unmade. Clothes were draped over a wooden chair, the only furniture other than the bed. A suitcase lay open on the floor, propped against the wall.

"Welcome to Chez Ralph's. Care for a cocktail? I'll ring room service," he said.

A week in the hole hadn't dampened Ralph's sense of humor.

"How'd you like to get out of here?" I said.

"You don't have to ask me twice," he said.

He threw the clothes in the suitcase and closed it.

"Ready," he said.

We left.

"Let's get you squared away," I said.

I'd seen no sign of food in the room.

"When was your last meal?" I said.

"It's been a while," he said.

Downtown, I pulled up at Curley's Inn, a diner on Douglas. Late morning patrons occupied a few tables. I chose a table away from others that provided a view of the door.

"You're in luck, gentlemen. The cook has prepared a rare treat, a lamb stew," the waitress said.

"Leftover Easter lamb?" I said.

"It's yesterday's, but it's fresh and tasty. You two beat the lunch crowd. It'll be gone before long."

Ralph nodded, and I ordered two bowls and two glasses of iced tea. The waitress moved away.

"We'll eat first, then get spiffed up. Where's your suit?" I said.

"The rest of my clothes are at my folks' place," he said.

The door opened, and a man entered. The slender man moved toward a stool at the counter. He caught my eye and grinned and came our way.

"Willie!" I said.

Willie slapped his palm down on the table.

"'Lo, Pete," he said.

He moved his hand away, and a shiny silver dollar lay on the table.

"Does that look familiar?" he said. "You gave me that coin."

"That was almost a year ago," I said.

"Goin' on," he said.

"Have a seat, Willie." I said.

Willie sat down, and I introduced the two men to each other. I caught the waitress's eye and held up three fingers. She gave me a thumbs up.

Willie and Ralph gave each other the up and down.

"Haven't we met?" Willie said.

"Don't think so. You look familiar, though," Ralph said. "What's with the silver dollar?"

When Willie picked up the coin, his hand twitched. The twitch subsided, and he twirled the coin through his fingers.

"I needed a drink," he said, "like I always did. This stranger here spoke to me, spoke to me like I was a man, not a bum. He offered to buy me a meal. I was hungry, all right, but mostly I was thirsty. That drink was more important than food. He said if I'd eat with him, he'd buy me a drink. So, I did. After we ate, he palmed me that silver dollar."

The waitress brought iced tea. Ralph squeezed lemon into his tea. The spoon shook in Willie's hand when he lifted it from the sugar bowl, once, twice, then stirred his tea. He lay down the spoon and spoke.

"It felt cool in my hand, that coin did, cool and solid. I squeezed it, and that cool metal warmed my palm. I'd never had a silver dollar, you see. I didn't want to spend it. I didn't want to lose it. I squeezed it all afternoon, then, I squeezed it that night. The next day, I still needed that drink, but I still had that coin. That was the first day."

Willie sipped his tea.

"The dollar's still with me, day and night," Willie said. "Sometimes it's just me and that dollar."

"For nearly a year," I said again.

"Goin' on," he said again.

The waitress brought steaming bowls of stew and a platter of bread.

"'Ain't got nobody in all this world, Ain't got nobody but ma self…'"

Ralph recited Langston Hughes.

"Every day is that first day," Willie said. "I still need a drink, and I still have the dollar."

He dipped a slice of bread into his stew.

"The Shimmy Shack," Ralph said. "That's why you look familiar. You used to hang around the Shimmy Shack."

Willie looked at Ralph and nodded.

"Yeah, I did," Willie said. "That was some time ago."

"Shimmy Shack?" I said.

"A roadhouse in the sticks," Ralph said.

"Not much of a road, not much of a house, the way I recall," Willie said. "Course I wasn't sober all that much at the time."

"We go there. The law leaves us alone," Ralph said, then flashed a grin. "I should take you there, Pete. You need to see the place. We'll have a bottle of beer. A bottle, not a glass. I'd never trust a glass at the Shimmy Shack."

He laughed and spooned his stew. Ice clinked when Willie lifted his glass.

"How are you getting along, Willie?" I said.

"Day to day. Men like me, lost in the bottle, we've come together. We share a place. Fellows come and go. Anyone's welcome long's he's sober and stays sober. If he backslides, he's gone. No booze, no drugs, that's the rule."

"Are you working?" I said.

"Nothing steady. I load a truck, mow a lawn, clean an attic. Steady work is hard to find."

Ralph dipped bread into his stew.

"I know a guy," he said. "He runs a warehouse. I did some work for him, uncovered a thief who stole some tools."

"You're a detective, like Pete?" Willie said.

Ralph hesitated, so I spoke up.

"He is," I said. "We're working together at the moment, but Ralph has his own agency, just like me."

"This warehouse guy complained he couldn't find decent help," Ralph said. "Too many workers cash their paycheck and go on a bender, fail to show up the next day."

"Sounds familiar," Willie said. "I probably know some of those folks."

Ralph tore a blank page from my book and borrowed my pencil.

"Tell him you talked to me," Ralph said.

Ralph wrote down Leo Little, L.L. Storage, and the address on Mosley.

Chapter 19

Waldo sat atop his stool at the Hotel Eaton. The customer chair was empty. He munched on a sandwich, his nose in a book. He read something and shook his head. Footsteps urged him to mark his place and close the book. He laid his sandwich aside.

"Hi, Pop," Ralph said.

Waldo rose to his feet and embraced Ralph.

"It's so good to see you," he said.

He clasped Ralph by the shoulders, held him at arms' length, then pulled him in for another hug.

"So good to see you," he said. "You know you don't have to live in that jail cell you rented. We've got room for you at home."

"He's not going back to the cell," I said. "We'll find something. I'll leave you two for a few minutes."

Waldo held my hand in both of his.

"Thank you," he said.

"We'll get to the bottom of this, Waldo," I said.

I turned toward the barbershop. Waldo's book lay next to his stool, *It Can't Happen Here,* by Sinclair Lewis. I'd read the cautionary tale. Lewis wrote about the perils of living under an authoritarian government.

"What do you think, Waldo? Can it happen here?" I said.

"I suppose it can," Waldo said. "It will if we let it happen. We can't do that. Some politicians try to rewrite the Constitution. Others ignore it altogether."

My mind flashed to Dr. John R. Brinkley and dwelled on the possibility of a convicted fraud leading the country. The barber's chair was occupied, so I passed by the shop and continued to the front desk.

"Is Jeff around?" I said.

The clerk dialed the phone. A moment later the house detective appeared, and I motioned toward the lobby.

"I need a favor, on the Q.T.," I said. "Can I get a room for a few days, strictly off the books? No room service. No maid service. No one goes near it."

"Give me a minute," he said.

Jeff huddled with the hotel manager at the desk. He returned with a key.

"Third floor, end of the hall," he said.

"Thanks, pal," I said. "I owe you one."

I returned to the barbershop. A gentleman admired his reflection in the mirror. He lowered his fedora onto his fresh haircut, paid the barber, and left. I went inside.

"Take the chair, Pete. Let's lower those ears."

Gus draped me with a cloth and went to work. He threw his head back and looked me over before he moved behind me. He snipped and clipped, then he came around front again and looked me over.

"Forty-five," he said.

"Forty-five. I'll bite," I said.

"I had my forty-fifth birthday in December," he said. "I figure we both live in the same neighborhood. You've gathered a little snow in the temples, same as me."

"Aren't you full of good news?" I said. "My forty-fifth is next month."

"Bingo. I thought so. I can feel it. The doctor tells me the ache in my shoulder will go away when I decide to put down the clippers. The doc had no suggestions on how I'd pay for groceries if I followed that advice."

"What do doctors know?" I said. "It's all guesswork. I asked my doctor how much time I had left, and he looked at his watch."

Gus shaved my neck and splashed on witch hazel.

"Come in on your birthday," he said. "I'll give you a free one."

I thanked him and settled up. Waldo had put a shine on Ralph's shoes. He did the same for me. Then, we said our goodbyes and left the Eaton. We drove to Waldo's place, and Ralph took only ten minutes to return in a pressed suit, grip in hand.

I handed him the key to the room at the Eaton and said, "This is your new address for a few days."

"The Eaton? Okay, what's next?" he said.

"We flush out Reggie Dexter."

Dexter the drug dealer had branched into construction, a legitimate front to gain access to politicians. Politicians in Kansas City controlled fiefdoms and maintained outside interests. Some dabbled in construction, some had interests in Wichita. It didn't stretch the imagination to picture Dexter schmoozing political figures, adding offerings to their coffers, in exchange for profitable contracts.

We drove to an address on Mead north of downtown. Craft Construction was housed in a structure that resembled a large garage. According to Bernstein, Dexter owned the company. I reached under the dash and retrieved my .38.

"Are you expecting trouble?" Ralph said.

"Probably not. When you poke a stick into a hornet's nest, it's best to be ready."

The manager behind his desk barked into a telephone.

"I don't care when they planned on finishing! Tell those idiots that slab has to be poured today before they knock off! Nobody leaves until the job's done!"

He slammed the receiver home and looked up. His eyes went from me to Ralph and back to me.

"Great. Frick and Frack, just what I ordered today. What do you clowns want?" he said.

"We're looking for Reggie Dexter," I said. "Is he around?"

"Never heard of him," he said. "Who's asking?"

I gave him my card. He glanced at it and tossed it into the trash.

"When does he come around?" I said.

"I said I've never heard of Dexter. I've never heard of you, either. Beat it."

"You know Dexter," I said.

"Are you calling me a liar?"

"Let's call it an honest mistake. For a moment there you forgot the name of the guy who signs your paycheck and calls the shots. It happens," I said.

The man lifted a wrench off the desk and tapped it in his palm.

"You're starting to annoy me fella," he said. "What makes you think I work for this Dexter?"

"You fit the mold," I said. "Loud and stupid."

He hurled the wrench at my head. I ducked, and the wrench shattered the window behind me. It clattered onto the concrete beyond. Heads outside the office turned and eyeballed the destruction. Busted glass tinkled onto the concrete. I pulled out my .38 and leveled it.

"Like I said, loud and stupid."

"What are going to do with that gun?"

"Behave yourself," I said. "Reach into that trash can and take out my card."

He looked at me, and he looked at the gun. Beads of sweat appeared on his brow. He swiveled his chair and reached into the trash can.

"Now when you see Reggie, give him that card. Tell Reggie I was asking after him. Tell him I'd like a meeting, just the two of us, and not with his pitiful flunky."

I dropped my gun into a coat pocket and turned. We hadn't reached the street before we heard the man bark into the phone again. The guy was having a bad day.

We returned to the Eaton. The restaurant chef fixed a plate with a ham sandwich and potato salad. The waitress filled a glass with iced tea. I paid for the chow, and we went up to the third floor. The room looked secure and comfortable. It included a bed and a bathroom.

"You'll be safe here," I said. "No one knows you're here. I'll pick you up in the morning."

Ralph pulled back the covers on the bed and ran his fingertips over the sheets.

"I always figured the other guy slept on sheets like these," he said. "I'll be just fine here, Pete. I'll be just fine."

I went back downstairs and stepped into a telephone booth.

"Sorry it's late," I said. "I've been on the go."

"I'm just running out the door," Lucille said. "An ambulance rushed my neighbor's husband to the hospital. It might be his appendix. I'm going to babysit her kids. I'll talk later."

We rang off. I left the Eaton and drove into the disappearing sun. I pulled my fedora low against the glare and crossed over the Arkansas River. At Seneca, I turned north and pushed my hat back. A few blocks later, I stopped in front of Tom's Inn.

I went inside and took a stool at the bar. Tom greeted me with a frothy glass of Storz on a coaster. He toted a tray loaded with four glasses of beer to a booth. Another customer asked for a refill. Mabel tottered out of the kitchen, delivered dinner plates to a table of four, and disappeared back into the kitchen. Tom wiped the bar.

"Busy tonight," I said.

"For a Monday," Tom said.

Someone at a table called for a pitcher of beer. A trio of men in khakis came through the door. Tables and booths were occupied, so they gathered at the bar. One man bumped my elbow and said, "Excuse me." I moved down a stool so they could sit together. Someone over my shoulder said something, and his tablemates guffawed. Loud voices competed with laughter.

I drained my beer and dropped a coin onto the bar. I waved goodbye to Tom and slipped out the door. My stomach rumbled, but the evening called for a quiet bite, not hubbub.

The sun dropped over the horizon, and a quarter moon appeared on stage. I drove south to Douglas and crossed back over the river toward downtown. A car's headlights reflected in the mirror. At Broadway, I made a left. and the headlights continued down Douglas. At Broadway and First Street, a glow came from inside the White Castle hamburger restaurant. I pulled over and tried the door, but it was locked. A guy wearing a paper hat came from the kitchen. The aroma of fried onions followed him.

"Sorry, we're closed," he said. "I'm just locking up."

"Any leftover burgers?" I said. "I'll buy what you've got."

"Just my dinner," he said. "Sorry."

A beat up Ford sedan pulled up next door in front of Gertrude Edler's School of Dancing. The school building was dark. No one got out of the car. The driver sat behind the wheel, and the motor idled. Restaurant lights went out, and a door slammed in back. I stood in the dark and eyed the Ford. Headlight beams played over my roadster. Shorts hairs on my neck tingled.

Shadows camouflaged me, but I couldn't remain in the shadows forever. Whoever sat behind the wheel wasn't waiting for a student to exit the school. Someone waited for me to make a move. Across the street, a crowd gathered under the marquee at the Orpheum Theater, chatting among themselves, buying tickets for the next show.

I eased my .38 out of my pocket. If I moved toward my roadster, headlights would make me an easy target for a gunman. If I moved toward his vehicle, headlights would blind me, and I'd still be an easy target. Shadows covered me, but shadows wouldn't stop a bullet. I had to do something.

I crouched low and dashed away from the headlights toward the corner of the building. A car door opened, and a gun fired, then fired again. Someone across the street screamed. I stayed low and ducked around the corner. I was in the open.

The door slammed and tires squealed. I stayed down and moved to the rear corner of the restaurant but had no place to hide. Parking stalls were empty. The car careened around the corner and sprayed shots in my direction.

"Get inside!" someone yelled.

I shot from one knee and busted glass tinkled. Another shot whizzed past me and thudded into the side of the restaurant. The Ford sped past. I came to my feet to take another shot, but I weaved, then dropped onto my backside. The Ford disappeared. I had to get to my roadster, but it was no good. Something burned. My shirt felt like it was on fire. My hand went down, and my fingers came back sticky, dark in the lamplight. I cursed the pain.

Thoughts swirled. Who's that screaming? Is someone crying? Would the Cardinals take it all? Fried onions. I smelled fried onions. A siren sounded in the distance.

Tuesday

April 11, 1939

Chapter 20

"So, angels smoke cigars. Who knew?"

"You're awake. What did you say? Angels smoke cigars?"

"You must be an angel," I said to the woman in white. "The stench doesn't fit. This can't be heaven. Tell me I'm alive."

"You are alive. You're in a hospital bed, and I'm a nurse." She twisted her torso at the shoulders. "See? No halo, no wings."

"I smell tobacco," I said, "rank tobacco."

"That's from the hallway. A man out there is smoking an awful cigar. I think he's a cop. He said to tell him when you wake up."

She adjusted the drip on a bottle of liquid dangling from a hook. A tube connected the bottle to a needle in the crook of my arm.

"Tell the cop I didn't make it," I said.

"He already warned me. He said you're too stubborn to die."

"How bad is it?"

"You were shot, but you'll survive. The doctor will talk to you."

"I'd give my secret decoder ring for a cup of coffee," I said.

"What's a secret decoder ring worth?"

"Less than the slug that put me here."

"I'll see what I can do," she said.

The nurse left the room. Lieutenant Thaddeus McCormick, homicide detective, came in.

"You're interrupting my hurkle-durkle," I said.

"That's my line, Stone. Quit complaining. What the hell happened?"

I moved to sit up, and a hot poker stabbed me in the side. I leaned back on a pillow and took a breath. I gave Mac a rundown of the previous night's events. A gunman in a car fired shots. I ducked and fired back. My bullet busted a car window. I gave Mac a description of the assailant who'd bumped into Lucille Friday night at the theater.

"It was the same man. I didn't see his face last night, and I didn't see it in Dodge City, but it was him. He's out there," I said. "He went after Ralph in Dodge. He came after me last night."

The nurse returned with two cups of coffee and handed one to Mac. Mac thanked her and pulled up a chair.

"There's good news on the assailant," Mac said. "We found a guy that matches your description. Rough looking cob, front tooth missing."

"He's behind bars?"

"He's in the morgue. A citizen found him in an alley off Mosley, some guy walking to work this morning. Your man was behind the wheel of the car, rear window busted out."

"I got off one round," I said. "It was a lucky shot."

"Slow down, Wyatt Earp. A .22 caliber bullet took out this guy. You carry a .38. Someone else popped your assailant, base of the skull, close range."

"That MO sounds familiar," I said.

"Bingo, detective. Moon and Boyd, aka, Smith and Jones went out in the same style. Ballistics is comparing the bullets. Five will get your ten they came from the same weapon."

"The guy with the .22 had no trouble getting close," I said. "Someone in a similar line of work?'

"Someone they didn't suspect, that's for sure," he said. "A gunman in Wichita is taking out the trash. We've got a vigilante in the city."

♦ ♦ ♦

The doctor studied my chart and delivered his assessment. A nurse stood at his elbow.

"The good news is you're alive. You were wounded in your torso, but no bone or organ damage."

"So, the bullet grazed me?"

"The bullet punctured you," he said. "It tore skin and muscle and exited. You lost blood, but we stabilized you quickly and stitched you together. You'll have to go slow, at least for a while. A bullet violated your body. Pace yourself for a few days. How do you feel today?"

"Like I'm ready to leave."

"You were groggy when you arrived. Do you remember everything?"

"I heard the ambulance. I remember being lifted onto a stretcher."

"We put you to sleep in the O.R.," he said and glanced at his chart. "You slept through the night. That's good. We did what needed to be done. The rest is up to you and Mother Nature. Go easy, understand?"

"No heavy lifting," I said. "Got it."

"The nurse will explain how to dress the wound. Follow up with your personal physician. He'll remove the stitches when it's ready. In the meantime, keep the wound clean and let it heal. You don't want an infection to set in."

The doctor left. The nurse gave me instructions, and she left, also. The clothes that survived hung in a locker. My shirt was gone. A bullet had torn a hole in my jacket. I'd need to replace it. My off-the-rack sack suit looked like a smart move. I slipped into my trousers without much trouble. Bending over for socks and shoes was no bargain, but I managed. I eased the tattered jacket over my undershirt and opened the door.

Agnes waited in the hallway.

"Oh, Pete," she said. "Mac called me."

"I'm fine, kiddo," I said.

"You are not fine. You've been shot. Do you know how serious this is?"

"I'm perpendicular to the world," I said. "That counts for something."

"Don't spoon feed me pap," she said. "You couldn't bluff a six-year-old in a game of Old Maid."

Agnes drove me to my place. My roadster was parked at the curb.

"You can thank Mac for that," she said. "He had a pair of uniforms ferry your car over. They left the key inside."

Together we navigated the stairs.

"Mac said he'd check on Ralph at the Eaton," I said. "I have to talk to Ralph."

"You have to talk to Lucille, first. I tried to call her, but she didn't answer," she said.

"What day is it?" I said.

"It's Tuesday."

"Lucille visits the beauty salon on Tuesday," I said, then I remembered our telephone conversation from the evening before. "Her neighbor's husband took ill. She may be looking after the children."

"I'll leave you to clean up, but promise me you'll call Lucille right away. She shouldn't be the last one to know."

"Okay."

"Promise me."

"Agnes, I'll call Lucille."

"Maybe I'll take you up on that offer you made me," she said.

"What offer was that?"

"To forgo my paycheck and play poker instead," she said. "I could use a raise."

Agnes left. I washed up and shaved and donned a clean suit. The one I'd worn was a wreck and would have to be replaced. In the kitchen, I stared at the phone and checked the clock. A call to Lucille could wait.

I drove downtown and parked on Douglas near the St. Francis intersection. Inside the Eaton, I ignored the stairs and took the elevator to the third floor. Ralph answered the door on the first knock.

"You should be more careful," I said. "At least ask who's there."

"Mac filled me in this morning," Ralph said. "The guy who was after us is dead. Dad knows, too. I thought Dad was knocking. I didn't expect you. Shouldn't you be in bed?"

"I'm too pert to loll in bed," I said. Ralph had packed his bags. "What's this?"

"I'm leaving. I'm going to find a place. I'll take my time and find something livable," he said.

Ralph carried his bags. We took the elevator down and stopped to visit with his dad. I went to the front of the hotel. The clerk at the desk sent a pageboy for the house detective, and when Jeff arrived, I gave him the key. His somber expression puzzled me.

"What is it?" I said.

"No maid service. No room service. Those were your instructions," he said. "No one goes near the room."

"That's right."

"Last night, after you left, Ralph came downstairs. He made a telephone call."

Jeff motioned to a phone booth.

"An hour later, a woman arrived. She went up the stairs. I tailed her to the third floor and peeked around the corner. She knocked on the door at the end of the hall, the door opened, and she went inside. She stayed all night. The night man on the desk saw her leave early this morning, five a.m."

I took several breaths before I spoke.

"Negro woman?"

"That's right."

"Who else knows about this?" I said in a soft voice.

"Just the night man," he said. "The restaurant hadn't opened, and the maids hadn't arrived."

"The manager?"

"If the manager hears about this, I'll lose my job," he said. "He was willing to help out a frequent guest of the hotel, but he thought he was offering a hideaway for protection not an assignation."

"That's what I thought, too," I said.

"The night man will keep his mouth shut," he said. "I gave him ten bucks, and his word's good."

I took out my wallet and slipped a sawbuck to Jeff.

"We go back, Pete," he said. "I wanted you to know. Handle it as you see fit. As far as I'm concerned, we're square."

"Thanks, Jeff," I said.

Ralph met me in the lobby. We exited the hotel and boarded the roadster.

"You should be in bed," Ralph said. "You don't look so good."

I said nothing and drove in silence for a number of blocks. I stopped at a diner.

"Have you eaten anything today?" Ralph said.

"Coffee and cigarettes," I said. "Let's go inside."

I ordered eggs and toast and coffee. Ralph pointed to a cinnamon roll and ordered a glass of milk.

"I had breakfast at the hotel," he said.

"Was that breakfast for two, or just for yourself?" I said.

Neither of us spoke until our food arrived. Ralph nibbled on his roll and stared at his plate. I had little appetite but choked down nourishment to keep my energy from flagging. Ralph raised his head.

"I'm sorry, Pete," he said. "It was foolish."

"You're correct on both counts," I said.

"Miriam's been staying with Stella, but there's tension between those two," he said. "She had to get out."

"She didn't have to meet you last night, not at the Eaton," I said.

"I'm sorry," he said again.

"You first met Miriam in Dodge. That's what you said. Were you telling the truth?"

"I don't lie to you, Pete. Amos talked about her. He told her about me. We met, and we both felt it, like we already knew each other. We talked, and the more we talked, the more that feeling grew. We spent the night together at the Trail Inn, in Miriam's room. That was after Stella suggested I might not be safe in my own room. Someone might trace me there. She was right. You traced me to the room."

"Your relationships are your business, Ralph. I'm not criticizing that. I'm upset at your timing. The point of putting you up at the Eaton was to maintain your safety. People I know and trust stuck their necks out to keep you safe. What if somebody had followed Miriam? You would have been vulnerable, not to mention Miriam and those people I mentioned."

Ralph lifted his milk, but his hand trembled. He set the glass down without drinking.

"I never wanted anyone to risk their necks for me," he said.

He went silent. I waited.

"I lay in that room on those crisp, white sheets that smelled so fresh, like spring itself. And that cozy, warm bed inside a grand hotel. I had to call Miriam. Sure, I wanted to see her, but it was more than that. I wanted to share that experience with her. For a few hours, we weren't looking in, wondering what it was like. For one single night, we held each other and looked out. We didn't have to wonder. We knew. That's what we did."

Ralph and I left the diner, and I dropped him at his folks' house. He needed time to find a new place and settle in. I needed time to cool off and put things in perspective. It wasn't difficult to see the situation from Ralph's viewpoint, but that didn't excuse his actions. Endangering the lives of others was no small matter. Three potential assassins had come for us. Three potential assassins were dead. Would there be a fourth?

My pert feeling had passed. The car parked at my place on Lewellen was one I recognized. I killed the motor and sat behind the wheel for several long moments, mustering the energy for what came next. The door at the top of the stairs opened before I reached it. The beautiful blonde's expression flipped from exasperation to compassion.

"Oh, Pete," Lucille said. "You look just awful."

"Thanks, sweetheart. It's good to see you, too," I said. "Your hair looks nice."

"Oh, my hair. Okay, I went to the beauty shop. That's no excuse for not calling me. You were in the hospital, and I didn't even know it. I came right over as soon as I heard, and you weren't even home. You're impossible."

I lowered myself into a chair.

"I've steamed and stewed and rehearsed for hours, all the things I intended to say," she said. "You're ready to collapse. Have you eaten anything?"

"I had eggs," I said.

She ignored that and said, "I'm going to make soup."

She moved to the stove and lectured from the kitchen. A pot clanged on the burner.

"All the things I keep bottled up inside. I swear, Pete. Sometimes, I love you, and sometimes I hate you. Okay, maybe I don't hate you. I was so frightened when I heard the news, from Agnes, by the way, not from you. I wanted to belt you one. Then, you appear, looking like you're a step ahead of the grim reaper, and I'm so grateful you're alive. I love you, Pete Stone. I don't hate you. I love you. Did you hear me, sweetheart? I said I love you."

My whispered, "I love you," was the last thing I heard.

Wednesday
April 12, 1939

Chapter 21

Lips brushed my forehead. My eyes opened.

"Hungry?"

Smiling gray eyes and pink lips hovered above. Blonde pin curls peeked out from a blue, short-brimmed hat. The scent of bath powder stirred me. I sat up and wrapped my arms around her waist.

"Starved," I said and leered. "What's on the menu?"

She bent down and kissed me.

"Not that, darling. You're incorrigible. First, you're out cold, then you're eager to pounce. Get up and come with me. Bacon and eggs are ready. I'll sit with you before I leave."

Lucille had taken a position at The Wichita Art Museum. She started as a part-time volunteer. The museum had opened four years earlier, and as the museum added to its growing collection, it grew busier and added personnel to its staff. Lucille's position remained part-time, but now it came with a paycheck.

"Aren't you eating?" I said and tucked into my breakfast.

"I had toast and coffee while you slept," she said. "I ate supper last night, alone."

"I remember nodding off in my chair, that's it."

"I put you to bed. You played along, but you were out of it. I checked under your bandage. It's coming along. Does it hurt?"

"It's better today. Sleep was what I needed. I collapsed because I pushed it."

"Imagine my surprise," she said.

A copy of *The Wichita Eagle* lay folded on the table.

"What's in the news?" I said.

Lucille scanned the headlines.

"The city commission elected a new mayor. The city manager resigned," she said.

"Anything on baseball?"

The telephone rang. Lucille laid the paper aside and reached for her purse.

"I'm off," Lucille said and kissed me goodbye.

The voice on the phone was gruff.

"If you're still in bed, we're going to have words," Mac said.

"I was shot," I said. "Maybe you didn't hear."

"I called your office. You were on the street yesterday," he said. "We're meeting the medical examiner in an hour. Be there, St. Francis morgue."

I dressed and left my place with time on the clock, so I stopped at the office. Agnes was worried. She needed to see I was alive, maybe give me a tongue-lashing for not calling Lucille. I braced myself and crossed the threshold. Agnes rose from her desk and embraced me. She hugged me in silence. Then, she looked up at me.

"I don't know whether to laugh or cry," she said. "I never know what to expect from you, Pete Stone. You exhaust me. I talked to Lucille. She said you'd passed out."

"Just a needed snooze. Lucille spent the night and made breakfast. Now, I have a date. I'm on my way to see Mac at the morgue."

She smiled.

"That's the place for you, all right. Go ahead then," she said. "Just make sure when you walk in, you walk out."

St. Francis Hospital was located at Ninth and Emporia, north of my office. I used the Emporia Street entrance. On the other side of the glass door, a nurse wheeled an elderly man in a chair, his leg extended in a cast. I held the door for them to pass through.

"Fresh air," the man said to me. "Still, the best medicine in the world."

The temperature dropped inside as I went down the stairs to the basement. McCormick and a shorter man dressed in a white coat huddled together. Harsh light glinted off the tile floor. Another man stood at Mac's elbow, his back toward me, and shifted his weight from foot to foot. Mac looked my way, and the other man turned.

"Willie," I said and shook his hand.

"Stone, this is Dr. Walter Bryce, medical examiner," Mac said.

We shook hands.

"And this is the fellow who discovered the deceased in the alley. I thought you'd want to meet him, but you've obviously already met."

Willie shifted his feet and rubbed wiry arms that resembled pipe cleaners. His short-sleeved denim shirt did little to warm the man.

"How's that nick?" Mac said. "Is it giving you trouble?"

"I'm better," I said.

"Okay, let's look at the body," he said.

Dr. Bryce tugged on the drawer, and metal rollers whirred. The drawer braked to a stop, and an icy clang reverberated off tiled walls. The doctor lowered the sheet to the corpse's shoulders. An untidy tangle of black hair atop a coconut skull fell short of batwing ears. A nose bent to starboard beneath a low brow and a gap-toothed grimace completed the caricature of a man never troubled by an original thought.

"Cletis Rackley, formerly of Sedalia, Missouri, recent alumnus of Leavenworth prison, in for armed robbery, extortion, and general mayhem. Accused but not convicted of murder in the death of a cousin who Rackley claimed had owed him money. Witnesses testified that the cousin came at Rackley with a butcher knife, and Rackley plugged him between the eyes with a .45. Jury ruled self-defense."

McCormick read from his notes. Willie looked on with wide eyes, hands twitching at his sides.

"Willie?" I said.

"I got a case of the heebie-jeebies," he said.

"Why don't you wait in the hall," I said. "I'll be through in a minute."

Willie stepped away.

"Is this the man?" Mac said.

"He bumped into Lucille outside the Miller," I said. "He dropped this into her purse."

I unfolded a handkerchief and revealed a single tooth. The doctor held the handkerchief with thumbs and forefingers and placed it atop the sheet. He picked up the tooth and slipped it into the gap in the dead man's maw.

"Looks like a fit," he said.

He dropped the tooth into a small envelope and passed back the handkerchief.

"Keep it," I said.

The doctor tossed the handkerchief onto the sheet.

"I made the face only once—on Friday night," I said. "I didn't see the face when I slugged him in a dark alley in Dodge City or when I fired a shot through the window of his vehicle on Monday. It was this guy, though, three times."

"The .22 slug in his skull matches the two we took out of Smith and Jones, all fired from the same gun," Mac said.

"A murdered man in a bathtub, then three dead killers," I said. "Has Miriam Johnson claimed her brother's body?"

"I released the body yesterday," Dr. Bryce said. "The sister was having him cremated."

"Was she with another gal?" I said.

"Yes, a real beauty. I dealt only with the sister, though."

"Stop by the station later," Mac said.

I left Mac with the medical examiner and caught up with Willie in the hallway.

"Let's get out of here," I said.

Outside, Willie stopped on the sidewalk. He bent at the waist, hands on his knees. Then, he stood and drew in a great gulp of air.

"I'd sooner snuggle with a snake than visit that place again," he said. "How does that doctor fellow stand it?"

"You're shaking," I said. "Let's get coffee."

We crossed the street to a café. The man behind the counter frowned at the Negro who came through the door. The man caught my glare, and his frown melted. A voice from a booth to the right said, "What the hell, Frank?" Frank looked toward the voice and offered an almost imperceptible shake of his head.

"Two cups of coffee," I said, "hot and fresh."

"Yes sir," Frank said and hopped to it.

We took a booth to the left, in the corner. Willie spooned sugar into his cup, blew on it, and sipped.

"Thanks for this," he said. "I drink a lot of coffee and still can't seem to get enough. It doesn't replace the bottle, but it has to do."

I passed a cigarette to Willie and lit his and one for myself.

"How's it going, Willie? Did you get that job at the warehouse?" I said.

"Thanks to Ralph," he said. "Mr. Little praised Ralph and hired me right off. He asked after Ralph, wondered if he was doing well. He also mentioned a body in Ralph's apartment. Was that the body?"

"No, that was another body," I said.

Willie shook his head and said, "Another body. My, my. I told him I didn't know anything about a body, and I said Ralph appeared to be fine. He asked if I knew where Ralph lived now, but I didn't know that, either."

A couple of workers in hard hats and khakis came through the door. They started our way and paused. They turned and found seats at the other end of the diner. One man looked toward Frank. Frank looked back and shrugged.

"How's the job?" I said.

"It's not every day, only part-time, but it's a job. Mr. Little likes it that I work hard. As long as I show up and do the work when he needs me, I figure he'll keep me on. I was headed to the warehouse when I came across that man in the alley."

"The alley is off Mosley?" I said.

"That's right, between my place and the warehouse. I walk down that alley most every day."

Willie's forehead wrinkled. He lowered his cup onto the table and stared into it, eyes on his cup. He drew on his cigarette and exhaled a cloud of smoke.

"What is it?" I said.

"Mr. Mac asked me questions. He asked if I knew that man lying in the morgue, if I'd ever seen him."

"What did you say? Did you know him?"

"No, I never saw him before, and I told him that, but something struck me. We walk along Mosley, me and my roommates, that is. You recall I said we go to meetings? We meet downtown, men like us, men trapped in the bottle, same as us. We talk, and we listen, and it helps, you know? Especially at night. Nighttime's the worst time to be alone."

Willie crushed out his cigarette.

"Those meetings run late. Some nights it seems like that ole sun's never gonna come up."

I remained silent.

"I've never seen that man in the morgue," he said, "but I've seen that car. I recollect seeing that car."

The vehicle that had idled in front of the dance school was a Ford sedan.

"That's a common automobile," I said. "The streets are crawling with Fords. How can you be sure you saw it?"

"It was late at night, after one of our meetings. That car was parked at the warehouse. We walked home like we always do, and that car was sitting under a lamppost, right outside the warehouse."

"What time was that?" I said.

"Midnight, maybe later."

"Was that the only car parked there?"

"It was the only one under the lamppost."

"That could've been another Ford sedan."

"It was the same car. It had the same dings and dents," he said.

A pair of uniformed cops came in and took stools at the counter. One cop wore a smug look. He swiveled his stool and gave the place the once over. He looked at the back of Willie's head, rested his eyes on me, and frowned. Frank poured coffee for the cops and served them each a slice of apple pie. He came our way and refilled our cups.

"Thanks, pal," I said. "You make a mean cup of coffee. We'll be back."

Frank's eyes went wide, but he said nothing. Willie wrinkled his brow. Mr. Smug Look at the counter lowered his fork and heaved his frame into an upright position. He fixed his eyes on mine and strolled to our booth. A name tag on his uniform identified him as Vic Harris.

"Did I just hear you say you'll be back?" Harris said.

"The coffee's great," I said. "Say, that pie looks good, too. Maybe we'll try some of that."

"Do you know who you're talking to?" he said.

"Unless I miss my guess, you're Vic Harris," I said. "This gentleman with me is Cool Papa Bell, the greatest baseball player in the Negro Leagues. He's fast, and he can hit. Maybe you've heard of him."

Willie's mouth fell open.

"And I'm Jacob Ruppert. Maybe you've heard of me. I own the New York Yankees," I said. "I'm always on the lookout for fresh talent."

Vic Harris struck me as a Neanderthal who didn't read the newspaper or anything else. I doubted he knew that Jacob Ruppert had died three months earlier.

"This man's colored!" Harris said.

I stared at Willie for a long moment and looked up at Harris.

"Officer Harris, I believe you're correct," I said. "Still, he is fast, and he can hit."

"Listen, Ruppert, or whoever you are. My partner and I come in here every day at this time, see. We like this diner. We like it just the way it is, no coloreds. So you and your pal, what's his name—."

"Cool Papa Bell," I said.

"Whatever. You and your pal, you finish your coffee and beat it," he said.

"Officer Harris, your attitude is inexcusable. Dishonoring a man over his skin color is offensive, but slighting a baseball player of this man's stature is more than I can abide."

Harris laughed.

"What're you gonna do? Call the cops?" he said.

"No, of course not. I'm going to place a call to New York City. They don't call my team the Bronx Bombers for nothing, you know. My players' bats hit more than home runs. Unless you return to your stool immediately, I'll sic some very heavy hitters onto you. You shan't be pleased with the outcome."

The cop's frame shook. Consumed by outrage, consumed by doubt, his pea-sized brain struggled to process a thought. He spun and walked away. Willie leaned across the table.

"You are one crazy detective," Willie said.

"More like fed up," I said. "Tell me about that car."

Willie glanced over his shoulder at the cops, then leaned back.

"That car I saw has an odd dent on top of the front fender, driver's side. That's what I remember, that fender. Something came down hard on that fender, a hammer, or a pipe maybe. It left a deep, narrow dent."

Willie identified the Ford I'd seen Monday night. It had that dented fender.

"That's the car, all right," I said.

"I saw that car at the warehouse," Willie said.

♦ ♦ ♦

"I have a few questions," I said. "Can we talk?"

"We already talked," Leo Little said. "Lieutenant McCormick was here, too. I've told you everything I know."

"Something new came up. This won't take long."

"Look, I didn't hear anything. I don't know anything. I was asleep. It's a quiet neighborhood."

"Quiet, sure. Except for one lousy murder, that is. Do you know Cletis Rackley?"

"Never heard of him," he said.

"I think you have," I said.

"You calling me a liar?" he said.

I chastised myself. It wasn't Leo Little's fault that I was a rat lost in a maze, running down passageways and bumping my nose onto walls.

"Rackley tried to kill me this week. He nearly succeeded."

"So, that means I should know him?" he said.

"An eyewitness spotted Rackley's car parked at your warehouse. It was late at night. Can you explain that?"

Leo Little answered in an even, measured voice.

"I don't know Cletis Rackley. I leave the warehouse after I lock up at night. I leave lights on to discourage theft, and the property's posted against trespassers, but folks ignore those signs. If someone parks a car after hours, there's not much I can do about it."

Two men had finished loading a truck. Little instructed them to return the next morning, and they left. Little looked at his watch.

"One last question," I said. "Do you know Reginald Dexter?"

"Craft Construction?" he said. "He's out of Kansas City. I know him by name."

"He's not a customer?"

"What's it to you? I'm tired of talking. You toss names around like they're birdseed. I told you I know Dexter by name. Why don't you roll your hoop down the road and leave me be? I'm busy."

Saturday
April 15, 1939

Chapter 22

Searching for a clue is like panning for gold. You have to sift through a lot of sludge before you strike that yellow nugget. Ralph and I had asked after Reginald Dexter, so far with no results. Leo Little flinched when I asked about Dexter, but only my suspicion connected the two men. I had no hard evidence to go on.

Lucille stayed at my place for a few days and acted as live-in nurse and maid. She changed my bandages, dressed my wound, and warned me to take it easy. She cooked and dusted and instructed me to raise my feet when she swept the floor. She kissed me when I went out and greeted me when I returned. Her love was kind, generous, and stifling. A guy accustomed to being a bachelor wasn't used to the hovering. Even a baby chick grows weary of a mother hen's attention.

My place offered a bed, a bath, a stove to cook a meal, and a comfortable chair at the end of a hard day, ample furnishings for one but too tight for two. Temperature in our little nest rose to a fever pitch.

"Pete, let's move to my house. I have more room," Lucille said.

"I have a better idea. Let's go out and kick up our heels," I said.

"You know better than that," she said. "Your heels belong on the floor."

"Okay, no kicking," I said. "Waltzes only."

"Oh, Pete, do you feel up to it?" she said.

"You've given me plenty of care, the best."

"Waltzes only, no jitterbugs," she said.

She drove to her place to fancy up. I shaved and dressed and left to pick up Lucille. I crossed over the river and drove west to First and Clarence. She exited the front door before I reached her porch. I stopped on the walk and watched her approach. The fading light haloed an angel.

"What is it?" she said.

"Magic. You're Florence Nightingale, then you're Jean Harlow. I'm crazy over a chameleon."

She pecked my cheek and wiped away the smudge of lipstick with her hankie.

"You're sweet," she said. "You do know that both of those women are no longer living?"

"Gone but not forgotten," I said. "They live on in my heart."

Lucille wore a blue satin dress and high heels. Silver earrings dangled beneath blond curls and complemented a silver pendant necklace and bracelet.

"No doubt about it, you're the blonde bombshell. Odds are someone mistakes you for Jean Harlow tonight," I said.

We boarded the roadster, motored to the edge of town, and kept rolling. The roadhouse was not beyond the eyes of the law, but neither was it in the city's backyard. Cops rarely came by. The bartender spotted me and raised a hand.

"Pete Stone, private eye," he said, "fighter of evil, imbiber of demon rum. Make that bourbon."

Lucille laughed.

"On the money, Rudy," I said.

"And for Miss Harlow?" Rudy said.

Lucille spun her head toward me.

"You two cooked this up!" she said.

"Wait a minute. Don't tell me," Rudy said. "I read it in a fan rag. Jean Harlow's drink is a sweet rum martini. I knew somebody drank demon rum."

"You can't be trusted," Lucille said to me.

Rudy laughed and said, "Last time you were here, you drank gin and tonic. If you're feeling adventurous, try that sweet rum martini. It really was Harlow's drink, and you're a ringer for the gal. The first one's on the house."

"Try it, sweetheart. You already lost the bet," I said.

Lucille's mouth fell open. The bartender and I shared a laugh.

It had been a while since we last visited Green Gables. Lucille sipped her martini and declared it wonderful. We took a corner table for two and dined on pork chops, applesauce, and roasted vegetables. The entrée was tender and juicy. I lost count of Lucille's "oohs and yums." For dessert, Lucille had chocolate cake, and we each had coffee.

After our meal, the music drew us up the stairs. A pianist, a bass fiddler, and a drummer backed a female vocalist who sang jazz standards. The drummer I'd seen in Kansas City had returned to Wichita.

"You know that drummer," Lucille said.

"Ivan S. Baker," I said. "I saw him recently. He gets around."

Ivan joined us on the break and ordered a Shirley Temple, ginger ale with a garnish.

"I don't booze during the gig," Ivan said.

The poet/drummer, a recent graduate of Wichita University, wasn't in a combo, but he stayed busy with temporary gigs. When the call came, he answered, and the more he answered, the more his phone rang.

"It takes time to establish a reputation," he said. "When I don't play, I write."

We listened to jazz, danced to the slow tunes, and enjoyed a quiet evening outside of our same four walls. On the dance floor, I squeezed Lucille and whispered in her ear. Later, in the bedroom, I took Lucille in my arms and squeezed again.

"One more dance," I said.

"A slow dance," she said.

We held each other for one more waltz, long, slow, and tender. Afterwards, we whispered in the darkness and fell asleep in each other's arms.

Sunday
April 16, 1939

Chapter 23

The white, frame house near Ninth and Water had a welcome mat on the porch and bars on the windows. The front door was barred as well, along with a dormer window overhead. The welcome mat played the role of oxymoron to the secure fortress.

Ralph had called me at home that morning, and when he didn't get an answer, he dialed Lucille's number. Ralph knew where to find me. He was a detective. We hadn't spoken since Tuesday, the day he left the Eaton Hotel and I delivered him to his folks. Since then, he'd found his own place, and he wanted to talk. That afternoon, I stopped by for a visit.

I peeked through the bars into the house, and a blur in black and tan crashed against the window. A snarling Doberman, front paws scratching at the glass, bared his fangs and growled. No one from inside appeared to investigate the disturbance, so I stepped over the welcome mat and down off the porch.

Stairs ran up the south side of the house. I walked that way, and a flock of startled sparrows flew out from a cedar tree. At the top of the stairs, I knocked on the door. A curtain ruffled in a window, a chain rattled, and a bolt clicked. The door opened.

"If you have a dog in there, tell me now," I said. "I'm unarmed."

"You met Suez," Ralph said. "Come in, no dogs here. Suez rules alone. He doesn't play well with others."

"Who names a dog Suez?" I said.

"That would be my landlady," he said. "She has a twisted sense of humor. Zeus is a common name for a big dog, but this gal's not common. Suez is Zeus spelled backwards."

"And dog is god spelled backwards," I said.

"Bingo. She quotes the Bible like a preacher, drinks like a barfly, and cusses like a sailor. She invited me in for a drink and drained a bottle of elderberry wine. Then, she stared at her empty glass and railed against the evils of alcohol. She never slurred a word."

"Quite a gal," I said. "Your place looks livable."

"I barely make the rent," Ralph said, "but it'll do."

"That hundred bucks that came in the mail? It's gone?" I said.

"Not quite. A good bit of that stayed in Dodge City," he said. "The cost of living goes up when Hollywood drops in."

"Who else is in the building?"

"The landlady and Suez. This is her only rental."

"How about Miriam?" I said.

"I want you to know I'm sorry about that, Pete. You were right, and I was stupid," he said. "I never should have called Miriam. That was wrong."

"Seeing Miriam isn't wrong. I was concerned with your safety at the Eaton, that's all. That's behind us, Ralph, over and done. Let's move on," I said.

We sat at the kitchen table. Ralph sipped coffee and lowered his cup.

"Let's go for a ride," he said.

"I have something to talk about," I said.

"I know just the place," he said.

Ralph directed me to drive north and west to the outskirts of the city. Twenty-first Street reached the Arkansas River, and Ralph pointed down a dusty road that ran north. I left the city street and bounced onto a road that wound alongside riparian trees, cottonwood, hackberry, walnut, and others, a forest growing on the riverbank.

"My roadster's going to complain about this," I said, "not to mention my back."

"Road graders don't much bother to come down this road," Ralph said. "Some things are easy to ignore."

Across the way lay acres of green, winter wheat and fallow fields. A red-tailed hawk clasped a rodent in its talons and winged from the ditch. A meadowlark on a fencepost seemed disinterested in the predator and its prey.

We approached a farmhouse on the right. A colored man in a straw hat and bib overalls watched from his porch. We drove past the farmhouse, and Ralph said, "Slow down," and then, "Turn here."

He pointed left, to a road that went into the trees. I suspected where Ralph was taking me, but I didn't know why. The narrower and bumpier road wound through trees to the edge of the river and ended in a clearing. A faded green Chevy pickup with a rusted right fender and vestiges of red paint on the passenger door was parked in the clearing.

"Last night, there would have been plenty of cars here," Ralph said.

I pulled up and looked overhead. Birds fluttered and tweeted on leafy limbs. We stepped out of the roadster, and Ralph helped me button down the top.

"This way," Ralph said.

We followed a footpath along the riverbank and reached the shack, weathered barn wood covered with a tin roof. A drape fell over a window opening that held no glass. A hinged door stood ajar. The shack looked to be on its last shimmy.

A man outside sat on a chair tipped back against the wall. An assortment of empty chairs, straight back, Adirondack, and others formed a circle beneath unlit lanterns hanging on posts. Ashes smoldered in a fire pit at the center of the circle. The man on the chair stood up and moved toward an outhouse with a crescent moon carved into the door.

"This place jumps on a Saturday night, when the weather's right," Ralph said. "A fiddle, harmonica, washboard, guitar, whatever folks bring, men and women. There's always music."

"I can see why the law leaves you alone out here," I said. "A man's got to have a powerful thirst to trek back here."

"A powerful thirst, yeah," Ralph said, "but not for whiskey alone."

Another structure lay further along the trail, beyond the outhouse.

"What's back there?" I said.

"That's private. It belongs to the guy who owns all this. He lives there, I suppose. No one goes back there unless they're invited, or they pay. Let's get a beer."

Ralph led me inside. The open door provided the only light. A short, stocky man, bent over at the waist, sat on a stool behind a makeshift bar of stacked crates. He snoozed with his head in the crook of his arm. His snore and the buzz of flies and mosquitoes provided musical entertainment at the Shimmy Shack.

"Hey, Mule, you open for business?" Ralph said.

Mule groaned and lifted his head. He wiped slobber from his chin with stubby fingers and peered at me with a frown.

"You the law?" Mule said.

"He's with me," Ralph said.

Mule faced Ralph and didn't lose the frown.

"What you be bringing the law into my place for?" he said. "You crazy, boy?"

"I'm private, and I don't want trouble," I said. "Ralph's my pal."

"Give us a couple of beers, Mule. We'll drink them outside," Ralph said.

Mule looked at me and back at Ralph and shook his head. He reached into a cooler. Chips of ice floated in water covering brown bottles. He popped the tops on two bottles of Pabst. Ralph tossed a couple of dimes onto the crate.

"Enjoy your beverages, gentlemen. Then leave," Mule said.

We went outside and selected a pair of Adirondacks.

"That fellow hasn't come back from the outhouse," I said. "Maybe he fell in."

"He's biding his time out there in the trees. He'll come back after we're gone," Ralph said.

"I hope Mule doesn't hold a grudge," I said. "I'd hate for the executive committee to revoke your membership."

"He'll get over it."

I took a pull on the Pabst. Elm and maple seeds wafted and whirled in the wind. Whirligigs landed on us and around us.

"Why are we here, Ralph?" I said.

"So you could see. I admire you, Pete, always have, but you have no idea what it's like to go through a door and have someone tell you to get out, sometimes with words, sometimes with looks or gestures."

He sipped his beer.

"For the record, I drink my beer at Tom's Inn. Tom always welcomes you, Ralph," I said.

"Yes, he does. I can't say the same for his customers. I wanted you to taste what it's like. I'm not making excuses, and you've put it behind us," he said, "but when I stretched out on those sheets at the Eaton, and no one told me to get out, I had to share that experience with Miriam. So, I did."

He held out his beer, and we clinked our bottles together.

"Now, we'll move on. We can both put that behind us," he said.

"Fair enough," I said.

I lit a Chesterfield.

"I spoke to Leo Little," I said. "Willie had seen Cletis Rackley's car parked at the warehouse late at night. Little says he didn't know Rackley. He says he would have been in bed, hits the hay early every night."

Ralph grinned.

"Something funny?" I said.

"Leo Little isn't a bad guy," he said. "He's not above telling a tale or two. Leo's been right here on more than one Saturday night. Mule and Leo are tight, longtime pals. Leo didn't care for Amos, but I understood."

"He knows Dexter by name," I said.

"Dexter's another story," he said. "Dexter's slippery, and he wants us dead. The question is why?"

"How close were you and Amos Johnson?" I said.

Ralph shrugged.

"We worked together and stayed pals after I left Dexter," he said.

"Foxhole buddies?" I said.

"What's that mean, foxhole buddies?"

"Foxhole buddies look out for each other, under fire and after the shooting stops. They remain loyal to one another. You and Amos worked together. After you moved on, you stayed pals."

Ralph said, "That sounds right. Even though I left and he stayed in that world, we looked after each other."

Ralph dropped his eyes and shook his head.

"Until the end. I wasn't there when it counted," he said. "Amos died, and I wasn't there for him."

"Don't beat yourself up, Ralph. Amos went his own way. You said you hadn't spoken to Amos recently."

"There was that phone call, the call that was cut off. I play that over in my mind. It could have been Amos," he said.

"Before that, when was the last time you spoke to him?"

"Some weeks, I suppose. Amos had a habit of showing up unannounced. It wasn't like we'd set a date and plan to get together. He'd just be there, then he'd be gone again."

"If Amos made a big score, would that come as a surprise?" I said.

"Where are you going with this?" Ralph said.

"What would a big score look like to Amos?"

"That's a good question. A big score for Amos might be chump change to another guy. Amos thought small. The big stuff went to those at the top. He'd never challenge a tall hog. Amos wasn't crazy."

"You spoke to Amos weeks ago," I said. "Do you recall that conversation?"

"He came to Wichita, and we drank a beer. We didn't discuss his business."

"Did you discuss yours?" I said.

Ralph leaned back and raised his eyes. A squirrel scampered up a cottonwood.

"Amos asked about my work, seemed interested. I'd tell him what I did, nothing private or personal."

Ask a citizen to rank occupations, best to worst, and he'll put doctor or lawyer at the top of the list. A private eye, if he makes the list at all, will be near the bottom. Ask that same citizen who he'd like to have a cup of coffee with, and the private eye comes out on top.

"Chump change wouldn't get Amos killed," I said. "Could he have had a partner, a partnership that went bad?"

"Amos worked alone," he said.

"Maybe he had something valuable and didn't know its value," I said.

"Possible. Let me snoop around," Ralph said.

I said nothing.

"It's best, Pete," he said. "We need to split up on this."

"You're a target," I said.

"And you're a target," he said.

"So we stay together," I said, "foxhole buddies."

"We split up," he said.

Mule appeared in the door of the shack.

"Don't be nursing them beers," he said.

Ralph and I could banter back and forth, but we'd be wasting our time. Ralph was right. A white man tagging along with Ralph would be in the way. Doors would close. Mouths would zip up. Ralph had to go his way. We both knew it, but knowing it didn't make swallowing it any easier. It went down like castor oil and left a bitter taste. I raised my empty bottle toward Mule.

"Thanks for the hospitality," I said.

Monday
April 17
to
Wednesday
April 19, 1939

Chapter 24

My doctor was a former Army Major, a seasoned veteran of the Great War who'd patched up wounded soldiers in France. Doc had experience, and he knew first-hand the damage a bullet could wreak upon a human being. He didn't say much about those war years, but memories haunted him. When he did open up, he delivered his message like a sermon to a sinner, chastisement tinged with anger.

He had me remove my shirt and undershirt, and he examined my wound.

"It's healing," he said and leaned in to remove the stitches. "Smart money says you've had help along the way."

He pulled a stitch, and I flinched.

"My gal nursed me, kept the wound clean and dressed. She also kept me out of trouble," I said.

"That makes you a lucky man on two counts. Listen to your gal. She's the smarter of you two. And listen to your doctor. Another inch, and that bullet would have caused some real damage. I almost wish it had. You'd be better off if you didn't rely on dumb luck. It's going to get you killed one day. This isn't your first gunshot wound, you know."

I'd taken a bullet to the leg the year before. The doctor placed a bandage over the wound, secured it with tape, and washed his hands. He spoke as he wrote on my chart.

"Leave it covered so your shirt doesn't chafe the wound. You can remove the bandage as soon as there's no irritation. Two bullet wounds in a year's time is a lousy average. Take care of yourself, detective. You're not getting any younger. You've got a birthday coming up."

"You're not the first person to remind me," I said.

"People pay attention to your birthdays," he said. "Every time you celebrate a birthday, somebody loses a bet."

The curtain came down on the dark season with Johnny Vander Meer's first pitch in Cincinnati. Baseball was back. The St. Louis Cardinals opened their season against the Pittsburgh Pirates, and I stopped in at Tom's Inn for the festivities. Fifteen thousand fans gathered under an overcast sky in Pittsburgh to watch the Bucs take on the Birds. A sizable crowd gathered around the radio in Tom's Inn to listen to the same game.

Tom pulled the stick and poured Storz beer. He moved from one empty glass to another, from one end of the bar to the other. He bounced around like a barefoot kid playing hopscotch on a summer sidewalk.

Opening day brought nostalgia I didn't try to shake off. Dwelling on the past is a fool's game, but I indulged myself on opening day. For a couple of hours, I shagged fly balls, played catch, and knocked the horsehide into orbit. I ran like I could run forever across green, green grass in centerfield.

Carrying a platter of steaming franks, Mabel tottered out of the kitchen and beamed at cheers from the peanut gallery. Someone called for mustard, and other voices chimed in. Mustard, beer, and baseball—everything a hotdog needed.

We shelled peanuts and smoked cigars and placed friendly wagers with nickels, dimes, and quarters.

"Nickel says the next pitch is a fastball."

"A dime says it's a curve."

"I'll take that bet."

"Groundball, he's out."

"No, a pop up."

"My nickel against your dime, he gets a hit."

"This is the Cardinals year," Tom said over and over to anyone within earshot. By the sixth inning his voice began to waver. The Pirates owned a two-run lead over the scoreless Birds. Things looked up for St. Louis in the top of the seventh inning. Three Cardinal hitters got on base. Joe Medwick came to bat with the bases loaded and whacked the ball, plating a pair and tying the game. Johnny Mize came up behind Medwick and knocked in the go-ahead run. The 3-2 score held up the rest of the way. The Cards won their first game of the season.

Tom pulled the stick and whooped. "A round on the house!" he said, and fans bellied up to the bar. Baseball was back. Mabel shook her head and tottered back into the kitchen.

♦♦♦

On Wednesday morning I telephoned Ralph from my office. He'd uncovered evidence that Johnson was peddling his product in local clubs, but not much else. The people he spoke to, men and women, were saddened by the death of their dealer and equally concerned by where they'd get their next fix.

The newspapers I picked up from my desk belonged to earlier in the week. I'd fallen behind and scanned headlines. S. S. Van Dine, writer of detective novels featuring Philo Vance, had died. The coroner said his heart gave out. Van Dine was only fifty, too young to take the final bow. Writing detective novels sounded like risky business.

In Oklahoma, a banker took his own life and left depositors wondering why $55,000 was missing. Maybe banking was a risky profession, too. Also in Oklahoma, a tornado killed seven people.

Locally, Nelson Eddy would perform at the Wichita Forum in a couple of weeks. Band leader, Paul Whiteman, touted Chesterfield cigarettes in an advertisement. In another advertisement, S.G. Holmes & Sons offered suits for $13.95. I made a note to pay them a visit. Fourteen bucks would leave a hole in my budget, but I had to replace my suit riddled with bullet holes.

Poland and Romania agreed to an anti-German alliance. The situation in Europe heated up. A photograph of the USS Wichita, recently commissioned heavy cruiser, appeared in the Sunday edition. The Navy announced plans to parade its fleet off the coast of Virginia later that month. Officials assured the country that the display of military power had nothing to do with the conflicts in Europe. Only a sucker would take that bet.

I stood at the window and looked to the street below. A green bike leaned against a lamppost. A few moments later the outer door opened, and a youngster greeted Agnes.

"Hiya, Miss Agnes."

"Hiya, Rusty," Agnes said.

I opened my door, and Rusty and I repeated the Hiya greeting back and forth. Rusty handed me the latest edition of *The Eagle*.

"What's in the news?" I said.

"War and war," he said. "My dad says the news is no good. My teacher says the same thing. Are we going to go to war, Mr. Stone?"

The telephone rang, and Agnes said it was for me. The caller saved me from coming up with an answer to Rusty's question, an answer I didn't have. I went into my office and picked up the receiver.

"I thought cowboys knew when to duck," a voice said.

"I did duck, right into a bullet. How'd you get the news?" I said.

"I'm a bookmaker. I know everything," Aaron Bernstein said. "You're too old to be in gunfights. The odds of you growing old just went down. Do you feel up to placing a bet?"

"I'd bet against myself, but who'd bet on me? If you called to yank my chain, I'm hanging up. I'm chasing a hot lead."

"Hot lead? Even money says you're reading the newspaper and giving Agnes a hard time."

"No bet," I said.

"Listen, Pete, Dexter's onto you," he said. "He knows you've been asking after him."

"Good. I'll hear from him."

"Dexter and I crossed paths the other day."

"He showed up at the El Capitan?"

"Not even close. Try the B'nai Jehudah Temple," Bernstein said. "It turns out your favorite bookie and your archenemy are both Jewish."

"That makes no sense. You said Dexter cozied up to the German American Bund," I said. "The Bund is the sworn enemy of Jews."

"True and true," Bernstein said. "Dexter's working an angle. One of his goons gave me the word, a guy who's into me for a chunk of dough. The Schmo laid a bundle at fourteen to one on a hopped up nag in the fourth at Fairmount. The trainer had dosed the ride with cocaine. The nag led the field out of the gate and dropped dead on the first turn."

"That's tough for the goon and worse for the horse, but what does that have to do with Dexter?"

"I cut the guy a deal. He'll pay off the bet, and I'll eat the vig. He swallowed the offer. In return he spoon-fed me the inside scoop on Dexter's ties with the Bund."

"You took a hit if you made nothing on the bet," I said.

"I'll make it up next time. The guy's a born loser."

"So, what did you learn?"

"It turns out that Reginald Dexter isn't his real name, not the name he was given at birth. He changed it."

Aaron Bernstein told me about Dexter's past.

Friday
April 21, 1939

Chapter 25

Agnes came in with a cup of coffee. She set her cup on the desk and sat down in the customer's chair. Afternoon sunshine cast shadows over her face. I adjusted the curtain on the window. She leaned back in the chair and crossed her arms.

"Something's on your mind," I said.

"Nothing escapes you, detective," she said.

I lit a cigarette and said, "Shoot."

"You might want to rephrase that. There's been enough shooting," she said. "I'm in the dark, Pete, and I don't like it. You usually let me in, but you're playing your cards close to the vest lately. I'd like to know why. When I took this job, I was to be more than your secretary. I was to be your right arm, your assistant, beside you on every case. Let me in. Talk to me."

"You are in. I'm not blocking you out, Agnes."

"You're holding back, not telling me everything. This started with a body in Ralph's apartment. That sent the snowball rolling down the hill. A hit man named Rackley tried to kill Ralph. He put a bullet into you. Four people are dead, Johnson and three hired guns. What's Ralph involved in? What are you involved in? How did Reginald Dexter get into the picture?"

Agnes was right. I had held back.

"If I had answers, I'd tell you," I said. "Amos Johnson's body was a message for Ralph to give up what Johnson had. Ralph doesn't know what that is. Ralph met Amos Johnson when they worked for

Reginald Dexter. That's the connection. Dexter knows I'm looking for him. Keep that information in the office. I don't want Lucille to hear about Dexter. As far as she's concerned, he belongs to the past."

"I won't say anything to Lucille. What's the history there?" she said.

"Dexter and I crossed paths shortly after Lucille was widowed."

"I remember that."

"I helped the Wichita police boot Dexter out of town. Lucille worries. As far as she knows, he's gone and good riddance to him. I don't want to dredge up unpleasant memories, that's all."

"Fair enough," Agnes said.

The telephone rang, and Agnes answered.

"Speak of the devil," she said into the phone. "No, he's right here."

"It's Lucille," Agnes said to me and handed me the phone. Then, she left my office.

"What have you been saying about me?" Lucille said.

"What I always say, sweetheart. I love you, and I can't stop talking about you."

"That and a buffalo nickel buys a Coca-Cola."

Lucille said her sister was in town and planned to spend the night. She invited me to join the pair that evening for leftovers and girl talk. I declined, and she giggled. After she rang off, I donned my fedora, and headed for the door.

"Lock up the office when you're ready, Agnes," I said. "I'm going to see a man about a suit."

S.G. Holmes & Sons was located on Douglas a couple of blocks west of my office. Clouds formed on the horizon, but I chose to walk. Pedestrian traffic picked up in the late afternoon. I stretched my legs and took in fresh air.

The business's founder, Sam Holmes, had passed on several years earlier, leaving management of the store to his son, Dan. An eager salesman greeted me when I darkened the door. Dan spotted me from the back of the store and waved. My mind flashed to Ralph Waldo. He harbored a simple wish to walk through the door and be served like any other man. The salesman rested his chin on a thumb and forefinger and looked me over.

"Forty-one, regular," I said.

He steered me toward his finest suits, but I mentioned the advertisement in the newspaper. He veered toward another rack.

"Yes, right this way," he said.

I browsed while he lectured about fabric, cut, style, and other things I ignored. A navy blue number in lightweight wool caught my eye. The color and style suited me, so I tried it on in the fitting room. The jacket was a perfect fit, but the pants needed to be taken in and cuffed. The tailor measured my inseam, made chalk marks, and stuck pins in the right places. He promised to have the suit ready early the following week. The clerk at the register totaled the bill, $13.95 plus 28 cents for the governor, for a total of $14.23. I paid up, thanked the salesman, and walked the couple of blocks back to Douglas and Emporia.

The temperature had dropped, and I buttoned down the top on my roadster at the corner. By the time I rolled through downtown and crossed the river, a fog was rolling in. Motorists turned on their headlights. I pulled up at Tom's Inn on Seneca. Vivid neon signs in the windows flashed "Storz Beer" and "Open."

"The Birds held off the Cubbies until the first inning," Tom said and placed a beer on a coaster. "The bums committed three errors today. Can you believe that? How can major league ballplayers boot the ball three times in a single game?"

Tom muttered and pulled the stick over a pitcher, then delivered the beer to a party of four sitting at a table. A loss to the Cubs was tough for Tom to swallow. The Chicago Cubs were hated rivals of the St. Louis Cardinals. Some folks referred to the games as the Route 66 rivalry, although mutual animosity existed long before the highway was completed. That was in 1926, the year the Cards won the World Series.

"We hit the ball. We got eleven hits, and we still managed to lose the game," he said when he returned to the bar.

Mabel appeared at my elbow.

"Pete, before Tom starts crying in your beer, how about something to eat? I have a pot of Hungarian goulash bubbling on the stove," she said.

"The perfect dish to ward off a chill," I said and pecked her on the forehead.

Friday night business was steady. Tom served beer, Mabel served food, and patrons came and went. Tom and I hashed out baseball, and mildly debated which team was better, the Yankees or the Cardinals. Our disagreements were friendly. In the end, we clinked our glasses and swallowed our beer but never our pride.

The big hand on the clock was poised over the twelve and the little hand over the nine when the door opened. Two men in dark suits came through the door and swiveled their heads. Their eyes roamed the room and settled on the bar. They took stools, one to my left, the other to my right.

"Beer," one said.

Tom poured two glasses and served the men. Each man lifted his glass and drained it. The man to my right tossed a fin onto the bar.

"Let's go," he said to me.

The men stood up.

"Pete?" Tom said. "Is everything all right?"

"It's okay, Tom," I said. "I've been expecting them."

Chapter 26

We stepped outside. Thick fog brought a damp chill. I pulled up my collar. The pair led me to a sedan at the curb, a dark Cadillac with shiny whitewalls. One guy opened the back door.

I moved to get in, and he said, "Hold it. Raise your arms."

I held out my arms while he frisked me. I didn't carry a gun.

"Get in," he said.

He followed me inside and closed the door. The Caddy had that new car smell.

"Leather seats," I said. "Nice."

The other guy got behind the wheel and U-turned from the curb. He steered the Caddy south to Douglas, then turned east toward downtown.

"Nothing beats a Cadillac," I said. That got no response. "My Cadillac's on back order. I expect it any day now. The dealer was fresh out."

The stoics stared straight ahead. I took a different tack.

"Which one of you Rockefellers is into Aaron Bernstein for a pile of dough?" I said.

That brought a snicker from the driver.

"Not a word, Lou," the guy next to me said.

Lou laughed and neighed like a horse. Then he gasped and gargled and rolled his head to the side. I grinned at the antics and looked to my right. Veins on the other guy's neck bulged.

"I mean it, Lou! Shut your yap!"

Lou laughed and neighed again. The car continued to the east. We passed through downtown and kept rolling. Some blocks later, we neared the city limits. We crossed over Oliver and went on. We reached a lighted sign that read, "Eastborough."

Eastborough was established a couple of years earlier, a small community hovering on the edge of Wichita, incorporated as its own place, a mayor and a city council, a municipal court and a police department, the works.

Lou braked the Caddy at the Eastborough limits and proceeded at a slower speed. He turned on Hampton and rolled onto a circular driveway. Pebbles crunched beneath the tires. Had Reggie Dexter taken up residence in Eastborough? If so, I had to tip my fedora to the man. He would remain active in Wichita without actually being in Wichita, and live in peace away from the scrutiny of the Wichita police. He'd run his businesses from the sidelines, like a baseball manager directing players from the dugout.

Lou pulled up at a stone and brick structure that boasted pillars, bay windows, and dormers. A chandelier glowed within. An enormous chimney hinted at a fireplace in an ample chamber, large enough to house the Wichita Symphony Orchestra, should it pop in for a gig.

"Let's go, Stone," my escort said.

We went inside, and the fog and chill melted behind us. Logs crackled in the fireplace. I breathed in the wealth and ambience. Paintings hung on the walls, and sculptures were scattered here and there. I recognized paintings, a Robert Henri portrait, a rolling hills scene by Thomas Hart Benton, and haystacks in a field by John Steuart Curry. A Bruce Moore bust rested atop a pedestal. Only a fool would question their authenticity. Stunning art took one's breath away and leant an air of coziness that belonged to a museum. The only warmth came from the fireplace.

"Wait here," Lou said and disappeared down a hallway. I looked up at the crystal chandelier that dangled above me and stepped to the side. I didn't anticipate that the glistening glass would crash to the floor, but if it did, my remains would nestle nicely in a thousand matchboxes.

"This way," Lou said.

He led me down the hall and through a doorway. A smaller fire burned in a smaller fireplace. Flags hanging on stands framed the fireplace, the American flag on one side, a swastika opposite. Mounted photographs decorated the walls.

A figure to my right rose from a chair. I ignored the figure and studied the photographs. Several had been taken two months earlier when the German American Bund rallied in New York City. A shot from above in Madison Square Garden showed seats filled with people, twenty thousand according to reports. A photo of Bund leader, Fritz Kuhn, showed him at the podium, eyes wide, mouth open, fist in the air. Another photo captured Kuhn shaking hands with Reginald Dexter. The pair wore smiles that would freeze a snowman's heart.

"I didn't figure you for a man interested in the Bund," Dexter said.

"To each his own," I said.

According to Aaron Bernstein, Reginald Dexter worked an angle. He'd been born Reinhold Dresner, the youngest child of a Jewish family in Dresden, Germany. He was orphaned as an infant and sent to America to be raised by an aunt and uncle. The aunt and uncle changed their name from Dresner to Dexter at Ellis Island. They did the same with their new arrival from Germany.

Years later, Dexter, nee Dresner, embraced the German American Bund. Fritz Kuhn ran the Bund and hobnobbed with Adolph Hitler when the opportunity arose. The thought made my guts churn.

Dictators all used the same MO. First, they seized the mind, then they severed the spine. Bow to a dictator, and you were neutered forever. Brains and backbones separated humans from the lowest forms of life. I wasn't giving up mine, not without a fight. Nobody would seize, sever, or neuter this private eye.

"My testicles are mine, not a billy goat's," I said.

Dexter raised his eyebrows.

"You are a strange man, Mr. Stone," he said.

"I could say the same about you," I said.

"Have a seat," he said.

I lowered myself onto a wingback chair facing Dexter who sat in a similar chair. A low table separated us. The fireplace to my left brought welcome warmth to the room.

He'd put on some weight but remained dashing. His dark hair was slicked back. Any gray had been masked with dye as had a thin, dark mustache. He wore an open-collared shirt beneath a silk smoking jacket that hadn't been hanging on the sale rack. The wrap had set him back more than $13.95. A red jewel sparkled on the ring he wore on this right hand.

"You're a bourbon drinker," Dexter said.

On cue, a woman appeared at the doorway. She caught my eye, and a vessel throbbed in my temple. She carried a tray laden with crystal tumblers, an ice bucket, and a bottle of Four Roses. Dexter and I rose when she entered. She wore a blue, floor-length gown, silver slippers, and a string of pearls. She lowered the tray to the table. The scent of Tabu perfume lingered in her midst.

"Thank you, Stella," Dexter said. "Stella, this is Mr. Pete Stone. Mr. Stone, Miss Stella Grace."

"How do you do, Mr. Stone?" she said.

She acted as if we'd never met. I played along.

"Fine, thank you, Miss Grace. How do you do?" I said.

"That will be all, Stella," Dexter said.

Stella Grace left the room, closing the door behind her.

"Well, we meet again, as you hoped we would," he said as he filled tumblers with ice and poured bourbon. "You've been spreading my name around trying to draw me out, and you have done so. Here we are. It's been some time."

He handed me a glass and lifted his.

"To your health, sir," he said.

I raised my glass and said, "That's a peculiar toast, coming from a man trying to have me killed."

Dexter sipped bourbon and lowered his glass. He removed a cigar from a humidor on the table.

"Cuban tobacco?" he said.

"No, thanks," I said and lit a Chesterfield.

He snipped the end of the cigar, held a match to it, and puffed. Smoke wafted up to a ceiling fan. He watched it dissipate, then shifted his eyes toward me.

"Mr. Stone, why on earth would I wish to have you killed?" he said.

"I've been meaning to ask you that very question," I said. "Maybe you can also tell me why you had Amos Johnson murdered and why you loosed assassins on Ralph Waldo. Those are a few of the questions jostling for position in my mind."

Dexter drew on the cigar. He raised his glass with a steady hand and savored a swallow of Four Roses.

"You recall we met some time ago," he said. "You also recall that meeting did not go well."

"No, it didn't. The cops threw you out of town. I helped them do it."

"Yes, I was urged to graze in greener pastures, so to speak. That's true. Perhaps you believe I harbor animosity toward you for what happened then. You might even believe I wish to see you dead. Well, Mr. Stone, hear me well. I want no such thing. Does that surprise you?"

"What you say is no surprise. Does it surprise you that I don't believe a word of it?"

He dropped cigar ash into a tray.

"Try this," he said. "When I left Wichita I went to Kansas City, a fortuitous move, I must say. I won't bore you with details. Let's just say business has been good, better than it ever was in Wichita. The pastures were, in fact, greener. I have you to thank for that."

"I'm thrilled. If things are so swell in Kansas City, what are you doing here?" I said. "What's this little cottage, your summer home?"

Dexter smiled.

"Kansas City is swell, to use your vernacular, but there are always new and profitable opportunities elsewhere. Why should a man limit himself?"

"Limitations build character," I said.

"I prefer to think of it as free enterprise."

"No one deserves it all."

"We differ on that point, but we're not here to argue. Men are dead. Other men are in danger. Let's agree that this killing must stop. As you know, Amos Johnson worked in my employ. He plied his trade in Kansas City, but he freelanced. How and why he met his death in Wichita I do not know. Whatever precipitated his demise had nothing to do with our mutual employment arrangement."

"Mutual employment arrangement. You make Johnson sound like a diplomat, an ambassador spreading good cheer and bonhomie on your behalf. He peddled drugs."

"Amos Johnson filled a need in the marketplace, as do I," Dexter said. "Arguing the morality of my business gains us nothing. He worked for me, and he was rewarded for his efforts. His death comes as a blow to me."

"I don't believe you," I said. "You'll measure the minutes it takes to replace Johnson with an egg timer."

Dexter reached for my glass. I crushed out my cigarette. He refreshed our drinks and leaned back in his chair. He drew on his cigar and stared at its glowing tip.

"You possess a cop's mentality. That's why you don't believe me," he said. "It's that mentality that limits you. Your thinking is useful in your line of work, I suppose, but it's limiting."

"How so?"

"To someone in law enforcement, the concept of innocent until proven guilty belongs in the courtroom, nowhere else. To a cop everyone is a suspect. He believes no one is innocent. He believes everyone has something to hide."

I laughed and said, "Are you telling me you have nothing to hide?"

"No. I'm telling you that I'm innocent. I'm innocent of these murders and innocent of the threats you've received," he said. "Until you accept that fact, Mr. Stone, your investigation will be stymied, limited by your narrow focus on me."

The man sounded earnest, as do the best liars.

"Someone has hired assassins to kill you and Ralph Waldo. I am not that someone," he said.

"I wish I could believe you," I said.

"What is my motive? I have no motive for committing these crimes," he said.

"How well did you know Johnson? What can you tell me about him?" I said.

"Johnson was dependable, eager. He made money, and from what I gather, he spent what he made. He ran with a fast crowd, musicians and entertainers, and amused himself with women drawn to that scene. He had plenty of money, and he wanted more."

"That sounds familiar. Why should Johnson limit himself?" I said.

"Indeed. I don't intend to lecture the dead. I'm merely suggesting that his eagerness brought him to Wichita for a reason. Perhaps that eagerness led to his death."

Dexter rose from his chair and moved to the fireplace. He laid a log on the fire, stirred the ashes with a poker, and returned to his chair.

"My interests in Wichita are legal and aboveboard. As you know, I'm in the construction industry. That is not a secret. Opportunities for ownership have recently opened up, and I've taken advantage of those opportunities."

Something I'd read in the news came to mind.

"The Pendergast family is in the construction business," I said. "Does Tom Pendergast have interests in Wichita?"

"I'm not associated with Tom Pendergast," he said. "Pendergast and his minions are on a downhill slope. His reign in Kansas City politics is approaching its end."

"The end of a reign. That presents new opportunities," I said.

"Tread lightly, Mr. Stone," he said. "Don't pry into things that are none of your business. You're a fan of baseball, I believe. Keep your eye on the ball."

"That sounds like a threat," I said. "Politics is politics, and business is business. I don't give a tinker's dam for either. A man is a man until he crosses a line. Then, he becomes a rat. I'm after a rat."

Dexter lowered his glass and pierced me with a stare. He reached into a pocket and drew out a wad of cash. He placed three Ben Franklins on the table.

"I'd like to retain your services, Mr. Stone."

"Forget it. I don't sell out to you," I said.

"My money's good," he said.

"Not for me," I said.

"For a lousy gumshoe, you ride a high horse," he said. "You must understand that you and I have a common enemy."

"A common enemy doesn't make us foxhole buddies, Dexter," I said. "Your evil thrives in shadows. The gumshoe strives to make shadows safe."

"So, we reach an impasse. Hear me out. Prying into my business interests is time wasted. It won't get you closer to the answers you seek. Turn your attention elsewhere. Broaden your scope. That's all I ask. Find the person who's committed these crimes, Mr. Stone. Find the person who threatens you and Ralph Waldo. I'm not asking you to find me innocent. I'm asking you to find who's guilty. Call this expense money, not a retainer. You won't be working for me. You've been paying the bills out of your wallet. A detective doesn't last long doing that. Think of me only as a benefactor, not your employer."

I looked at the bills on the table.

"We understand each other, then," I said. "I solve the case, but I don't work for you."

"Understood," he said.

"One other thing," I said. "Ralph Waldo works with me. Half of this goes to him. How do you feel about a Negro working on the case?"

Dexter peeled off a fourth C-note and laid it on the table.

"Four is easier to divide than three," he said.

Chapter 27

Dexter's goons dropped me off in front of Tom's Inn during the ten o'clock hour. The lights were on in the tavern. The Four Roses Reggie had poured hit me like a heavyweight's haymaker. I didn't need a drink, but I went inside.

"The detective returns," Tom said. "I was worried about you. Who were those guys?"

"Nobody to fuss over. Just hired help," I said.

He offered a beer, but I declined.

"I'm going to work," I said.

"Now, on Friday night?"

"I'm going on a stakeout. I have to see a fellow. Is Mabel still in back?"

"No, she left for home. Are you hungry?"

"I need coffee," I said. "A thermos full if you can."

"Just a minute," he said.

Tom went into the kitchen and returned a moment later.

"Mabel left a pot of coffee on the stove," he said and handed me a thermos bottle.

"Thanks, pal," I said. "Give Mabel my thanks, too."

Outside, I inhaled a lungful of foggy air and climbed aboard the Jones Six. The fog over the city turned downtown into a graveyard. I reached Mosley at walking speed and inched toward the alley in fog so dense I could hardly make out the roadster's hood ornament. The sun had been in bed for hours, and the light of the moon was a rumor. A streetlamp across the street cast an eerie glow.

The alley ran behind an abandoned building shrouded in fog. It was just as well. I'd eyeballed the structure earlier, and it didn't beg to be admired. Methodical vandals had broken each pane of glass. Graffiti artists had scratched the walls with witticisms that featured an exhaustive vocabulary of four-letter words. Beyond the alley, a path continued on through a field of ragweed, dandelions, and such.

I removed the lid from the thermos bottle and poured coffee. The beverage warmed my insides and kept me from dozing. I lit a Chesterfield and replayed a baseball game from my youth, the one where I pitch a no-hitter and slam a homer for the winning run. This time, a pretty girl in the bleachers cheered me on and fell into my arms after I crossed home plate.

The fog eventually gave way to clouds that threatened rain. I'd buttoned the roadster's top into place earlier to ward off the damp, evening chill. I peered into the shadows and checked my watch. The big hand snuck up on midnight.

When the bourbon and coffee caught up with me, I stepped behind the roadster to relieve myself. A drop of rain plopped onto the brim of my fedora, then another, and another. Faraway voices grew louder. Figures appeared out of the shadows. I came from behind the car. The figures drew near, spotted me, and went silent. Shapes froze in the glow of the streetlamp.

"Willie?" I said.

One figure came forward.

"Pete? Pete, is that you?" Willie said. "Lord almighty, you scared us to death."

"It wasn't my intention," I said.

The other man walked up.

"This alley. First a dead man, then a ghost," the man said. "This is one spooky neighborhood."

The rain picked up.

"Hop in the car, fellas," I said. "I'll drive you the rest of the way.

Willie introduced me to his pal, Spider. Willie directed me north a couple of blocks, then east. I pulled up in front of a rambling house secluded by towering trees. The rain became a downpour. Lightning flashed, and thunder clapped.

"You saved us from a good soaking," Willie said.

"Do you work tomorrow?" I said.

"Yeah, most every day lately. Trucks being loaded. Really busy."

"More trucks than usual?"

"It seems to be," he said. "Some of the men say they've never been this busy. That's fine by me. I can use the money."

"I spoke to Leo Little," I said. "He told me Amos Johnson peddled drugs behind the warehouse. He also told me one of his employees dealt with Amos and ended up dead, overdosed on heroin. This was before you started working at the warehouse, but I wondered if anyone ever talked about that?"

Spider stirred in the back seat and coughed. The rain beat on the top of the roadster.

"I think I'll go on in," Spider said.

"Spider, do you know anything about this?" I said.

Spider went silent.

"Speak up," Willie said. "It's okay. I know this man."

"I can't be talking to no white cop about a dead man," Spider said, "less'n I want to end up dead myself. My momma didn't raise no fool."

"This man's trying to solve a murder," Willie said.

We listened to the rain, poker players at the table, waiting to see who'd fold.

"You got a smoke?" Spider said.

I passed around cigarettes and matches.

"His name was Silas," Spider said. "We don't use last names so much. He lived here until he didn't. We kicked him out. We had to. This was before your time, Willie. The only rule we have is no using, no alcohol, no drugs. Silas couldn't obey that rule. He'd slide. We gave him chances, but he always went back to the needle."

Spider drew on the cigarette and gathered his thoughts.

"He left the house. Not long after, he was dead."

"They ruled it an overdose," I said.

"Yeah. Another case closed by the men in blue," Spider said.

"You don't believe it," I said.

"Silas never overdosed himself," Spider said. "The man used the needle, but he knew what he was doing. If he died from H, someone did it for him. Someone overdosed Silas. That's what happened there."

The rain eased into a steady drizzle. The door opened, and Spider disappeared into the night. Willie stayed behind.

"Leo Little told me he never met Cletis Rackley, but you saw Cletis's car parked at the warehouse. You saw the body in the car and again at the morgue. Have you noticed any rough looking characters hanging around the warehouse, characters that don't belong?"

"The fellows at work are a rough bunch," he said.

"I mean an outsider or a visitor Leo might talk to behind closed doors."

"There could be someone like that. I wouldn't know, though," Willie said. "Mr. Little don't tolerate snooping. He's touchy about that. One day a guy asked him what was stored behind a locked door. The next day that guy was gone."

The hour was late.

"Thanks, Willie. Run along and get some rest," I said. "You'll have another truck to load in the morning."

"There'll be a truck to load all right. We clean off that loading dock every day before we leave. The next morning, there's another load on the dock waiting to be loaded."

Willie opened the door, then paused.

"Say, next time you see Ralph, tell him Mr. Little was asking after him."

Saturday
April 22, 1939

<h1 style="text-align:center">Chapter 28</h1>

The fog and rain had moved on and left a blue sky and yellow sun in its wake. I washed up and shaved while the coffee brewed. My wound hadn't troubled me lately, so I removed the bandage and slipped into a fresh shirt. I breakfasted on coffee and a cigarette, stepped out onto the porch, and closed the door.

A robin and a cardinal competed for top billing in the maple tree at the curb. A mourning dove cooed a countermelody to the sharp chirps and trills. Bells interrupted the chorus. I went back inside and answered the telephone.

"Hello?"

"Mr. Stone?" a feminine voice said.

"Guilty," I said.

"This is Miriam Johnson," she said. "I'm sorry to bother you at home on a Saturday morning, but I wondered if you'd meet with me. Would that be possible?"

"Anything's possible," I said. "I can be in my office in ten minutes."

"Would you mind meeting me here?"

She gave me the name of a café on South Broadway.

"I'm on the way," I said.

At the bottom of the stairs, I tipped my fedora to a young mother who pushed a stroller along the sidewalk. A small boy squatted at the curb, fascinated by the gutter awash with rainwater.

Water ran to the corner and spiraled down a drain. The boy floated a boat fashioned from twigs and squealed as he ran after it.

I took a giant stride off the curb, unbuttoned the top on my roadster, and climbed in behind the wheel. Light traffic on a Saturday posed no problem. City streets glistened after the rainfall.

I pulled up at the café on Broadway. Blinds covered the windows, and the lights were turned down low. When I went inside, I understood why. The clientele ranged from bums and hookers to the plain, old down-and-out. Those who once were, and those who never would be. The eyes of a drunk held terror at the prospect of facing another day of sunshine, city noise, and no booze.

A Friday night Cinderella had failed to board the carriage before it turned into a pumpkin. She sat alone at a table and nursed a bruise under her left eye. Her dress was stained and wrinkled. She'd managed to hang onto her shoes. Hanging onto her dignity was another matter.

Her hands shook when she placed ice on a napkin, and the cube fell to the floor. I spooned ice from her glass and placed it on the napkin. Then, I twisted it into a knot and placed it on her cheek. She mumbled something that might have been, "thanks."

I spotted Miriam sitting alone in a booth.

"Aren't you the gentleman?" she said.

"Always, m'lady. How's the coffee in this joint?"

"Surprisingly good. I had eggs and toast, earlier. They've stayed down."

"I'll stick with coffee," I said.

The waitress filled my cup and refilled Miriam's.

"I was afraid you wouldn't see me," she said. "Ralph told me you were upset over our night together at the Eaton Hotel."

"I hope he explained I wasn't upset at you, personally, just the circumstances."

"He did, and I do understand."

"Ralph wanted to share his experience with someone, and he chose you. Do you two have something together, or is that question too personal?"

"Ralph is sweet. He knows I care for him, but there's nothing in Kansas for me. I'll be going back to the coast."

"To pursue your acting career," I said. "Have I seen you on the screen?"

She frowned.

"My roles have been small. No, you wouldn't have seen me. I've been cast as an extra, that's all. I answer cattle calls along with dozens of others. We work for a day or two at a time. I barely earn enough to cover my rent. I wouldn't be able to dine in a fine restaurant like this or have the dough to watch a film in a theater, if I didn't waitress or clean rooms. Few people of my color make it to the big screen."

She sipped coffee.

"That may change, though," she said.

"How so?"

"Mr. David O. Selznick is producing a film that Hollywood is already calling an epic. It's called *Gone with the Wind*. It'll be released late in the year. Have you heard about it?"

"Not the movie, but I've read the book. It's by Margaret Mitchell. That should make quite a movie. Plenty of action, greed, and betrayal. Not to mention a great love story. It'll be a hit."

"It'll have a great cast, too," she said, "including Negroes, lots of Negroes."

"The story takes place during the Civil War, southern plantations," I said.

"That's right. Do you know Hattie McDaniel? She's famous, and she's Negro, and she's landed a big role. And guess where she was born? Right here in Wichita. I can't hope for a big role, but I intend to be in that movie," she said.

"Hattie McDaniel starring in an epic motion picture. That's a stretch, a Hollywood producer sticking his neck out, trying something new," I said.

"What do you mean?" she said.

"So many movies are like the last one, the same old thing. I figure a producer to be a coward, a fraidy-cat. The guy who looks both ways twice and wears a safety harness in his Barcalounger."

"Not Selznick. Selznick has guts," she said. "I'm almost ready to leave. The coroner released Amos's remains, and I've had them cremated." She gazed over my shoulder at nothing. "I guess that's all I have left to do."

"Why did you want to see me?" I said.

"You met with Reginald Dexter last evening," she said.

"That's right, I did. And if you know that, you've spoken to Stella Grace. Ralph told me you were living with Stella."

"I was living there, no more, but yes, I did speak to Stella," she said. "May I ask what you and Mr. Dexter discussed?"

I offered a Chesterfield to Miriam and lit hers and mine. I flicked my cigarette over an ashtray.

"I hope David O. gives you a part, Miriam. You deserve it. You're a terrific actress, and you play your role well."

"That doesn't sound like a compliment," she said.

"Why ask me what Dexter and I discussed when you already know the answer. You've spoken to Stella. She was listening in on our conversation. Or am I wrong?"

She drew on her cigarette.

"You're right. Stella told me what you talked about. What I want to know is, do you believe what Mr. Dexter told you about his innocence in the murder of my brother?"

"What do you believe?"

"Lies drip off that man's lips so easily people believe he's telling the truth," she said.

"Did Dexter have your brother murdered, and if so, why?"

"If Dexter did order his death, I couldn't prove it," she said. "As to why, I've been thinking about that since I first heard Amos was dead. Why?"

"Dexter isn't as innocent as he'd have me believe," I said. "He believes he's innocent, though. The man truly thinks he is not guilty of any wrongdoing. What does Stella Grace think?"

"I wonder that myself," she said.

"Who is Stella Grace?" I said. "She says she knew Amos as a child."

"We grew up together. We're from the same neighborhood. She's telling the truth. We've known each other since we were kids."

Miriam sipped coffee and lowered her cup.

"I say I know her. All these years, and I don't know what goes on inside her," she said.

"Why is she with Dexter?" I said.

"I tried to warn her away from him, not that I blame her. You saw Dexter's home. Where do you live? What's your home like? Do you live in Eastborough? Do your neighbors live in another world? Dexter has another home, you know, in Kansas City. It looks over the Country Club Plaza.

"Dexter does what he wants, goes where he wants. Doors aren't closed to him, not for long. If a door is closed, someone opens it for him. A woman who grew up with little finds that attractive. A woman appreciates being treated well. If that woman is beautiful, and white, she gets what she wants."

"Is that why you called me, Miriam? To tell me how well off Dexter is?" I said.

She leaned over and stared into my eyes.

"My brother's death must be avenged," she said. "The police found the bodies of the men who killed Amos. Those men were guilty, and they got what they deserved, but they were following orders. The police are satisfied they have Amos's murderers, case closed. You're willing to go deeper, to find the real guilty party. Don't let Dexter sway you. If it was Dexter, bring him down. Find the truth."

"I intend to find the truth," I said. "I intend to stop these attempts on Ralph Waldo's life, along with mine. Anything you can tell me about your brother would help. Amos knew something or had something, something someone wants. What was your brother mixed up in?"

She looked around the room.

"I'd like a glass of water," she said.

The waitress brought water, and I declined a refill on coffee.

"We grew up poor," Miriam said, "like most everybody in that neighborhood. Folks these past years talk about the Depression. We wouldn't have understood what that word meant back when I was a kid. When you grow up with nothing, you got nothing to lose. That's poverty, not a Depression. This Depression hasn't changed my life."

Miriam drank water and set the glass on the table.

"On his first day of school, Amos came home with a bloody nose. He was just a little tyke. He tried to swipe a bigger boy's sandwich, and the boy beat him up. Amos was six-years-old, and he was hungry. He didn't cry, though. That little boy took his beating like a man. Right from the start, teachers labeled him a troublemaker, and they treated him as such.

"Amos discovered that adding and subtracting numbers and learning his ABC's did nothing to fill his belly. At first, he played hooky. Momma punished him for it, but he didn't care. He hated school and kept playing hooky. Finally, Momma just wore out. She quit chasing after him, and he quit going to school altogether. He fell in with boys like himself, troublemakers who were streetwise and book stupid. On the street, that's where he learned his lessons."

"Your family drew a tough hand," I said. "It still doesn't tell us why Amos was killed."

"Amos fell into crime," she said. "He watched for an opportunity to take something and pounced when it appeared. He was a scavenger, a thief, but he wasn't violent. As far as I know, Amos never owned a gun. He took what he could and didn't resist when he got caught. He broke the law, but he didn't fight the law. When he got caught, he served his time, and when he got back on the street, he started right in again. He sold drugs, but he started as a thief. Whoever killed Amos is after something he stole."

"You sound certain about that."

Miriam sipped more water.

"I spoke to Amos," she said. "He called me in California. This was several weeks ago. He was excited. He didn't tell me why. He wanted me to ask, but I wouldn't do that. I didn't want to know what he'd done. He wanted me to know he was doing well. I could tell from his voice that he'd made a score."

"Did he do that, call you when he made a score?"

"He sought approval, a pat on the head, from the time we were kids. Our daddy was gone, and Momma never praised him at all after he quit school. Now, she's gone, too. He turned to me, his big sister. He needed someone to believe in him, to believe he was a success."

"Stella was there during those early years," I said.

Miriam gazed back into a memory.

"As bad as we had it, Stella might have had it worse. I knew who my daddy was, even if my memories are few. Stella lived with her mother, just the two of them. The two of them and whatever gentleman came calling that night, that is. Stella never knew who her father was. The fact is, her mother didn't know, either, not for certain.

"Amos and I were too young to know about that, and we wouldn't have cared if we did know. A father was something that happened to other people, like the Depression does today. Momma kicked my father out of the house. I don't remember that. One day he was there. One day he was gone. Momma never spoke about him after that and grew angry if I asked about him.

"Momma didn't care for Stella, the little white girl. Stella was a beautiful child. She and Amos were born about the same time, and Amos was crazy about her. Momma warned us to stay away from her, but Amos ignored her like he always did. He was only three or four when he called Stella his sissy. Momma tanned his hide with a switch."

I lit cigarettes for us. Two men in dungarees took a table nearby. I leaned closer to Miriam.

"The night Amos called, did he finally tell you what he stole?" I said.

"He would have. I didn't let him. I told him I loved him, and I hung up the telephone."

Monday
April 24, 1939

On Monday morning, the three of us huddled around the desk in the Wichita Police Station: Detective Lieutenant Thaddeus McCormick, myself, and the toxic stogie Mac clenched between his teeth. The closed door muffled rumbling voices and ringing telephones beyond. The closed door also squelched the possibility of a draft wafting through with fresh air. My eyes watered, so I stood up, raised a window, and fanned my fedora.

"Why don't you strangle that thing before it chokes us both to death?" I said.

Mac looked at the stogie he held between thumb and forefinger, then looked at me with raised eyebrows.

"What's wrong with my cigar?" he said.

I dropped a White Owl on his desk.

"Try this. Babe Ruth smokes a White Owl," I said. "His wife swears by them."

"You know, you owe me this cigar," Mac said.

He pinched the tip of his stogie, and the ash fell into the tray. He laid the stub aside for later. He lit the White Owl and blew a cloud of smoke. I lit a Chesterfield and did the same. Any poor soul who darkened the doorway would be on his own for a breath of fresh air. I pulled my chair close and gave Mac a rundown of recent events. Mac listened and nodded before he spoke.

"Dexter's crafty," he said. "He keeps business interests in Wichita, but he's too smart to manage anything hands-on. Better to hire underlings for the day-to-day. That residence outside of town comes as news, though. I suppose the chief could drop a suggestion to the Eastborough police, ask them to keep an eye open, but to what end? Dexter isn't breaking any laws as far as we know. Until he does, we all have better things to do."

"Do you have anything new on the vigilante murders?" I said.

Mac grunted something unintelligible.

"We have matching bullets. The two men who killed Johnson bought it in the park, late at night. The park was closed, no witnesses. We took fingerprints from the bridge rails, and there were footprints on the path. Too many to be useful and nothing that points to an assassin. Cletis Rackley was killed in the alley. His fingerprints were on the car along with those of your pal, Willie. Maybe the assassin wore gloves. Willie's footprints were outside the car along with others, adult-sized and kid-sized. The alley is well-traveled.

"Uniforms canvassed the neighborhoods near Mosley. All was quiet. Nobody saw a thing. Nobody heard a thing. Everyone was cozy in bed, little birdies nestled in their nests. The only night owls are predators and their prey. We're stretched thin. Frankly, without a public outcry, there isn't much pressure to go on. When one bad guy shoots another bad guy, John Q. doesn't care one way or the other, so long as a bullet doesn't come his way."

"Suppose Dexter is square," I said. "Suppose this has nothing to do with him. The sister, Miriam, points to Dexter, probably because she doesn't care for him. She also admits her brother was a thief in addition to his drug dealing."

"Dexter's still not off the hook. He's involved in more than drugs," Mac said.

"Ralph backs up Miriam's story about Johnson's thievery. He was a small-time crook," I said. "Suppose Johnson did commit a heist. What's gone missing recently?"

Mac grabbed his cigar, cough-laughed onto the back of his hand, and struggled not to choke. He blinked at me through watery eyes and wheezed and coughed again.

"Stone, never let it be said you aren't good for a laugh."

"Okay, call me the court jester, and you win the Oscar for your performance," I said. "How about giving me a straight answer?"

Mac leaned back in his chair and looked up.

"Well, let's see," he said. "Shall we start with auto theft? Someone on the other side of that door could give you a list of a dozen or so open cases. How about breaking and entering? That should keep you busy. Jewelry, paintings, heirlooms—just to name a few hot items."

Mac leaned over his desk.

"You name it, we've got it," he said. "If it's valuable, there's a chance it'll go missing—and often does."

Mac enjoyed another laugh at my expense. A snippet of Shakespeare came to mind, "The robbed that smiles steals something from the thief." Mac was right. If it's valuable, it can go missing.

◆◆◆

Agnes greeted me at the office with a message from Aaron Bernstein.

"He has business in Wichita. He'll be stopping by tomorrow afternoon," she said. "He says you still owe him a dog and a beer."

"Only if there's baseball," I said. "A dog needs mustard, beer, and baseball, the trifecta."

I'd asked Ralph to come to my office, and when he did, I dropped a pair of C-notes on my desk.

"What's this?" he said.

"We have a benefactor. I met with Dexter," I said.

"Dexter hired us? I don't believe it."

"This is expense money, not a retainer," I said and explained we didn't work for Dexter. "Dexter claims Amos made dough working for him, but his earnings didn't satisfy him. He wanted more."

"There's nothing wrong with that," he said.

"I also met with Miriam. She called me," I said. "She said Amos was a thief, and someone's after what he stole."

"I can't buy that. Amos was small time. Amos wasn't a bad guy, not in here," he said and bumped his chest with a fist. "Amos wanted a better life. Tell me who doesn't. He lifted a little here and there, penny-ante stuff. He'd pocket a comic book, a candy bar, like he did when he was a kid. He never grew up."

"Miriam spoke to him by telephone. She said Amos was excited. Maybe he'd graduated from the penny ante to the big time. What do you think?"

"If he did, he never told me about it."

"But?"

"I wonder if that wasn't his dream," Ralph said.

◆ ◆ ◆

The St. Louis Cardinals didn't play that day, but Tom had pent up chatter to vent. The Birds had completed a home stand against the Cubbies, winning one game and losing two to their rivals. Their only win on Saturday was a lopsided 9-0 affair. On Sunday, the Birds rallied from a 2-6 deficit and almost took the game but fell short in a 5-6 loss.

Tom poured Storz beer into a glass and set it down in front of me. He leaned over and shook his head.

"Twice we lost, Pete, twice to the Cubs. Close games, too. You don't win a pennant by losing close games. We scored sixteen runs in those three games—sixteen runs and gave up only ten. We scored six more runs than the Cubs did, and they still took two out of three games from us."

"The Cardinals have played four games," I said. "There's a 150 games left to play. The season's young. Tom, if you lament every loss, you're going to be ten years older before the World Series even starts."

"The Birds should have won those games," he said.

I tossed a nickel onto the bar. Tom picked it up.

"What's this for?" he said.

"Fill a glass and cry into your own beer," I said.

He dropped the nickel, and it clanked onto the bar. Mabel came to the rescue with a tray from the kitchen. I got off the stool and took it from her.

"Mabel, this tray is heavy," I said.

I placed the feast on the mahogany bar, two bowls of chili and a third bowl brimming with soda crackers.

"You shouldn't work so hard," Tom said.

"Somebody has to work. I hear you two whining at each other clear into the kitchen. That's enough baseball talk. Eat," she said.

An intoxicating aroma of hot chili topped with onions wafted through the tavern. Heads raised and swiveled around us.

"Say, I could go for a bowl of that," a guy at the end of the bar said. A voice at a table over my shoulder said, "Here, too," followed by another voice, "And me."

Mabel hustled back into the kitchen. Tom and I spooned chili and sipped beer. We chatted more baseball, but we kept our voices low when we did.

Tuesday
April 25, 1939

Chapter 30

Sometime during the wee hours, pieces came together. Sunlight hadn't peeked through the blinds. Floors creaked, and leaves rustled, but morning noises remained in abeyance. No car motored along the street, no dog barked, no door slammed.

Not yet awake and no longer asleep, I lay silent in the tweener time. The truths and the lies, the promises kept and the promises broken, the stuff of dreams butted up against the realities of failure, all carried a stench and tasted of grit, fodder for life in the city.

It began with drugs and escalated from there. Silas, the man with no last name, died of a heroin overdose. He bought heroin from Amos Johnson, and the drug took his life. Willie's friend, Spider, claimed someone else had wielded the needle that killed Silas. A figure in the shadows ushered Silas to his date with the grim reaper.

Who had done it and why? What was the motive? What made Silas a target for murder? Maybe Spider was wrong. Maybe Silas did die of an accidental overdose. It happened. Drugs carried a risk that went with the territory.

Heroin itself raised a question. Silas used the needle, and heroin was addictive. He needed regular fixes. That took money. Where did a common laborer earning low wages come up with the dough to finance his habit? Users turned to crime to get the money to satisfy their needs.

Amos Johnson telephoned his sister, Miriam, not long before he died. He wanted his big sister to know that he was a success. He needed to tell her he was on top of the world. He needed her approval. Miriam had always been there for him. On that day she wasn't. On that day she hung up the telephone.

Johnson needed approval, someone to tell him he was a good boy. He played the tough guy, but the child inside needed a pat on the head. Who did he turn to?

A door slammed, and a dog barked. The clocks chimed me out of bed. I started a pot of Eight O'Clock Coffee, washed up, and shaved. I splashed bay rum on my face and savored the scent and the sting. A fresh shirt under my navy blue suit from S.G. Holmes & Sons and a maroon silk tie did the trick. I returned to the land of the living.

At the kitchen table, I lit a Chesterfield and sipped coffee. When the clocks chimed eight times, I dialed the operator and waited while she made the connection. The telephone rang. If a male answered, I'd hang up, but I doubted a man would answer. I was right. The voice that spoke was female.

"We need to talk," I said, repeating the words she'd used in Dodge City.

She agreed. A man's voice in the background asked who was on the telephone.

"A salesman," she said. "He's selling life insurance."

"Hang up," the voice said, and the phone went dead.

I smoked another cigarette and pondered my conversation with Mac. Valuables went missing. Of course, they did. Without light-fingered thieves, a private eye would soon be out of business. Miriam said that when Amos got caught stealing, he accepted his punishment, and started right in again after he served his time. Amos didn't score a single heist and call it a day. Amos was a serial thief.

I boarded the roadster. From Lewellen, I motored east to Waco and turned south toward downtown. Willie had reported increased activity at the warehouse. His crew cleared the loading dock each day. When the warehouse opened in the morning, material waited to be loaded. Leo Little was moving inventory. He'd been asking about

Ralph. I intended to visit Ralph and deliver the message in person following my meeting in the office.

I turned left at Central and drove over to Broadway where I turned right and rolled past the stunning Cathedral of Immaculate Conception, a church built early in the century. Sunlight glistened on towering crosses mounted atop domes.

Down the street, I passed the Orpheum Theater on my left and White Castle burgers on my right. In the next block, script lettering in the window of an establishment caught my eye, "Nifty Nut House." I pulled over at the store with numerals, 155, above the door. Inside, a pleasant aroma and a smiling gentleman greeted me.

"I'll bet you're Mr. Muckenthaler," I said.

"Call me Ed," he said.

I shook Ed's hand and gave him my name. Lucille had treated me to an assortment of roasted nuts and warned me the merchandise was irresistible.

"Three sacks," I said.

I'd treat Agnes and Lucille, too. Ed Muckenthaler scooped a mixture of cashews, walnuts, almonds, and other nuts into a trio of sacks and taped them shut.

"Come back," he said.

"Count on it," I said.

Moments later I climbed the steps of the Lawrence Block Building. A twinge in my side spurred me. I paused at the third floor landing and inhaled a deep breath of air. Then, I opened the door with the sign on pebbled glass that read, "Pete Stone Private Investigator."

Agnes sat behind her desk and looked up.

"Something smells nice, twice," she said.

I placed a sack on her desk.

"Twice?" I said.

"Twice," she said and thumbed toward the door to my office. "These nuts will be delicious, Pete. Thank you. Percival will enjoy them, too."

"Give hubby my hello," I said.

"A woman is in your office. She said you called her. I don't know her game, but she doesn't spare the perfume," Agnes said. "I gave her coffee. My guess is she'd prefer something stronger."

My office door was closed.

"Do I get coffee?" I said.

"Sure you do. It's fresh and hot and at your elbow," she said. "Just pour your own. I'll be busy."

"Busy?" I said.

"Someone has to man the firehose," she said. "Believe me, brother, when you get a load of this dame, you're going to need it."

Agnes chuckled. I opened the door to my office and caught a whiff of Tabu. The lady sat in the customer's chair, back to the door. Smoke curled above her head. She spoke without turning.

"So, this is how a private eye lives," Stella Grace said.

"Only the good ones," I said. "Top floor, penthouse."

Stella sniffed at that remark and crushed out her cigarette. I placed my coffee on the desk. Without looking at me she rose from her chair and glided toward a window. She fingered a string of pearls around her neck and took in the view of downtown Wichita. I stood at my desk and took in the view of Stella Grace. She wore a black and white number that fell to slender ankles above black high heels. A wide-brimmed hat matched the heels. The scent of her perfume would rouse Rip Van Winkle from slumber.

Where was Agnes with that firehose? Tuesday was the day Lucille visited the beauty shop. Somewhere at that moment my gal was getting her hair done, making herself beautiful. Stella's voice interrupted my thoughts.

"I grew up in a third-floor walkup," she said. "It was not a penthouse. Cold running water, heat in the summer, air conditioning in the winter. We got whatever the window let in."

"For me, it was a sod house in western Kansas," I said. "I don't recommend it. This has been a week for dredging up memories better forgotten. Would you care for more coffee?"

"No, thank you," she said. "I'm not the first to bring up the past, I take it? Have you spoken to Miriam?"

"She called me before she left for Hollywood. If she left for Hollywood."

"She hasn't yet. I'm not convinced Miriam has a future in motion pictures."

"Maybe she's dragging her feet. Maybe Ralph has something to do with that," I said.

"There's a spark there," she said. "Sparks make it exciting, but they do little to put food on the table. I wonder, does a private eye live any better than a film extra? No offense."

"None taken," I said. "Don't I get points for my dapper new duds?"

That brought a tight-lipped smile to her face.

"You, on the other hand, have found a soft place to land," I said.

"I get by," she said.

She returned to her chair and removed a cigarette from a silver case. I leaned over and lit it. Her dark brown eyes followed me as I leaned back.

"Your suit looks nice, or should I say you look nice in that suit?" she said.

"Thank you. As for you, you're doing better than getting by."

Her smile started at the lips and moved up to her eyes. She uncrossed her legs and crossed them again the other way.

"I no longer live in a third-floor walkup. Thank you, by the way, for playing along with my little ruse the other night. I had no reason to hide our earlier meeting, but Reginald doesn't need to know I traveled to Dodge City."

"So, a seat at the table comes with a leash?" I said.

"Reginald takes care of me," she said.

"I'd say he takes good care of you."

"He gives me money to stay close, not enough to go far," she said.

"Is that why you agreed to meet with me today? So you could thank me for putting one over on Reginald?" I said.

"I don't suppose you'd tell me what you and Miriam discussed?" she said.

I sipped coffee and lowered the cup.

"What is it with you dames? These nicks and scratches on my carcass didn't come from falling off the turnip truck. You've talked to Miriam. She told you what we talked about. What is it you really want to know?"

Those dark eyes flashed.

"What did Miriam say about Reginald?"

"She doesn't care for the man."

"Does she think Reginald had Amos Johnson murdered?"

"She'd make me believe that, if she could. She wants to believe it, too. Maybe she does, but she can't prove it," I said. "How about you? Did dear old Reggie have Amos murdered?"

She ignored my question.

"Miriam loved her brother," she said. "She's not thinking clearly."

"She says the same about you," I said. "She says you're the one not playing it smart. She tried to warn you off Dexter."

"She doesn't know Reginald, not like I do," she said. "Amos Johnson was a petty thief. Miriam was right about that. Amos was also a babe in the woods. When a baby wants something, he takes it. Amos didn't think about the things he did. He just acted, period. Amos lacked the brains to pull off that big score Miriam talks about. You're wasting your time traveling down that road."

I lit a Chesterfield. Stella's assessment of Amos Johnson matched my own.

"Johnson was murdered. Dexter claims it wasn't over drugs. You claim it wasn't over a heist," I said. "Where does that leave a bumbling private detective? Was it over a dame? Am I to believe a jealous lover took out Amos? No dice. You might as well tell me it was an overdue library book."

"The men who killed Amos are dead," she said. "Isn't that enough for you?"

"You know those goons were hired help, lady. I want to know who called the shots. What is it with you and your boyfriend? Why the concern over a two-bit gumshoe wasting his time on a case no one else wants to touch? No one else cares about the murders of druggies and assassins, not even the police."

"Does that surprise you? Druggies and assassins are dead. White or colored, it doesn't matter. Nobody cares. Why do you care?" she said.

"Why don't you? Two of those assassins killed Amos. The third tried to kill Ralph, not to mention yours truly," I said.

"And those men are dead," she said.

"Why are you afraid of the truth?"

"Did Miriam talk about our childhood?" she said.

"She had a tough beginning," I said. "You all did. Amos fell in with a tough crowd."

"Amos and I were close, born only weeks apart," Stella said. "Miriam was Amos's big sister, but she acted the big sister for both of us. We grew up with no fathers. I never knew my mine, and their father ran off about the time Amos was born. The three of us had our mothers and each other. That was it. We played together and looked after each other. Mother welcomed Miriam and Amos into our home, but I was not allowed to visit theirs."

She lifted her empty cup.

"I've changed my mind. May I have more coffee?"

I refilled our cups in the outer office. Agnes watched me with raised eyebrows. I shrugged and went back to my desk.

"It wasn't until I was older that I understood why I wasn't welcome around their home," Stella said. "My mother was a beauty. She was also alone and poor. Men sought her company. I discovered when I was older that one of those men who visited my mother was Miriam's father."

The Seth Thomas banjo clock ticked. A fly buzzed the window, circled over the desk, and buzzed the window again.

"And you and Amos were born weeks apart," I said.

"Mother did what she had to do to keep us from starving," Stella said. "I don't fault her or judge her. We had food, shelter, clothes. We survived. Did Amos and I share the same father? I can't answer that. Mother never told me. Maybe she didn't know. It doesn't matter. I intend to remain childless, so that question will remain unanswered. Amos and I were as close as a brother and sister can be. He did not commit a grand heist."

"Why are you telling me this?" I said.

"Because it's the truth," she said. "Don't you want the truth?"

"It's the truth, but it's not the whole truth. Amos did not commit a grand heist, you say. Fine. Something was stolen," I said.

'Yes, something was stolen," she said. "Of course, that's why you called me."

She lifted her cup, sipped, and lowered it to the desk. She fixed her eyes on me and opened her purse.

Chapter 31

I figured whatever was stolen had ended up with Stella. I didn't know what that was. Unsure of what she carried in her purse, I leaned forward, ready to pounce.

"Relax," she said.

She pulled a leather wallet out of her purse and tossed it onto the desk. The long, breast pocket wallet looked familiar, a twin to the one I'd seen on Leo Little's desk. I opened it and looked inside. It appeared to be empty, but a lump indicated an object stowed beneath a flap. I lifted the flap and pulled out a narrow notebook. There was nothing else inside the wallet, no cash, no identification, no photographs, nothing.

"That's the way it came to me," Stella said. "Amos gave it to me after he'd removed the cash, the only thing he wanted. He clutched the money and crowed like he'd just cracked the combination to Fort Knox."

I opened the book and scanned notations, names, initials, lists of materials, item amounts, dollar amounts, and arrows pointing this way and that. Bank receipts were tucked into the back of the book.

"I've seen the cousin to this wallet. Leo Little keeps it in his cage. Amos stole this one from Little," I said.

"Amos didn't steal it. His customer's the one who stole it, the one who died," she said.

"Silas?"

"That's it, Silas. He had no money, and he needed a fix. He stole Little's wallet. He fumbled it when he handed it to Amos, he was shaking so bad."

"Leo Little must have been careless," I said. "I've watched him lock the cage when he steps away."

"According to Amos, it happened quickly. Silas came up with an excuse to leave the warehouse when Little was out of the cage. Silas spotted the wallet and lifted it as he walked out the door," she said. "Amos said Silas didn't even open it. He was so desperate for a hit, he handed it over, took the heroin, and hustled off."

"Little told me Silas returned to the warehouse, and he fired him," I said.

"Little lied. Silas grabbed the drug and disappeared," she said. "That's what Amos said."

"That fits. A man desperate for the needle wouldn't hang around until quitting time to use it," I said.

"The silly fools. Silas needed a fix. He was stone-cold broke and ready to beg Amos, then the wallet appeared," she said. "Silas had an opportunity to steal, and he took it."

"Little knew who took it," I said. "Little found Silas and shot him, not with a gun, with a needle. He didn't find the wallet on Silas, but he knew who had it. Little hired gunmen to track down Amos and get the wallet. We know what happened then. How much money was there?"

"I have no idea. It doesn't matter. Little wasn't after the money," she said.

"No, he wasn't after the money," I said.

I thumbed the book and read the notations. Stella smoked a cigarette. The fly had given up on the window. I didn't recognize all of the names in the book. The ones I did recognize belonged to a city councilman, a county commissioner, and a city cop, Vic Harris, the guy who tried to roust Willie and me from the café. Arrows with dollar amounts pointed toward names. Other arrows connected names.

Those arrows pointed toward more than money and names. They pointed to crimes. How many and what kind was open to speculation. There would be an investigation. Stolen goods? Bribes? Payoffs?

Notations and arrows alone wouldn't lead to arrests. Police would have to follow the arrows and connect the dots. They had reports of what was stolen. They'd call on city hall and investigate construction bids approved, contracts awarded, and most importantly, who'd given favors to whom. The police would also be interested in why one of their own was listed in the book.

That would come later. As for me, the book was the gold nugget in the sludge, the motive for the killings and attempted assassinations, the reason Ralph Waldo and I had been looking over our shoulders. I fought to keep my voice even.

"You've been sitting on this for weeks," I said. "Why?"

"Something snapped when I saw Amos's body," Stella said. "He was tortured. He died slowly."

"He also died with his mouth shut," I said. "Little would have come after you if Amos had talked."

"Yes, that's right. When Little didn't come after me, I was afraid he'd go after Ralph. I didn't know Ralph then, but Amos talked about him. I warned Ralph to leave town. You stepped in with your investigation, and I tried to warn you, too. I told you to leave it alone. You didn't."

"That doesn't explain why you held onto this book," I said.

"I wanted Little to die slowly, like Amos died," she said.

I recalled Stella Grace's MO.

"You sent a letter to Leo Little and signed it, ad astra per aspera," I said, "To the stars through difficulties."

"I told him I'd return the notebook in exchange for $5,000," she said. "I enclosed a bank receipt so he knew I wasn't bluffing."

"You kept the book for money," I said, "blackmail."

"I never wanted a dime. I wanted Little to squirm. I wanted Little to suffer. I wanted him to feel what Amos must have felt before he died."

I lit a Chesterfield. She took a cigarette from her purse and lit it with a silver lighter.

"No dice, sister. Your timing's off. Amos was alive when you received this wallet. You didn't keep it to make Little squirm. You kept it because you wanted dough," I said. "You blackmailed him."

"My first thought was money," she said. "You're right. I recognized the value of what I had. I still don't understand why Little had such a book. Why would a criminal keep a diary of his crimes?"

I looked over the list of names.

"This is Little's insurance policy, his get out of jail free card," I said. "Schemes like this don't remain secret when this many people are involved. One mistake, one errant comment, one weak link, and the chain snaps. When that happens, the guys at the top shield themselves behind lawyers and lies. They all point fingers to the guy at the bottom, the little guy."

Stella smiled at the pun, then frowned.

"After Amos turned up dead, all I wanted was revenge," she said.

"Amos turned up dead in Ralph Waldo's bathtub," I said. "Leo Little figured Amos gave the wallet to his buddy, Ralph. I came into the picture when I discovered the body. Little hired a third assassin, Cletis Rackley, to take out Ralph and make sure I didn't get in the way."

"I did what I could to keep both of you safe," she said.

The elephant in the room could no longer be ignored.

"You took out the assassins," I said.

Stella's expression didn't change. She was a seasoned poker player not revealing a tell. Whether she held a full house or a busted flush, she wouldn't lay down her hand until I called. She raised her cigarette to her lips with a steady hand and blew smoke toward the ceiling.

"The police are going to have questions," I said. "You'd better have answers. When this tower topples, you're going to be buried under a pile of rubble."

"Any suggestions?" she said.

"A vigilante with a pistol would be wise to get rid of it. The police aren't busting their tails looking for this person, but if a .22 pistol fell into their lap, they'd be obliged to examine it. They'd want to know if it matched with the slugs they have in evidence."

"Suppose you had such a pistol," she said. "What would you do?"

I glanced toward the window.

"That river that runs through the city washes away all manner of sins," I said.

Chapter 32

I drove toward the white, frame house near Ninth and Water that had a welcome mat on the porch and bars on the windows. Ralph deserved to be in on this. Little had been asking after Ralph, according to Willie. Willie had asked me to pass that message along to Ralph. I had not done so. My plan was to take down Leo Little, to hand him and his notebook over to the police and let them deal with the fallout. Ralph and I would be side-by-side when that happened. That would end the attempts on Ralph's life, and it would mark the end of my investigation.

I climbed the stairs and knocked on the door. No answer. Ralph wasn't at home for lunch. My watch told me that lunch hour had come and gone. Back downstairs, a dog growled, and a woman spoke.

"Sit, Suez," the woman said.

The lady on the porch held a taut leash that stretched to the collar of a Doberman Pinscher. The Doberman obeyed her command and rested on his haunches. Lucky for me. If the dog had charged, he'd have brought the woman and the leash right along with him.

"You must be Ralph's new landlady," I said.

"And you must be who?" she said.

The lady didn't slur, but she weaved, aftereffects from a noontime tipple of elderberry wine, perhaps. I introduced myself.

"I'm looking for Ralph. Have you seen him or do you know where I can find him?" I said.

She raised her free hand and tilted her head toward the skies.

"'Vengeance is mine; I will repay, saith the Lord.'" She lowered her head. "Romans twelve, nineteen."

The Doberman punctuated her pronouncement with a growl.

"Who is seeking vengeance?" I said.

"That son of a bitch with Ralph," she said. "They went up those stairs. They went into Ralph's apartment together. They made one hell of a racket, those two. They wrestled like she-bears protecting cubs. They tore that room apart . . . 'and behold, a pale horse! And its rider's name was Death.' Revelations six, eight."

"Who wrestled with Ralph?"

"That bastard in the bow tie, that's who!" she said. "If it's Ralph you seek, find that bastard in the bow tie!"

"Did you hear anything they said? What did they say?"

She raised her arm again.

"No more Bible verses, lady," I said, but it was too late.

She stared heavenward. The Doberman growled, and I hightailed it for the roadster. The landlady started in on the Proverbs. "Envy thou not the oppressor . . ." I gunned the engine before she finished.

◆ ◆ ◆

The door was unlocked at L.L. Storage, but no one was inside. The inventory appeared to be intact. No one had moved it or loaded it onto a truck. Either the crew had been dismissed or they'd taken a hike. I opened the door to the office with no windows and found the same desk and chairs I'd seen before, nothing else. Another door led to a toilet.

One door remained, and it was locked. It had to be the door Willie had mentioned, the door that cost a curious worker his job when he asked what was stored behind it. Cracking the lock was a snap but not worth the time it took. The six by eight room was empty. Whatever it once held was gone.

The cage was unlocked. The desk and stool and a few office supplies remained. Records and paperwork were gone. Leo Little left in a hurry and took everything with him but the inventory. The materials left in storage belonged to various businesses. Stolen goods, if any, had been shipped out and liquidated. The only thing belonging to Leo Little was the building itself, a sagging, bent-at-the-knees structure that had outlived its usefulness.

I drove over to Ninth and Cleveland in the McAdams neighborhood. Only one unit in the four-unit apartment house looked lived in, the landlady's place, lower left. Curtains were drawn over the windows in the unit to the right, Little's place. His Packard was nowhere in sight.

I stepped onto the porch and peeked through the curtains. The door to my left opened, and the landlady frowned, hands on hips.

"He ain't here no more," she said. "He's gone, too, same as the others. Ain't nobody here except me, thanks to you. You've brought nothing but trouble, you have. Everything was peaceable until you showed up. Now, everybody's cleared out. Now, nobody wants to rent a room in this place. So, you go on. Git. Clear out now."

She slammed the door. The lady had a point. Murder discourages a potential tenant. It gives a prospect pause. I had a bigger concern. Leo Little had pulled up stakes and taken a powder, and he'd taken Ralph with him.

◆ ◆ ◆

Leo Little had planned his exit well. He knew the warehouse was the first place I'd look, and when I found him gone, I'd try his home. He stowed his stuff in his Packard, got ready to leave town, then lured Ralph into his web. He suspected Ralph either had what he was after or knew where to find it. He tossed Ralph's apartment and came up empty.

That left Little homeless, out of business, and desperate. He'd flee Wichita, but he had work to do, and he wouldn't get far with a hostage in tow. He needed to question Ralph, torture him if necessary, and he needed an out of the way place to do it.

I drove downtown and parked at the corner of Douglas and Emporia. I needed firepower, and my gun was in my desk.

"He's in your office," Agnes said when I opened the door.

"Who's in my office?"

"Aaron Bernstein. He said he'd be here today, remember? Something about a dog and a beer?"

Agnes was right. Bernstein had said he'd come by. I entered my office. Bernstein stood and grinned. He looked at my mug, and the grin evaporated.

"Talk to me, cowboy," he said.

I opened the bottom drawer of my desk and removed the Smith & Wesson .38. I loaded cartridges into my gun and gave Bernstein a rundown of events. I dropped extra cartridges into my pocket. Agnes stood in the doorway and took it all in.

"I have a gun in my car," Bernstein said.

"I can't ask you to do this, pal," I said.

"You didn't ask. I'm in," he said.

Agnes fidgeted and said, "What's with the guns? Where do you think you're going?"

"It's called the Shimmy Shack, not much more than a pile of lumber out in the sticks," I said. "Little is tight with the owner. That's from Ralph. I don't know if Little is there or not, but it fits."

"So city boys in suits stroll into the woods and shoot up the place? That's your plan? They'll be waiting for you. Haven't you heard of home-field advantage?" she said.

"We'll sneak in," I said. "I'm a gumshoe. Ralph's in trouble. Let's go."

Chapter 33

Long shadows followed us into the country. Daylight dwindled. Dim light and shadows might work to our advantage, provide an opportunity to sneak in unnoticed. Darkness could also work against us, shield a shooter who aimed a shotgun or a rifle.

I pulled into the clearing and spotted a lone vehicle, a Packard. Clothes and papers peeked over the rear window.

"Bingo. That's Little's car," I said. "They're here."

Bernstein pulled a long-barreled Colt .45 out of his coat.

"Now who's the cowboy?" I said. "How do you conceal a Peacemaker in your suit?"

"I don't conceal it. I hold it in plain sight. Pointing this barrel to a spot between a man's eyes is all it takes," he said. "Even a tough guy's bowels loosen."

Bernstein's words triggered a memory of Hamilton Bell. The retired Dodge City lawman used a similar approach back in his day and never shot a man.

"Where is this shack?" Bernstein said.

I gestured toward the path in the trees.

"We walk," I said.

We got out of the roadster, and a car engine rumbled behind us.

"Get down," I said.

We crouched low and waited. The dark sedan pulled to a stop. Several figures exited the car.

"Stone, is that you?" a voice said.

Lieutenant Thaddeus McCormick approached the roadster followed by two cops in uniform. Each cop wore a bulletproof vest, a holstered firearm, and carried a shotgun. I shook hands with each man.

"How'd you get here, Mac?" I said.

"Agnes sounded the alarm. She called and said you and Bernstein were going to pull a cockamamie stunt. It looks like she was right."

"How'd you find us?"

"You mean how'd I find the Shimmy Shack? I'm a detective. I know everything," he said.

"We're outside the city limits," I said.

"Oh, damn," he said. "Is that Little's car?"

"That's it. Little has Ralph inside somewhere, probably in the shanty out back. No other cars. That leaves the owner of the place," I said.

"Mule," Mac said.

"Mule," I said.

Mac retrieved a bullhorn from the sedan.

"Let's get in there," he said.

Shadows fell over the trail. I took the lead followed by Mac, the two cops, and Bernstein in single file. Something ahead slithered over the ground and disappeared into the undergrowth. One of the cops swore at a sandbur that stung his ankle. We stopped at the edge of the clearing and peered into the shadows, scanning the outline of the Shimmy Shack behind the assorted chairs. Lanterns on posts were unlit, and no fire burned in the pit. The shack was dark.

We inched forward and took cover behind the shack. A scream froze us in our tracks. It was too dark to see the shanty beyond the outhouse. Mac looked around the corner and raised the bullhorn.

"Give it up, Little! We've got you surrounded!"

A shotgun boomed. Pellets sprayed into the shack and the brush behind us. Mac took cover. A voice yelled from the darkness.

"You're out there with that lousy private eye! You and your popguns!"

Mac nodded to the posse and said, "Make some noise. Don't hit the shanty."

The cops blasted their shotguns, shot after shot. Bernstein fired his Peacemaker, and I emptied my .38. The barrage echoed in the night, a Fourth of July celebration in April. We stopped shooting to reload. I emptied my pocket and reloaded the .38 with my remaining bullets. The cops fired their shotguns again.

A voice screamed, "Stop! Stop shooting!" and footsteps grew louder. "Don't shoot!" A figure appeared, arms up over his head. Mule had lost his swagger.

"I ain't a part of this!" Mule said. "I don't want nothing to do with this!"

Mac frisked Mule and cuffed him.

"Sit," Mac said.

Mule dropped like a sack of cement and stared up from the dirt.

"Is Ralph Waldo alive?" Mac said.

Mule nodded up and down and said, "Yes. He's alive. Leo singed him with a hot coal once or twice, but he didn't kill him. He tried to get him to talk. The man's alive. I told Leo I wanted nothing to do with this. I told Leo to get out, but he's gone plum crazy. He's got a gun doing the talking."

"Give us the layout," I said.

"I never wanted no police. No sir, I never wanted no police," Mule said.

"The layout," I said.

"Ain't nothing but one room. One door, one window. There's a woodstove, a chair, and a cot, that's all. Your man is tied up on the cot."

"And the woodstove's burning," I said.

"That's right," he said.

"I'm going in," I said.

"You can't go busting in there," Mac said. "You'll get Ralph killed."

I peered into the gray and tried to recall the shanty I'd seen in daylight.

"How high is the roof around back?" I said.

"It slopes. Not much over six feet," Mule said.

"What are you thinking?" Mac said.

"I'm going down there. I think I can draw him out. You men cover me. Make noise so Little can't hear me."

"I'm going with you," Bernstein said.

"I'll give you two minutes of cover before we move in," Mac said.

I hunched low and went down the path with Bernstein behind. Mac yelled into the bullhorn, "We've got Mule, Little. Come on out!" The cops blasted their shotguns. Bernstein took cover behind a cottonwood in front of the shanty. Shotgun blasts continued.

Around back, I grabbed a low hanging eave and pulled myself onto the roof. Smoke curled overhead. I removed my jacket and stuffed it down the chimney. I leapt to the ground ahead of the blast from inside. Smoke belched through a hole in the roof. Inside the shanty, Ralph coughed and Little swore.

The cavalry charged ahead. Leo Little came out with his hands up and stared down the barrel of Bernstein's Peacemaker. I untied Ralph while the cops doused the fire in the stove. A burn on Ralph's bare chest looked painful, but he was not wounded otherwise.

Bernstein remained fixed, an ice-cold grin plastered on his mug and the Peacemaker pointed between Leo Little's eyes. The man stared into the gun barrel and trembled. A foul smell told us the bastard in the bow tie had soiled himself.

"Never fails," Bernstein said.

Saturday
April 29, 1939

Chapter 34

The St. Louis Cardinals led the Chicago Cubs in the late innings at Wrigley Field. Lon Warnecke had tossed a one-hit, no-run gem, and the Birds backed up their pitcher with seven hits and two runs of their own. Tom turned up the radio broadcast. He glided from the bar to the tables and back to the bar, topped off glasses with Storz beer, and chanted, "This is their year, boys. This is their year."

We sipped beer and bantered among ourselves. Ralph Waldo looked over his shoulder and took in the room. Mac pulled out a cigar. Aaron Bernstein reached for the humidor in his suit coat.

"Try a Cuban," he said.

Bernstein to the rescue again. My fourteen-dollar suit went up in smoke during the fracas in the forest. Not Bernstein. The fashion plate stepped out of the woods brandishing a Peacemaker and wearing a grin, without a wrinkle or a crease in his duds.

Mabel shuffled out of the kitchen carrying a tray of steaming hotdogs. I lifted her burden, and she pulled a jar of mustard from her apron.

"Eat up, gentlemen," she said.

"Hotdogs served with mustard, beer, and baseball," I said to Bernstein, "as requested."

"Your marker is canceled," Bernstein said. "We're square on the books unless you'd like to let it ride. There's a fresh pony in the race."

"I'm in," I said.

Bernstein leaned forward.

"Reginald Dexter cozied up to the German American Bund and played Fritz Kuhn for a sucker. That was his angle. That gathering in Madison Square Garden attracted a lot of attention. Reggie was there. His money bought him a ticket into the Bund's inner circle. He became privy to how things were run.

"This is on the Q.T. for now, but it'll hit the news. Fritz spent a lot of Bund dough on a dame. He's on the hook for embezzlement and tax evasion. The mayor of New York City has ordered an investigation into Bund finances. Smart money bets Dexter whispered into the mayor's ear, and the mayor unleashed the hounds."

I sipped my beer and lowered my glass.

"Dexter did something decent," I said. "That's a pair of words I never thought I'd use in the same sentence, Dexter and decent."

"Dexter made the smart move," Mac said. "That construction company he owns stands to gain when our investigation is completed. There'll be new players on the field."

Ralph Waldo grimaced.

"How're you feeling?" I said.

"I'm fine. Just a twinge," he said.

"Has Miriam left for the coast?"

That brought a smile.

"Not yet," he said.

"Leo Little will pay," Mac said.

"I walked right into it," Ralph said in a low voice and shook his head. "During my investigation, I heard he was looking for me. I went to see him."

"Don't kick yourself, Ralph," I said. "We've got him."

"Kickbacks and bribes are not uncommon, but murder is," Mac said. "The players at City Hall are ready to spill. Lawyers are advising their clients to say whatever it takes to separate themselves from the murders."

Mac's eyes met mine.

"That leaves Stella Grace," he said. "We haven't questioned Stella Grace yet. I don't suppose you'd have anything to offer?"

"Someone in this town acted as vigilante," I said. "Someone watched over Ralph and me, gumshoes in the shadows. You have no prints, no smoking gun, and no suspect. You won't hear from that vigilante again. Let it go."

Mac frowned. Ralph looked over his shoulder.

"Relax," Bernstein said. "You're among friends here. You belong."

The ballgame ended, and Tom turned off the radio. He filled our glasses.

"The Cardinals took one from the Cubbies, boys. Someone make a toast. Pete?" Tom said.

I met the gaze of each man, each friend, each ally, a struggling detective, a smooth bookie, and an honest lawman, gathered together under the roof of my favorite bartender where we all belonged.

I stood, and they raised their glasses.

"Gentlemen," I said, "a Negro, a Jew, and a Scotsman walk into a bar."

"Hear! Hear!" Tom said.

We clinked our glasses and drank.

THE END

A Tip of the Fedora

Readers and fans share thoughts and ideas on Pete Stone's adventures. I appreciate hearing from each one.

Roger Heineken first brought the premiere of *Dodge City*, the movie, to my attention. He forwarded an article by Susan L. Sutton, "Dodge City, Kansas; Hollywood for a Day," that piqued my interest and provided a look at the events prior to and on April 1, 1939.

Tracy Million Simmons, Meadowlark publisher and native of Dodge City, forwarded websites and articles to explore. She steered me toward a former high school classmate, John Askew, who is a local Ford County historian. John drove my wife and me over highways, city streets, and backroads in his pickup truck as he shared his rich knowledge of the area.

Megan Welsh, Director of the Convention & Visitors Bureau, gave us a tour of the Historic Santa Fe Depot & Harvey Hotel, including a guest room that remains just as it was when the Warner Brothers Special rolled into town.

David Rogers at the Dodge City Public Library disappeared into the archives and returned with an armload of photographs and articles covering the era and the grand premiere of the movie. He also allowed me to use a computer to research additional library articles.

I'm grateful to the kind and generous people of Dodge City who shared their time and stories with me.

Our friend, Brandy Briggeman, learned that the Nifty Nut House, a favorite stop in Wichita, opened its doors for business in the 1930s. Pete and Lucille enjoyed their treats back then, just as we enjoy their treats today.

Other resources include microfilm copies of *The Wichita Eagle* and *Dodge City Daily Globe*, *People and Places of Dodge City*, Vol. I & II with photographs by Troy Robinson, et.al., and Boot Hill Museum.

As with all books in the *Shadow* series, Tracy Million Simmons does the layout and design. Photographer, Dave Leiker, provides the artwork. I appreciate the beautiful work they do. Feel free to judge my books by their covers.

Monica Graves, Tracy Million Simmons, and Cheryl Unruh each read early drafts of *Shadows Deep* and provided comments and advice that improved the story. Thank you, all.

Readers often wonder about the next adventure, and I wonder, too. Does Pete Stone have more to say? Will he speak to me again? As long as a reader asks, "When's the next one?" I'll keep listening for his whisper.

Michael D. Graves
Emporia, Kansas

Michael D. Graves created the character of Pete Stone as a memorial to his grandfather. The first and the third in the series were selected as Kansas Notable Books: *To Leave a Shadow* (2016) and *All Hallows' Shadows* (2021). *All Hallows' Shadows* was also the J. Donald Coffin Memorial Book Award winner by the Kansas Authors Club in 2020 and a silver medalist in the Midwest Book Awards in 2021.

Mike's writing has appeared in *Cheap Detective Stories, Thorny Locust, Flint Hills Review,* and *105 Meadowlark Reader.* He is an author of *Green Bike, a group novel,* along with Kevin Rabas and Tracy Million Simmons. He lives with his wife in Emporia, Kansas. They are both members of the Kansas Authors Club.

When life conjures its riddles, Mike turns to back roads and baseball for answers.

Pete Stone Private Investigator Series
Set in 1930s Wichita, Kansas

Book 1: To Leave a Shadow

A 2016 Kansas Notable Book

Paperback: 204 pages

ISBN:-0692567791   ALSO on Kindle & Audio

Pete Stone hasn't always been a private eye. He lost his dairy business at the toss of a coin when the depression hit. His children grew up, as children do, and his wife left him for a chinchilla farmer. Pete has learned to like his solitude. When Mrs. Lucille Hamilton walks through his door searching for her missing husband, Pete is the only one who believes her husband's death wasn't a suicide.

Book 2: Shadow of Death

Paperback: 264 pages

ISBN: 978-099680165   ALSO on Kindle

When a cop killer strikes Wichita, Pete Stone, Private Investigator, is on the case. He has to be. He wakes up in jail, battered and bruised, and accused of a murder he's almost certain he didn't commit. Pete must prove his innocence before he's abandoned by his clients, his friends, and one special lady. When Stone is not getting knocked around by cops, he's getting roughed up by love.

Book 3: All Hallows' Shadows

2020 J. Donald Coffin Memorial Book Award Winner

2021 Kansas Notable Book

2021 Midwest Book Awards Finalist

Paperback: 226 pages

ISBN: 978-1734247732   ALSO on Kindle & Audio

When a young woman is stabbed to death in Wichita, the police capture a suspect and put him behind bars within hours. Detective Pete Stone is hired to prove that the suspect is innocent, but Pete Stone has his doubts. Isn't being caught standing over the body with a knife in hand evidence enough? When additional bodies turn up murdered by weapons with similar strange markings and cryptic verses, Pete realizes the clock is ticking. He must uncover the truth before the real villain strikes again, on Halloween night.

Book 4: Shadows and Sorrows

Paperback: 236 pages

ISBN:-1-956578-03-4   ALSO on Kindle & Audio

Pete Stone and Cocky Wright met on a baseball field, a pair of boys with skinned knees and lots of moxie. They developed a loyalty and a friendship that lasted long after time stole their youth., Cocky is dead, his widow and daughter are in danger, and shady characters are after something he was hiding. All Cocky left behind was a key and lots of questions. Was he dealing secrets to the German American Bund? Was he a threat to the safety of the country? Was his death an accident or murder? When his pal's ghost whispers, "You got moxie, kid," Pete Stone knows he must find the answers. He must uncover the truth and save the reputation of his friend.

Book 5: Human Shadow

Paperback: 280 pages

ISBN: 978-1-956578-40-9   ALSO on Kindle

Pete's Pal, Professor Ethan Alexander, has a friend in hot water, and Ethan is eager to get Pete on the case. Pete is convinced the friend is guilty, but he values friendship and loyalty and agrees to help. The investigation leads Pete to call on the help of a few old friends, as well, and trouble with his lady-friend encourages him to pause and examine more than just the suspects at large. Are his intentions enough to turn the relationship around? Will he find Ethan's friend before the cops do? Some stories, like friendships, are deeper and filled with more complications than can be seen and heard in the moment.